I0735053

MARY CRAWFORD

Freedom

HIDDEN HEARTS BOOK 9

COPYRIGHT

Published on January 28, 2018, by Diversity Ink Press and Mary Crawford. Author may be reached at MaryCrawfordAuthor.com.

ISBN: 978-1-945637-36-0

Cover by Covers Unbound

HIDDEN BEAUTY SERIES

Until the Stars Fall from the Sky
So the Heart Can Dance
Joy and Tiers
Love Naturally
Love Seasoned
Love Claimed
If You Knew Me (and other silent musings) (novella)
Jude's Song
The Price of Freedom (novella)
Paths Not Taken
Dreams Change (novella)
Heart Wish (100% charity release)
Tempting Fate
The Letter
The Power of Will

HIDDEN HEARTS SERIES

Identity of the Heart

Sheltered Hearts

Hearts of Jade

Port in the Storm (novella)

Love is More Than Skin Deep

Tough

Rectify

Pieces (a crossover novel)

Hearts Set Free

Freedom (a crossover novel)

The Long Road to Love (novella)

Love and Injustice (Protection Unit)

Out of Thin Air (Protection Unit)

Soul Scars (Protection Unit)

OTHER WORKS:

The Power of Dictation

Vision of the Heart

#AmWriting: A Collection of Letters to Benefit The
Wayne Foundation

DEDICATION

To those who see difference
and find love, not limitations.

CHAPTER ONE

PHOENIX

One thought is running through my head as I do a last-minute check of my bike. I have twenty-eight days to make it from Gainesville, Florida to McMinnville, Oregon. If I take the most direct route, it means I need to drive 105.857 miles per day. My boss, Tristan Macklin, wants me to go to Identity Bank's new facility to see if I'd feel comfortable there.

I'm still reeling from my performance evaluation. I don't know what to think. On one hand, Tristan said he would like to see me advance in the company. Yet, he criticized the way I interact with my coworkers. He was gentle, but the message was still clear. I guess I don't really understand why I need to be more social. I'm just a game debugger. I'm really good at that. I'm not so good at making friends at work.

The new job would mean I'd get a promotion, but I like my job now. Tristan reviewed the time I've taken off since I started. He was not happy. He told me working three years straight with no vacation time was not good for me. When he found out I like to take road trips on my motorcycle, he told me to take a month-long trip and go across the country.

Most people would take a plane for this type of trip, but I've never been able to bring myself to fly. Of course, Tristan thinks this is funny because he owns his own plane and can't understand why anybody wouldn't jump at the chance to fly. He even offered to spring for first-class tickets. I don't know how to explain to him how uncomfortable I am in new situations. Some people are nervous flyers, but my anxiety goes far beyond that. So, I'm setting off on an adventure to go across the country. I'm trying to buck my natural tendencies and just go with the flow. It is so far beyond my usual approach I'm not sure if I'll be able to accomplish my mission. But, I'm tired of people pigeonholing me because I like my life to be structured and routine. Maybe it's time for a new approach.

On this trip, I'm challenging myself to be spontaneous and ride by the seat of my pants. Barring any complications, I've built in enough time in my schedule to stop and see things I've never seen before. Over the past month I've spent a lot of time convincing myself this isn't the most radically stupid plan I've ever come up with.

I tighten the strap on my helmet and get onto Interstate 75 to begin the journey of a lifetime. After only about thirty minutes, the road noise starts to irritate me. I pull over to the side of the road, insert my earbuds and start my favorite playlist on my phone. It's a good thing I've got extra batteries for my phone. If traffic continues to be this heavy, it'll be a long trip.

As I check my rearview mirror before pulling back out into traffic, I see a weird white blur. I look behind me to see if I can interpret what I just saw. Much to my horror, there is a Golden Labrador Retriever running across the lanes of traffic. Before I can take my next breath, he runs into the path of a vehicle. Instead of stopping, the pickup weaves into the other lane of traffic and takes off. No one else seems to notice the dog was hit. I make a U-turn on the shoulder and make my way to the grassy area where the dog has come to rest. My heart is racing as I get closer to the dog. I don't even know what I'm going to do. I don't have any first-aid skills to use on humans or animals. But, I can't just leave him there to die — assuming he survived the collision. My parents are watching my dog while I'm on my road trip, but if Gizmo were hurt, I'd want somebody to stop.

When I reach the puppy, I can see his coat is stained with blood. The sight causes my stomach to lurch. I've never been steady around blood. Swallowing hard, I move closer. The dog sees me and lets out a weak cry.

I let him sniff my hand before I take a bandanna out of my back pocket and place it over his wound. The poor dog is shaking like a leaf. Then again, so am I.

With my other hand, I pull my phone out of my pocket and use Google to find the closest veterinarian. It brings up a website called Hope's Haven.

As I am waiting for someone to answer the phone, the puppy stops wagging his tail. His eyes seem to roll back in his head. Crap! I should've done Boy Scouts or something useful when I was a kid. I don't want this dog to die in front of me.

Finally, someone picks up the phone. "Hopes Haven, this is Zoe."

"Umm … hi, I am calling to get help. I just saw a dog get hit by a car and he'll die unless I can get help. I don't know how to fix him," I explain in a burst of words.

"I'm not sure our facility is the best place. We train dogs at Hope's Haven," Zoe answers.

"Please, you have to help me. I don't know who else to call," I reply as traffic whizzes by.

"Of all the weekends for Dr. Stuart to be out of town," she mutters to herself. "Okay, tell me where you are."

"I'm not real sure, I was headed north on Interstate 75. I think I passed the High Springs exit a little ways back.".

"I don't know how much I'm going to be able to help you. Are you going northbound or southbound?"

"I'm northbound. I'm on the side of the road it's just me and my bike."

"I am in Alachua. I guess that puts me ten or fifteen minutes away from you. I'm driving the work truck."

"Please tell me you've got first aid stuff with you. I don't think this little guy has much left."

"I honestly don't know. I'm sure there's something in here. My boss doesn't go anywhere without being prepared for the worst. It's kinda how the dog rescue business works. I'll be there as quickly as I can."

Before I can say another word, the phone goes dead in my hand. I stroke the puppy and mutter, "I'm sorry I can't help you, but help is on the way."

Finally, I see a pickup truck with a decal of a German Shepherd on the side. Unfortunately, Zoe parked on the wrong side of the highway. Without thinking, I jog across the freeway. Lucky for me, traffic is at a near standstill. When the truck door opens, I'm surprised to see a young woman who looks barely older than a teenager step out. Her hair is in a ponytail, and she's wearing an oversized football jersey.

"Are you Zoe? We need to hurry; the dog is hurt bad." I point to the other side of the freeway where the dog is crumpled in a heap.

"Yes, I'm Zoe."

"Good!" I grab her sleeve and begin to pull her back across the freeway.

"Wait! I've got to get the supplies out of the back," she protests.

"Hurry please. High Springs is only nine minutes from Alachua. It took you seventeen minutes to get here," I observe.

She pauses for a moment and narrows her eyes at me. "Look at this traffic. I got here as quickly as I could. Do you want help or not?"

Zoe struggles with the door to the canopy. I reach over and pull it open for her. She disappears inside for a few moments before she emerges with a large first-aid kit.

"That's it? That's all you got? I don't know if it's gonna save the dog's life."

"What is it with you? I told you I didn't know if I could help. This is the best I've got. You seemed so desperate I figured I should try," she responds as we weave through the cars essentially parked on the I-75 to get to the other side where the puppy is crumpled in a much-too-still heap.

Before I can process what she's doing, Zoe strips off her jersey as she sprints the last few yards to the puppy. Kneeling in just her sports bra, jeans and Doc Martens, she covers him with her shirt.

"Oh, you poor baby! You're a bit of a mess," she coos as she looks over the dog. She glances up at me. "Do you know what happened? Did you hit her with the bike?"

Her question startles me out of my thoughts. "No! I didn't hit him. I just saw it happen. Some truck with custom rims hit him and drove off without stopping."

"I'm not sure I believe you, his injuries don't seem severe enough for a freeway accident. Are you sure?"

I study the rough pavement under my feet and kick around a little gravel. This conversation is way more confrontational than I expected. "Yes, I'm sure. As you already pointed out, traffic is awful. The truck wasn't going very fast."

"I Just think it's weird you can't look me in the eye when you deny that you hit this dog."

I shrug. "It's hard for me to look at people I don't know. It's kind of a thing with me," I confess awkwardly.

"What's your name?" She demands.

"I'm Phoenix. Phoenix Wolf."

"Well, I'll give you points for creativity. That sounds like a name that should come from a shape-shifter novel or something?"

"Whatever … it's my name. What's your name?"

"Zoe Hurlington," she answers as she checks the eyes and gums of the dog.

I can see goosebumps form across her back when a breeze kicks up.

"We need to get this dog to a vet. I can hold pressure

to the laceration on his flank, but that would mean you would have to drive the truck."

"Just a second, I'll be right back," I say as I run back to my bike.

Zoe looks up briefly and sees me headed away from her. "Hey! Don't ditch me here. I need your help. I can't rescue this dog without you. What are you doing?"

The tone of her questions makes me stop in my tracks and turn around to face her. "I'm trying to make it so I can help you. I told you I'd be right back."

"We need to get this dog to a vet," she insists.

I put my hands over my ears as a semi-truck whizzes by. I'm trying to stay calm but the ambient noise, together with her questions, are overwhelming me.

"I know. I can't drive the motorcycle and your truck at the same time. I don't think it will fit in the back with the canopy. Give me a second," I reply, frustration showing in my voice.

I walk my bike over to a clump of trees and pull things out of my saddlebags. At the bottom is my Xena — it looks like a boot that the traffic enforcement people use. I quickly attach it to my back tire. I start to cover it with a camouflage rain shield.

"Dude! Bring that over here. We need it for the dog."

"I've only got one," I announce.

"So? How do you think we're going to move the dog into the back of the pickup? I think that's more important than not getting dirt on your bike."

"That's not what I'm using it for. If I leave my bike here, I don't want it to be visible to everyone driving past."

"Okay! Fine! Do whatever you feel you have to do," Zoe says as she turns back to tend to the dog.

I shake my head and wring my hands in frustration as I try to process the information. I pick up the rain tarp and a sweatshirt. I jog back toward Zoe.

"You're cold," I state bluntly as I study her.

"Well, duh! I'm a little too busy to notice it."

I thrust the sweatshirt toward Zoe. "Here. This should help."

She looks a little surprised at my offer but slides the sweatshirt over her head. "Hold this so I can get the shirt on."

"I'm not really qualified to do this —" I protest

"Look, Phoenix. You and I are the only thing standing between this dog and death. Today you are qualified to hold pressure on the wound."

I squat down beside the dog and carefully place my hand over hers. "Is this okay?"

"I need to get my hand out of there, but as soon as I do that. I think you're good."

I let up for a moment while she removes her hand. She quickly stands up and goes over to the rain tarp. She lays it out on the grass and folds it into thirds.

"What are you doing?" I ask.

"Well, I don't see any stretchers around, so you and I will have to do this the old school way. I'm making a sling to carry this bruiser."

I look at the dog skeptically. "The dog doesn't look all that big. He looks kinda skinny for a yellow lab."

"True enough, I suppose. But, compared to my pug,

he is a bruiser."

"Maybe you should name him Bruiser."

Zoe drags the folded tarp over to where the dog is. She sighs. "Well, before we name this guy, we have to save him first. That may not be so easy. He might have internal bruising or fractures. We need to be careful when we move him because don't want to make any of his injuries worse."

"Are you sure we should move him at all? Isn't there a vet on-call at your place?"

"No, I'm a dog trainer. The vet we use at the rescue center is busy helping his wife have a baby." After arranging the tarp right next to Bruiser, she stands up and wipes the sweat from her brow. "I suppose I could call Sydney Austin. She fills in for Dr. Stuart."

"Why didn't we do that first?" I ask.

"I should have. But I was so focused on trying to figure out what was wrong with the dog, I forgot."

"Can you call him now?"

"I'll call her and have her meet us at Hope's Haven."

The puppy wags his tail weakly as if he understands real help is on the way.

"Hi Sydney? This is Zoe. I need you to meet me at Hope's Haven. We're bringing a dog in. He doesn't look so good, so bring as much of your medical stuff as you can. He seems shocky to me. The only injury I see is a pretty substantial gash along his flank."

Zoe chews on her fingernail as she listens to something on the other end of the phone. Suddenly, she brightens. "Okay, see you there."

Zoe puts her phone in her back pocket. She looks up

at me as she makes one last adjustment to the tarp. "You ever watch any medical shows or adventure shows? We are going to try to move the dog over to the tarp and use it as a makeshift gurney. If he was hit by the car, he might have a spinal injury. We don't want to make it worse. So, we'll have to work together and cooperate. I'm going to count to three and as gently as you can lift up his head and shoulders. I'll take care of the back end."

"Is that going to be an even distribution of his weight?"

"I can handle it. Just pay attention to your end."

"Okay, I'm worried about him sliding out of the sling," I explain.

"Ideally, I wouldn't move in this way, but we have no other options. It would take Sydney too long to get here to do a field assessment. So, we need to get him where he'll be warm and dry," Zoe clarifies as she looks up. I follow her gaze and notice a huge bank of rain clouds headed in our direction. "Oh great. This is going to be murder on my bike."

"I think we have more important things to deal with right now. Are you ready?" Zoe positions herself at the bottom end of the tarp.

I examine the dog carefully as I try to figure out how to grab him without causing more pain.

"I guess I'm as ready as I'm going to be."

"Okay, on the count of three, we're gonna lift him up and place him on the tarp."

"I hope I do this right," I say with trepidation.

"Anything would be better than leaving him here. Just try to be smooth. One, two, three," She counts down.

I take a deep breath and position the dog as carefully as I can in the middle of the tarp. Miraculously, he doesn't seem to be fighting us. It's almost as if he knows we're trying to help.

"Okay, that was the scary part. Now we simply need to carry him over to the truck. When you're driving, the brakes on this are a little touchy. So, please be careful because I don't want you to jerk us around in the back."

"All right, I'll be careful," I pledge feeling overwhelmed by the enormity of the tasks in front of me. I wanted to get out of my comfort zone on this trip. But, this is so far out of my comfort zone I don't even know what I'm doing.

CHAPTER TWO

ZOE

"YOU GUYS DID A phenomenal job getting this pup here," Sydney Austin hangs another IV off the grooming table.

"Thank you. But it wasn't really me. All the credit goes to Phoenix because he called it in," I respond.

"Where is he?" Sydney looks around curiously.

I roll my shoulder. "I don't really know. I thought he said something about cleaning up, but he's been gone for a while."

"You are braver than me. I'm not sure I would've allowed him to drive my rig. He's kind of rough looking."

"I like the long blonde hair and black leather. But he is a little odd."

"What do you know about this guy?"

"Next to nothing. He says his name is Phoenix Wolf. He drives a nice bike. When he talks, he doesn't always make much sense — but maybe he was just nervous about the dog. By the way, he's attached enough to this critter to name him Bruiser. If he likes dogs that much, I figure he can't be all bad."

Sydney sighs wistfully. "Yeah, there's nothing sexier than a guy who likes animals."

Freedom

We both jump when we hear the sound of a throat clearing behind us. "Umm … would you feel better if I came back?"

"No, that's not necessary. Dr. Austin was just about to tell me what's wrong with your Bruiser."

Sydney's curls bounce as she looks at me with surprise. "I was?" When she sees my look of consternation, she adds, "Oh yes, I was."

Phoenix stuffs his hands in his pockets and waits expectantly.

Sydney looks at Phoenix. "I didn't have a chance to introduce myself, I'm Dr. Austin. I understand that Bruiser is your dog."

Phoenix shakes his head. "No, I don't know this dog. I just saw him get hurt."

"Oh, in that case, I probably need to scan for a microchip," Sydney removes a portable scanner from her bag.

We all wait with tense expressions on our faces as she scans Bruiser. After a few moments, Sydney says, "Unfortunately, this pup does not have a microchip. After I get him cleaned up, I'll take a picture and post it on the local lost-and-found boards."

"Is he going to last that long?" Phoenix asks as he looks over at Bruiser.

Sydney nods. "I think he will. He seems to have an angel sitting on his shoulder because dog versus motor vehicle collisions rarely go well. It looks as if he only has bruising around his rib cage and the one laceration. I can stitch that up here, or we can go back to The Critter Clinic. I don't know what you guys plan to do with him —"

Sydney and I look over at Phoenix. He puts his hands up in front of him in protest. "Don't look at me. I don't know what to do with him. I'm on a motorcycle. I can't take him. I'm on my way to Oregon." Phoenix wrings his hands. "Maybe I shouldn't have rescued him if he's going to be homeless."

I whirl around to face him. "Do you realize Hope's Haven is a rescue organization? We take dogs all the time. Many are in worse shape than Bruiser. I train them to be service dogs or search and rescue dogs. I can't believe you were so quick to give up on him."

"What? I never said I gave up on him. I don't want him to be homeless and end up at a shelter. They might kill him there."

"Not if we have anything to say about it," I look at Sydney. "We can board him here if he doesn't need additional support."

"He seems to be coming out of his state of shock. His injuries don't look severe. I can take x-rays if you'd feel more comfortable, but he doesn't seem to be having any trouble walking down your hall. Even the bleeding from his laceration seems better. I'll still take time to stitch it up just so it heals evenly."

"Bruiser was really out of it on the side of the road. Is he likely to relapse? If you think he needs physical therapy, I can pay for that," Phoenix offers.

"It's possible he was just very frightened and his fear contributed to his symptoms. He isn't having any trouble breathing and doesn't appear to be in distress. I think having the fluids onboard from the IV has helped. If he's homeless, he might have just been dehydrated."

Phoenix moves closer to Bruiser and starts to stroke

his head. "Would it be possible for me to stay with him tonight just to make sure he's okay?"

Phoenix's about-face confuses me. How could he say he almost wished that he didn't rescue Bruiser and then suddenly be so concerned he can't leave his side?

"I don't know. I'll have to check with my boss. Right now, Dr. Austin needs to stitch up Bruiser before we do anything else."

Phoenix looks in Sydney's direction but does not make eye contact. "This is where I make my exit. I don't deal well with blood and guts."

Sydney chuckles. "Well, unless something goes terribly wrong, there won't be any guts involved in this one. I simply have to fix this flesh wound."

"Blood is not my thing," Phoenix answers with a shudder. "I'm going to see if I can find a taxi to take me back to my bike. When I get back, we can talk about where I'm going to stay." Addressing us both, he says, "Thank you so much for fixing him." There's something odd about the way he says that phrase as if it's somehow rehearsed.

"I'm just happy I could help and that it didn't turn out to be more serious," Sydney answers with a smile.

"Me too," Phoenix answers. "It looked dire there for a while."

"Don't you worry, we'll take good care of him at Hope's Haven. It's what we do. We take dogs people have thrown away and give them a chance to be productive and active." Pivoting back toward Sydney, I ask, "Do you know how old this dog might be?"

"Based on his teeth, I'd say he's less than a year old," Sydney answers as she takes out a suture kit and lays it on the tray next to the table.

When Phoenix sees the needle, he blanches. "Okay, that's my cue to leave, I'll be back later." He quickly leaves the grooming room. I hear the bells from our front door ring as he exits Hope's Haven.

Sydney cleans and stitches the laceration. I used to help out a vet tech when I was in high school. I stand at the head of the table and keep Bruiser distracted while she works. It is silent while Sydney finishes suturing the laceration. When she is done, she moistens a blue towel and cleans Bruiser up as best as she can without disturbing him. "I wouldn't want to traumatize your biker guy with Bruiser's blood," she says with amusement. "In vet school, it was always the guys who claimed to be the toughest who were the first to face-plant during anatomy and physiology classes."

"I don't know what to think about Phoenix. He's just so odd. See what I mean about his conversations not making a lot of sense?" I ask as Sydney strips off her gloves and picks up the wrappers from her equipment.

She shrugs. "He's a little unorthodox. But, I've dated guys who were way stranger than Phoenix. At least he seems to have his heart in the right place."

"I wonder if he's just really shy or has anxiety or something." I theorize.

Sydney looks thoughtful. "That's a possibility, but he reminds me a lot of my cousin. My cousin has Asperger's syndrome. He does that thing with his eyes. Sometimes it feels like he's staring right past me."

I take the hairband out of my hair and form a new ponytail. "You know, that would make sense. He told me he has a hard time looking at people he doesn't know well. In a weird way, he reminds me of Ketki."

"I don't know for sure; it just seemed that way to me," Sydney cautions.

"Oh, I would never say anything to him. I was just trying to figure out why our interaction seemed so strange. I wonder if I should let him stay with Bruiser."

"That's a question I can't answer for you. It all depends on how comfortable you feel around him."

"I can stay at Mitch and Jessica's place. That's not a problem. I'm not worried that he'll do anything to Hope's Haven. Tristan has this place decked out with monitored security cameras."

"I know you think he's cute. Are you going to be able to resist the temptation?" Sydney teases with a wink.

"Oh! Heck yes! I have sworn off guys and relationships forever. I'm done."

Sydney's eyebrows fly up in surprise. "Why would you say something like that? You are so young and beautiful."

I grimace and sigh. "Let's get Bruiser into a kennel. After we get him settled, I'll explain."

"Wow! There must be quite a story."

"You have no idea."

"This sounds serious. Are we going to need something stronger than soda to have this discussion?"

I shake my head. "I've been there and done that. I'm all out of tears. Now, I'm just mad."

I spread chicken salad on croissants and grab some chips. I walk over to the table where Sydney is sitting and give her a plate. "I made you work through lunch, so I better feed you."

"I appreciate it, but it's not necessary. I work through lunch a lot. So, you were going to tell me why the biker dude is not a temptation."

"I forget you were new in town when all this happened. My big brother Vincent is about to go on trial for kidnapping and rape."

"Oh no! Are you going to testify for him?"

"No. In fact, I have been subpoenaed by the prosecution. It's pretty much torn my whole family apart."

"Gee, that's too bad. It's not like you have a choice about testifying."

"You have no idea how hard this is for me. I grew up idolizing my big brother. In my eyes, he could do no wrong. Now, I have to testify against him."

Concern fills Sydney's eyes. "Did he ever do anything to you? I know that sometimes abuse can start in the family."

"No. Thank goodness he never touched me — at least not physically. I didn't know what he was doing to other women until after Katelyn ditched him at the altar. That was the beginning of the end of my brother. I don't know if he had a psychotic break or if he just hid it really well before the facade of his happy relationship crumpled."

"Did he hurt Katelyn?"

"I don't know. There was an ugly scene at the

wedding. Vinnie was trying to get her to come out of the bathroom and said horrible things to her. I hate to think about it, but if he would do that in public, who knows what he did to her in private?"

"Yeah, it's hard to know what people do in private."

"So, if my big brother can do something like that, how do I trust any guy?"

"I know it's hard to imagine it right now, but not all guys are total creeps."

"I understand that, but I'm not sure I'm ready to play the odds if you know what I mean. I think I'll just stay around here and work with dogs. At least they don't lie."

"I don't blame you. I'd be cautious too. So, what does that mean for Phoenix?"

I shrug. "I wish I knew. Phoenix seems safe — then again so did my brother before he kidnapped a girl and held her hostage. On the other hand, doesn't seem fair to punish Phoenix for things my brother did. I just wish there were easy answers."

"I don't know if this makes it any easier, but I generally have a pretty strong sense about people. Phoenix seems like one of the good guys. Even though he may seem a little strange, I don't get the feeling he's dangerous. Still, if you decide to let him stay, I would give Tristan a heads up so he can monitor Hope's Haven a little more carefully when Phoenix is around."

"That's a good idea. Tristan might loan me one of his guys in training. I think Mitch told me Tristan has a bunch of new employees at Identity Bank. Maybe he can spare someone to stick close to me."

I feel a little ridiculous making this call. I've only met Tristan once when he came to the celebration of Darya and Dr. Stuart's engagement. Still, if this debacle with my brother has shown me anything, it's that you can't always judge a book by its cover — or a guy by his manners. After Tristan picks up the phone, I attempt to articulate my request. "Hey, I've heard you have some new employees at Identity Bank. Would you be able to spare a couple of them to keep an eye on me?"

"What's going on Ms. Hurlington? Is there something I need to know? We monitor your feed from your surveillance cameras. Do we need to step it up a little?"

"You'll probably think I'm paranoid, but we've got a client who wants to stay and check on the recovery of a dog. Mitch and Jess are out of town. I'd just feel better if someone was watching my back," I answer.

"You want me to run a background check on this guy?"

"Umm … I don't know if I want to go that far. Wait. I think I do want you to run a background check on him because I'm not sure he gave me his real name."

"I see. If your gut is telling you something is off about this guy, you definitely need me to do a background check. What is his name?"

"Get this — his name is Phoenix Wolf," I answer skeptically.

After a couple of beats of silence, Tristan says, "Well, I don't have to run a background check on Mr. Wolf. I have a recent one in his personnel file. Mr. Wolf is one of my most talented game debuggers."

I sink down on the couch in disbelief. "Are you sure? This guy has long blonde hair. It's probably longer than mine."

Tristan chuckles. "Yep, that's him. He's supposed to be on his way to Identity Bank West. I wonder what happened. Last I talked to him, he had everything planned meticulously."

"Phoenix witnessed a collision between a motor vehicle and a dog. He's formed an attachment to Bruiser and would like to watch his progress."

"Phoenix has worked for me for a while. Although he is shy and awkward, I don't perceive any danger from him. However, if you'd like I can still send a couple of my guys over."

I chew on my fingernail. "I don't know if it's necessary. If you know Phoenix and can vouch for him it makes me feel better. Besides, if he's so shy, the additional people around will be hard for him. He is already nervous enough about the health of Bruiser. I don't want to make this any more difficult for him."

"Okay, I'll monitor things remotely for now. I might send Nick over to do a cursory check on things to make sure everything is fine."

"Thank you so much. I appreciate it."

"It's the least I can do. You do great work at Hope's Haven. I'll send you pictures of the guys I'm assigning to you so you know they're supposed to be around."

"In case no one told you this lately, you're a life saver. I'm sure Bruiser will be grateful. He's quite attached to Phoenix."

CHAPTER THREE

PHOENIX

"CRAP!" I MURMUR UNDER my breath. This is the second time I've entered a room while Zoe is talking about me. My timing sucks. I back out of the room and make some noise with my keys as I reenter.

Zoe looks startled as she puts her phone down on the table. "That didn't take very long. Was everything okay?"

"Yeah, it's fine. I'm surprised. I figured someone would try to take my bike. Apparently, no one saw it."

"That's good. Hey, I thought you said you were headed to Oregon. You didn't mention you work for Identity Bank."

My throat tightens before I choke out an answer, "No, I didn't. So, how do you find out?"

This time it's Zoe who looks away. She reaches down to pick up a paper towel which had fallen on the floor during Bruiser's treatment. Finally, she meets my gaze. "I called Tristan about some security stuff here at the training facility. I had no idea you worked there. Your name just came up in conversation."

"Somehow I find that hard to believe. Tristan runs a multimillion dollar company. He has no reason to talk about me. He couldn't possibly know you and I met."

Zoe blushes. "Okay, you're right. I called him to see if he wouldn't mind checking in on me. I'm a little nervous about having someone I don't know stay at Hope's Haven."

"Why didn't you say something when I asked you if I could stay?"

"I don't know. Things seem pretty awkward between us and I didn't want to make them worse."

"I know I look scary because of the long hair and the motorcycle clothes, but basically I'm just a boring, nerdy computer programmer. I'm sorry if I made you feel uncomfortable. I seem to do that a lot."

"Please don't think it's you. I have a lot of drama in my life right now. It's shaking me to the core. I'm a little more frightened of the world these days."

"I can stay somewhere else. Keep an eye on Bruiser for me," I offer. I don't know what to say. Zoe and I seem like flint and steel. Even normal topics of conversation seem to be contentious.

"No, you are welcome to stay here. Tristan vouched for you and said you are a decent guy. I'll take his word for it."

"If you're sure you don't mind, I'll do my best to stay out of your way. I want to make sure Bruiser makes it through the night. I feel oddly responsible for him."

"Many rescuers feel the same way. I know it's hard for me to let a dog go after I've trained it for months. They worm their way into your heart."

"That's interesting. I've been accused of not having a heart," I reveal.

"Why is that?" Zoe asks with a look of trepidation.

I swallow hard. "It's sometimes hard for me to interact with people. Most of the time, they think I don't care."

Zoe gives me a small smile. "I can relate. I would much rather be friends with a dog or cat any day."

"I have a dog. Her name is Gizmo. I had to leave her with my parents because I'm going to Oregon."

"Really? What kind of dog is Gizmo?"

"No one is sure. We found her wandering through my yard. We couldn't find her owner, so she ended up staying with me. I think she's some type of Border Collie, but she has something else too."

"Border Collies are really smart."

"I'm not sure Gizmo was blessed with smart genes. She is a little clueless. She can't figure out how to walk on a leash without getting tangled up."

"When you come back from Oregon, you should sign up for one of Mitch's dog training classes. He can probably get her straightened out."

"Would there be other people in the class?"

"Mitch usually has a small group of students when he offers a class."

I run my hand through my hair and untangle it from my collar. "Yeah, it's probably not my scene. I'm more of a one-on-one person."

Zoe scrutinizes me. "You said that before. What's wrong with you?"

Her bold question takes me by surprise. It's been years since somebody has asked me directly, most of the time they murmur behind my back. People are strange. They equate being shy and private with not being able to hear. I can tell you — those are two very different things.

I take a few moments to formulate a response. It's just that people tend to get weirded out when I tell them my story. Eventually, I decide I have nothing to lose. In a couple of days, I'll be out of here and probably never see Zoe again. It doesn't matter if she knows.

"Have you ever heard of Asperger's Syndrome? It's on the autism spectrum."

"Of course, I know about Asperger's. Haven't you met Ketki? She has autism too. She helps Tristan test software. I figured the two of you would work together all the time."

"What you mean by that?"

Zoe puts her hands up in front of her in protest. "Nothing! I don't mean anything bad by it. I'm just saying Ketki is working with Tristan and her step-dad, John, on making Tristan's games more accessible. She told me all about it when she was here the last time."

"I keep to myself and Identity Bank. That's one of the things I like about my job. It's just me and the computer. But, what you're saying makes sense to me because Tristan keeps telling me to meet other people within the company. Do you think he might have meant Ketki?"

"I don't know the answer to that. I don't hang out with Tristan a bunch. Tristan and Rogue are good friends with my boss — but I don't socialize with them often. Can't you just ask Tristan who he'd like you to meet?"

I sag against the wall. Feeling it against my back helps ground me. The fluorescent lights in the exam room are distracting me, and I'm having a hard time focusing on the conversation.

"Come on, let's go check on Bruiser in his kennel and grab something to eat," Zoe says before I have a chance to answer her question.

She leads me to a separate part of the building. At first, I am relieved to have the distraction. Then, she opens the door to the kennel room. I am assaulted with the sound of excited dogs barking and the smell of wet dog.

Zoe waves me into the room. "Come on; I put Bruiser back in the corner so he would have some privacy."

I stand frozen in the doorway unable to move.

"Phoenix, are you listening? I said you could come on in. The dogs are all caged, no one's gonna bite you," she quips.

"I can't," I hoarsely whisper.

"I thought you said you had a dog. I didn't expect you to be afraid of them," Zoe comments with a puzzled expression on her face.

"I'm not afraid of dogs!" I feel my face turn hot with embarrassment.

"Then what's the problem?" Zoe asks.

I stuff my hands in my pockets and rub my fingers over the golf ball I keep in my pocket. Rubbing on the bumpy surface helps distract my brain from the assault of sensory information. Taking a deep breath, I answer, "What isn't the problem? The dogs are so loud I can't think. One of these dogs must've been sprayed by a skunk. The lights are blinking. Can't you see that?"

"Oh! I'm so sorry. I should've thought about all that. Why don't you come into one of the adoption rooms? I'll see if Bruiser is up to seeing you. You should have said something I wouldn't have ever brought you back here. It's noisy even for me."

"This is why I don't hang out with other people," I admit, my voice laced with frustration. "This kind of stuff trips me up all the time. I know you probably think I'm totally weird. I guess all I can tell you is I'm not typical. That's why they call us neuro-atypical."

"Okay. I get it. Let me get you into a quieter space."

Zoe touches my elbow to guide me to the other room. My senses are completely overwhelmed. I flinch when she touches me.

"I'm sorry," Zoe mutters. "You didn't seem to mind when I touched you when we were working with Bruiser earlier."

"When I'm stressed, things are more overwhelming. Like you said earlier, it's not personal. I apologize for bothering you. I think I should probably just go."

"Where can you go?" Zoe asks. "In case you haven't noticed, we're having a rainstorm. That can't be good for your bike. You might as well stay until it lets up."

"I don't know if I can. I'm hanging on by my fingernails here."

Zoe opens the door to a small room. There is a large, overstuffed leather couch and a box of dog toys in the room. Instead of florescent lights, there is an old-fashioned looking lamp with a stained glass. The walls are painted a dark red color and there is a portrait of a German Shepherd wearing a service vest.

I take a deep breath and let it out. I shake out my

hands and relax. "This is much better. Thank you."

"This is the room we named after Hope. It's my favorite room too. Sometimes if we're not busy I'll sneak in here on my lunch hour and just read a book."

"Is Hope the owner?" I ask, curious about the idea of naming rooms.

Zoe giggles. "I guess it depends on who you ask. She is the four-legged founder of Hope's Haven. But, Mitch and Jessica actually own it."

"Oh, I see. I feel stupid for asking such a dumb question."

"It's okay — not everybody knows our back story. Jessica brought Hope to Mitch when she was injured. The two of them fell in love and got married. They just had a baby."

Small talk doesn't come easily to me. Zoe seems to sense I don't have anything else to say. She stands up and heads toward the door. "I'm going to go check on Bruiser. If he's up to walking around, I'll bring him in here so you can say good night."

"That's great. Thank you," I respond as I rest my head against the back of the couch.

After Zoe leaves the room, I put my hand back in my jacket pocket and work my golf ball over. I remember when my mom first got me worry beads. I used them so much, they were constantly breaking. As a joke, my dad said the most durable thing he could think of was a golf ball. As silly as the idea seemed, it turned out to be the most effective solution.

I don't know how to answer Zoe's question about why I don't just ask my boss what he needs from me. A million thoughts hit my head at the same time and I am too stressed to sort them out right now. I can't believe I actually told Zoe about myself. It's not something I typically explain. I don't know if she understands anything — but it seems like she might.

Before I can get too lost in my thoughts, I hear the sound of Zoe coming down the hall and an odd sound I can't identify. Zoe knocks softly on the door as she asks, "Are you ready for us?"

"I think I am," I respond.

Zoe opens the door and then maneuvers a child's wagon into the room. "I didn't know how much walking Bruiser should do, so I improvised. We use these wagons to carry around dog food."

I smile. "That was a good idea."

As soon Bruiser hears my voice, he gingerly jumps out of the wagon and climbs onto the couch. He lays his head in my lap and lets out a heavy breath.

"Look at that! He knows who helped save him." Zoe grins.

"Do you think that's actually true?" I reach down and stroke Bruiser's ears. They are so soft.

"I think it's true. Rescue dogs have something a little extra special. I don't know I might be reading into things, but they seem more grateful than other dogs."

I continue to stroke Bruiser's head. "That's weird. You wouldn't think a dog would understand something that complex."

"Hang around me a couple of days, and I'll show you all the things they can learn. I teach dogs to be the eyes for people who cannot see, the ears for people who can't hear, and to be the legs for people who cannot walk. I also teach dogs to find the lost and to comfort those who are left alone in the world," Zoe explains poetically.

Bruiser licks my hand and nudges me to pet him some more. "I wish you could train a dog to help me. Maybe if I was more normal, I wouldn't have to find a new place to work."

"I'll be right back," Zoe says abruptly. "I'm starving, and this sounds like a long conversation."

"Umm, okay," I stammer in the direction of Zoe's retreating back. I look down at Bruiser and ask, "Was it something I said?"

Bruiser just lays his head back down on my lap. I thought maybe he would follow Zoe. Maybe he's staying put because he doesn't feel well. As I'm waiting for Zoe to return, my stomach growls audibly. It has been a long time since I've eaten. Maybe that's why I have a persistent headache.

For a few minutes, I just sit there and stroke Bruiser. Something about the soft texture of his ears and the way he responds to my touch seems to take the edge off my stress. I'll be sorry when I have to say goodbye. I have to keep in mind that I have three thousand miles and twenty-eight days to get there. I don't know what I'll do once I get to Oregon, but I need to stick to some sort of plan.

Zoe enters the room as abruptly as she left. To be honest, it startles both Bruiser and me.

Zoe spreads a blanket out on the floor of the room. When she's finished, she digs through a large grocery sack. "I'm sorry, all I had was whole-wheat bread. But, I have peanut butter and jelly or egg salad. Which would you prefer?"

Freedom

"What do you mean?" I ask, baffled by her actions.

"We're having a picnic. What do you think it was?"

"I don't know. That's why I asked."

"You've never had a picnic before? Even when you were a little kid you didn't make blanket forts in the living room with your friends and have a picnic in the middle of a blanket?"

"No, definitely not, my mom is a huge germaphobe. She would never allow food to get that close to the floor."

Zoe's brows crease. "That's too bad. Picnics are fun. Come see what I brought. I've got sandwiches, chips, and some lemonade." She pats the blanket in front of her. "Come on down. There's lots of room. I can't eat all this food myself."

"I need to wash my hands. I've been petting the dog. You should always wash your hands after you pet a dog."

Zoe giggles. "Do you think I'd disagree with that? The bathroom is down the hall and to the left. We even have antibacterial soap."

I get up to leave and Bruiser follows me. I look toward Zoe as I try to figure out what to do.

She shrugs. "If he feels well enough to walk, Sydney didn't say he couldn't. She simply didn't want him to be jumping around and playing with other dogs."

"Is it okay if he leaves this room?"

"If it's all right with Bruiser, it's all right with me."

"Don't I need a leash or something?"

Zoe gracefully gets up from the ground. "If there's one thing we have around here, it's leashes of all shapes and sizes. I'll go get you one."

I stand and wait as Zoe leaves the room. Fortunately, she's back before I can over-think my situation.

"Just hold this loosely at your side so Bruiser knows where you want him. He might pull at first, but we can fix that on another day."

Zoe reaches down and connects a bright red leash to Bruiser's collar. His tail wags with anticipation. He seems to think something great is going to happen. I can't help but grin at the happy expression on his face. "I'm sorry to disappoint you, Bruiser. I'm not going anyplace exciting. I'm just going to go to the restroom."

"Did he try to get up when I left the room the first time?" Zoe asks with the contemplative look on her face.

"No, he just kind of took a nap on my lap," I respond as Bruisers sits. He is looking up at me expectantly.

"Lucky you! It looks like Bruiser has chosen his human being and you are it."

Chapter Four

Zoe

AFTER PHOENIX LEAVES THE room, I take a deep breath and blow it out. I've never met anyone who doesn't understand the concept of a picnic. Maybe it's a gender thing. I used to get together with my friends and hold picnics and tea parties. I thought everyone did that kind of stuff — but maybe not.

I appear to have issues connecting with Phoenix. Fortunately, Bruiser seems to have dialed into his wavelength. Honestly, I'm surprised. Many of the stray dogs who come into Hope's Haven are scared of men. The same can't be said for Bruiser. It's clear Bruiser is Phoenix's number one fan. I probably should have supervised the trip to the bathroom, but I didn't want to crowd Phoenix. Even if my decision was a mistake, I can't very well go chasing after him without it being obvious I am checking up on them.

I resume setting out the food. It's an odd thing to pack dinner for someone you don't know. Hopefully, I guessed right.

Phoenix and Bruiser come back in the room. I'm almost afraid that Bruiser belongs to someone. He has great leash manners. Unfortunately for Phoenix, it probably means Bruiser is not a true stray dog. Maybe he jumped out of the back of someone's pickup or escaped from a local tractor which was pulled over on the side of the road.

"Did everything go well?" I ask Phoenix.

"Well, it wasn't exactly rocket science, I just went to wash my hands."

"That's true — but you and Bruiser don't know each other well and sometimes it takes a while to develop that kind of partnership."

"It was fine. You could've told me there is a cat running around the building though."

I slap my forehead in frustration. "You know, in all the drama of today. I completely forgot about Firecracker. Sorry about that. How did Bruiser do?"

"He did okay, I guess. He was a little startled by the cat. But, then again so was I."

"That's a good sign. At least he is not aggressive toward cats. That will make it easier to find an adoptive home for him if we can't locate his owners."

"You wouldn't let him go back to the people who allowed him to run on the freeway, would you?"

"I don't know. The decision wouldn't be mine. That would be something that Dr. Austin and Mitch would determine."

"Well, if they threw him away like yesterday's garbage, they shouldn't be allowed to have animals."

"Since we don't know who he belongs to, we don't know what happened. I guess time will tell. Are you going to come in and have something to eat?" I ask as Bruiser and Phoenix stand in the doorway.

"What should I do with the dog?" Phoenix asks.

"Bring him with you," I instruct. "It's never too early to teach table manners."

"Seriously? Gizmo would eat everything in sight."

"You definitely need to get her into some obedience training. I suspect that Bruiser here already has the basics down. His heel command and leash manners are impeccable."

"I don't know if I should be happy or sad about that. Hopefully, if he has good owners, you'll be able to find them."

"If he has a human family out there, they're probably missing him. I'll ask Dr. Austin to put the word out to other local vet clinics."

Phoenix shortens up the leash and walks Bruiser over to the couch. "Up!" he commands.

Bruiser gingerly climbs up on the couch and lies down as he wags his tail enthusiastically.

"Good job!" I compliment. "Sometimes when dogs are in pain, they forget their training. Bruiser seems to listen to you well despite his injuries."

Phoenix shrugs. "I watch a lot of Animal Planet. I guess I picked up some tips along the way."

I hold out a paper plate I got from the break room while Phoenix was washing his hands. I place a bag of chips on the side of it and pick up a sandwich. I look up at Phoenix and ask, "PB & J or egg salad?"

"Please don't do that," Phoenix says with an anguished expression.

"Do what? I thought you were hungry."

Phoenix scrubs his hand down his face. "I am hungry, that's why I don't want you to put my sandwich next to other food. I have a weird thing about my food touching. It stresses me out."

"Really? They're just on the same plate; they're not even touching."

"Oh, I know. But they could touch. I suppose it's a lot like other people when they hear obnoxious sounds like fingernails on a chalkboard. If my food is touching, I find it hard to concentrate on anything else."

"Wow! How do you eat out at a restaurant?"

"I don't go often," he admits.

"Isn't that going to make it difficult for you to be on a road trip? It's not like you can carry around a refrigerator on your motorcycle."

Phoenix lowers himself to the ground, but he seems uncertain about what to do next. "I figure I'll have to be careful about ordering."

"I don't want to stress you out any more than you already have been today. So, feel free to use as many plates as you want to," I answer as I gesture to the stack of plates.

"Are you sure?" Phoenix asks.

I nod. "Knock yourself out. We have plenty."

"Thank you for not making me feel weird about this. A lot of people think if I just try it a few times, it won't be a big deal."

"Well, that's rude!" I exclaim as I hand him a bowl of grapes.

Phoenix takes a sandwich, some grapes and a bag of Doritos. He puts one item on each plate. Much to my surprise, Bruiser is peacefully sleeping on the couch. His soft snore sounds loud in the quiet room. Phoenix picks up a peanut butter and jelly sandwich and takes a bite.

"It's grape. I like grape jelly."

I smile. "I like it too. My favorite is apricot. My brother says I'm not normal. He says normal people like strawberry jelly."

"At least you're not as weird as me." Phoenix shrugs. "I don't think people know how much I wish I could do normal things. I wish there was some kind of service dog for autism."

"There are dogs like that. They haven't gained as much popularity as hearing dogs or guide dogs for the blind. However, they can be a lifesaver," I explain.

"What does a service dog for autism do? It's not like a dog could help me understand social situations, and he couldn't make me stop being weird about food," Phoenix argues.

"Maybe not, but when you start getting upset and uptight, I can train a dog to distract you. Many people with autism who have service dogs find it's easier to interact with people because you have a ready topic of conversation. Nearly everyone loves dogs and will talk about them with no prompting. It takes the stress off of you having to come up with something to say."

"Sometimes, that would be nice — especially at work. I'm notoriously bad at small talk. People think I'm rude, but I'm really not. When I talk to people I don't know well, I can get distracted by what they're wearing, their aftershave or perfume, or if they need a haircut. It makes it hard for me to concentrate on what they're saying. If people are joking between themselves, it's even harder. Sometimes I have trouble figuring out whether something is supposed to be funny."

"That must be hard. It reminds me of when I was in school and the teacher would have kids from the class read aloud in front of everyone. I hated it because I'm dyslexic and I can't read well. I'm also painfully shy in a group. So, reading in front of people was my nightmare. I used to try to get out of class by going to the nurses office just so I wouldn't have to face the shame of reading like a kindergartner."

"I can't imagine being dyslexic. It would make my job very hard."

"Yeah, it does. I also have dyscalculia which means entering sales into a cash register and making change is hard for me too."

"Wow! I love math so much I automatically do it in my head."

I shake my head in disbelief. "Well, you are welcome to all the numbers because I don't get along very well with them. Now you know why I am a dog trainer."

"Maybe you're not as normal as I thought you were," Phoenix observes.

I laugh as I lift my hair off my neck to show him a neon blue swatch of my hair. "No one has ever accused me of being normal. This is toned down from how I usually wear it. I decided if I was representing Hope's Haven, I should fit in a little better."

"But, you're different because you choose to be," Phoenix counters with a shrug.

I sigh. "Not always. Anyway if I could train you a dog to work with your autism, would you be interested?"

Phoenix puts down his plate and fiddles with the strings which tie off the quilt. "I don't know. I don't know if I'm ever coming back to Florida."

"Why? I thought you worked for Tristan. He says you are one of his most valuable employees."

"You could've fooled me. I think he's sending me to Oregon so he can fire me. He doesn't seem very happy with the way I relate to my coworkers. He said I need to interact more. I don't know if he understands. It's not like I can just turn the autism off when I'm at work. It's too bad though, because I really liked my job."

Choosing my words carefully, I respond. "I don't know Tristan all that well, but he doesn't seem to be that kind of guy. He has people with disabilities who work for him. John Ashford is blind. He has one of our guide dogs, Tuffy."

"I don't know what to think. He is opening a whole new branch of Identity Bank in Oregon. He wants me to check it out to see if I would like to work there."

"Is Tristan demoting you?" I ask skeptically.

"No, that's the weird part. He told me about all the things I needed to fix during my performance evaluation, but then he said I deserved a promotion. After the meeting was over, he told me it had been too long since my last vacation and ordered me to take some time off."

"I'm guessing that's why you're traveling across the United States on a motorcycle?"

"Yeah … um … I don't really fly."

"I understand. I don't like to fly much either," I say with a shudder. "I think you should ask Tristan what he meant by his suggestions. What little I know of Tristan, I think he probably meant to give you a promotion. Do you want to go to Oregon?"

My question seems to stop Phoenix cold. For several moments, he is silent. Bruiser must be able to sense something because he climbs off the couch and puts his head in Phoenix's lap. Phoenix reaches out and strokes his ears. "I don't know the answer to that."

"Then why are you on your bike headed across the United States?"

Phoenix shrugs as he continues to pet Bruiser. "I didn't want to tick off my boss. He already seemed like he was upset with my performance. I didn't want to give him another reason to fire me. I like my job."

"I don't know — it seems pretty drastic to ride clear across the United States to check out a job you don't actually want."

"I'm not sure if I want the job. But, this trip is more than just about that. It's about challenging myself to do things I haven't done before — you know like we talked about ordering food in a restaurant and not following a specific map calculated down to the tenth of a mile."

"I'm impressed. I don't know if I could just take off on a road trip. I really wish I could right about now. Things in my personal life are a complete mess," I remark wistfully.

"What's wrong?"

"Just nasty family stuff I would like to make disappear. I wish I could go back in time before I knew any of this stuff was going on."

"We could rent you a bike. You could come with me."

I gather up the remnants of our picnic lunch.

"You have no idea how much I wish I could say yes to that. Unfortunately, I have to stick around to testify against my brother."

Freedom

Phoenix's eyes widen. "Why?"

I throw away our garbage and then sit back down on the blanket. I hug my knees to my chest. "I don't know why I'm telling you this, but maybe I just need to talk to a decent human being. My family is redefining the word horrible right now. Each conversation is more frustrating than the last."

Phoenix regards me silently as he waits for me to continue.

"So, I'll tell you about it — even if you don't really want to hear it."

"I asked," Phoenix responds succinctly.

"Don't say I didn't warn you." I smile weakly. "This is long, ugly and painful."

Phoenix nods before he takes a drink of his soda.

"Okay, I told you that I have an older brother named Vincent. Most of us call him Vinnie although he recently chewed us all out for using his nickname. He considers himself a serious business person and wants to be known by his full name. Anyway, Vinnie was supposed to marry this woman named Katie. On his wedding day, he seemed to go absolutely crazy because Katie was wearing an ivory dress instead of a white one. Understandably, she decided she didn't want to marry my brother. The police tell me he was trolling underage girls online and tried to kidnap one to be his wife after Katie said no."

"Why would he do that?" Phoenix asks.

"I don't know! My whole childhood I worshipped the ground Vincent walked on. He is about seven years older than me and I thought everything he did was cool and amazing. This behavior makes no sense to me. I don't know when my brother turned into a creepy abuser."

"Was he that way when he was younger?"

"I'm not sure about that either. He and I never went to the same school together because he is so much older than me." I answer. But even as I say those words, I remember the gossip. "Whenever I would tell anyone Vinnie was my brother, people would get a strange, guarded expression on their face. Almost without fail, someone would ask me, 'Are you all right?' I didn't understand why everyone reacted that way."

"When did you put all the pieces together?" Phoenix asks. "I mean, you must've made a decision about him since you are testifying against him."

"I don't want to testify against Vinnie, but it's the right thing to do. He can't go around hurting people. That's wrong. I guess after I asked him about it and he dodged and denied my questions, I found Katie's story to be more believable. I remember the sidelong glances teachers would give me at school. Finally, I asked one of my friends to ask her older brother what it was all about. He told my friend that Vinnie had a reputation for slapping his dates around. I was shocked! This was the first time I had heard anything about Vinnie hurting people. My brother can be uptight and pious, but I never thought he would hurt someone."

"Sometimes, people surprise us, and it's not always good."

"Tell me about it. When I tried to ask my brother about it, he made it sound like the girls and women deserved what he had done. I couldn't believe he said something like that. No one deserves what he did to that poor young girl. He tried to force her to marry him. Who does that? I don't even recognize my brother anymore. He's not the hero I grew up with."

"I take it your parents have sided with your brother?"

I nod as I wipe away a tear. "Yeah, in a big way. Everyone is mad at me because I'm going to testify to what I know and what I overheard at the wedding. My mother especially thinks it's unseemly for me to tell the story publicly. My parents have a great deal of standing in the local community and they find this whole matter completely embarrassing."

"They should probably be mad at your brother for assaulting women."

I nod vigorously. "Exactly! You'd think so, right? But that's not the way they're taking it. Even though they were at the wedding too and saw what unfolded, they've rallied around Vinnie. I am the person who is on the outs even though I did nothing wrong. It makes me not want to trust anybody — especially the people I love."

"I can't say I blame you," Phoenix says. His eyes are filled with pain.

Bruiser climbs out of Phoenix's lap and comes over to me to lick my face. "At this point, the only creatures I trust on the planet are my dogs. I don't believe in anyone else. I probably never will," I admit before tears flow down my face.

Chapter Five

Phoenix

"WAKE UP, SLEEPY HEAD!" Zoe greets me through the closed door. "Bruiser wants to take a walk."

I'm groggy as I sit up and look around. I can't believe I fell asleep here. Usually, strange environments make me so edgy I can't rest. Yet, I seem at peace in this room. "I'll be right out." Quickly, I shuck my jogging pants and put on jeans and a T-shirt.

I roll up my sleeping bag and put my backpack over my shoulder. I awkwardly make my way past Zoe and Bruiser in the doorway. "I'm going to stop by the bathroom first," I announce and then cringe. Zoe probably didn't need to know that.

I quickly do the rest of my morning routine and meet them by the door to the dog yard. "Good morning. Wow! Bruiser looks a lot better this morning."

"I think the anti-inflammatory Dr. Austin put him on is helping. You're right. He's much perkier this morning. He is definitely ready for a walk."

When he hears the word walk, Bruiser sits at my feet.

"He sure is well-behaved. I bet he belongs to someone." I stroke Bruiser's head and attach the leash to his collar.

"I called some of the local vets and the rescue organizations around town. No one is familiar with Bruiser."

"Did you check online? Sometimes there are Lost and Found groups," I suggest.

Zoe nods. "Yeah, I spent quite a bit of time scouring the Internet this morning while I was drinking my coffee. So far, nothing."

I know I should probably feel terrible about the fact that we can't find Bruiser's family. Instead, I feel relieved.

"Do you think someone dumped him out of the vehicle on the highway? I didn't see anyone on the side of the road or anything."

Zoe shrugs. "Who knows? I've seen stranger things happen."

Bruiser whines to remind us we are supposed to be walking. I snap my fingers and Bruiser comes around and sits by my left side.

"What a good boy!" Zoe exclaims as she opens the back door. "I don't think Bruiser is a runner. But just in case, today we'll walk inside the fence."

As we walk by a bucket of tennis balls, Bruiser's ears perk up. I look up at Zoe and ask, "Can I toss him a few?"

"Nope. Remember Dr. Austin said Bruiser needed to take it easy because of the possibility he might have internal bruising?"

I stop and look at Bruiser. "Sorry, buddy you need to heal up a little before we can play."

Bruiser's ears droop comically. I glance up at Zoe. "Now I feel bad."

"Just think how happy he'll be once he gets a chance

to run and play again. It sounds like you and Bruiser would make a good pair."

I sigh. "I wish I could. But I have to get on the road to Oregon. Who knows how long I'll be there. Besides, I've already got Gizmo at home. I don't know if she would want to share me."

Zoe holds up her hand to catch raindrops. "Are you sure you want to take off today? It seems like it's going to be nasty out here. Look at all those black clouds."

"I've got rain gear," I explain. "If I postpone my trip every time there's bad weather, I would never get to Oregon. I've got two thousand nine hundred and twenty miles to ride."

As we walk around the yard, pausing for Bruiser to do his thing, "I hate to be nosy, but are you going to call Tristan and talk to him about your job before you go?"

I scrub my hand down my face. "I spent a lot of time last night thinking about that. You're probably right. I do need to check in. I hate talking on the phone."

"You can borrow my computer if you want to send him an email —" Zoe offers.

"I need to have this conversation with Tristan in person."

Zoe looks down at Bruiser who is sitting on my left side. "It seems like Bruiser has finished his business. Do you want some breakfast before you head back toward town?"

I shrug. "I don't suppose you have Cheerios?"

"Actually, I do. Would you like some?"

Before I can answer, my stomach growls.

"Well, that's one way to answer," Zoe smirks.

Freedom

Zoe digs some keys out from her fanny pack. We walk over to the house on the property, and she lets herself in.

"This is a nice house. Do you live here?"

Zoe laughs out loud. "Not officially — but I'm here so much that I might as well. This is my boss' house. He and his wife are out of town at the moment."

"Is it all right if we are here?"

"Yes, part of my duties include house-sitting for Mitch and Jess. They don't mind if I feed myself while I'm here."

"I eat a lot," I caution.

"I have yet to meet a guy who doesn't eat half a box of cereal at a time. That includes my dad, granddad, and brother."

"I'll leave you some money. You could buy another box of cereal for them."

"Seriously, it's no big deal," she dismisses my offer with a light laugh.

When we get inside, Zoe shows Bruiser a dog bed. He promptly crawls into the bed and closes his eyes.

I look at Zoe with alarm. "Maybe he's not as well as we thought he was. If he's tuckered out by just that short walk, there might be something wrong with him."

Zoe smiles at my remark. "I don't think I would worry quite yet. Bruiser seems like a pretty laid-back dog. He might just be one of those dogs who like to take naps."

Zoe walks over to the kitchen sink and washes her hands. As she starts to dry them, her phone rings. The tone is shrill and insistent. She rolls her eyes at me. "As much as I don't want to, I need to take this."

She walks into the living room. I'm not sure what I should do. I'm in a strange house, and I don't know where anything is. I wish I could be as comfortable as Bruiser. This home is a little much for me with bright colors splashed everywhere.

I sit down on a barstool and pull out my phone. I need to recalculate my plan to account for missing two days of riding time. I'm relieved to find that it only adds eight minutes of driving time to each day. I think I can handle that. As much as I love the freedom of riding my motorcycle, some things bother me. Road noise is terrible and sometimes, depending on my stress level, just the feel of the air against my face and hands puts me into sensory overload. That's why am trying to limit my driving time each day. Some days, I'm sure I will ride more. But there might be other days where I can't bring myself to get on my bike.

I am still studying maps when Zoe comes back into the room. Her entire demeanor has changed. She is no longer happy and bright. She looks like she's been crying. Crap! I'm terrible at emotions. Give me binary values any day.

"What's wrong?" I ask.

Zoe takes a paper towel from the roll on the kitchen counter and wipes her face. "I don't even know how to explain this. That was my mom. My mom and dad are threatening to evict me from my apartment if I don't speak to my brother. I have nothing to say to him, but I need a place to live."

"Can they do that?" I ask.

Zoe nods sadly. "Unfortunately, they can. My

parents own the building."

"You shouldn't have to talk to him if you don't want to. Can you find somewhere else to live?" I ask.

"No. If I decide to leave Wellington Manor, my parents will do everything in their power to destroy my reputation, and no one in town would rent to me."

"That sucks," I state simply.

"It does," Zoe agrees with a teary smile.

"What are you going to do?" I ask.

Zoe shrugs. "I guess I have to take a call from Vinnie. I don't know what else to do."

"I'm sorry," I reply softly.

"I am too," Zoe says as a tear slides down her face.

In an uncharacteristic move for me, I ask, "Is there anything I can do?"

"I can't think of anything," Zoe admits. "But if I come up with something, I'll let you know."

I try not to drag my feet on the pavement as I walk into Identity Bank. To me, it feels just like when I was a kid and was called into the principal's office for my 'disruptive' behavior. I wasn't a bad kid. Not really. It's just that people didn't understand what I was going through — kind of like today. I could be on a fool's mission. I just don't know. But not knowing my future with Identity Bank is torture too. At least after today, I'll have some answers.

Zoe wanted to come with me but she had to work at

Hope's Haven. I'm surprised she even wanted to try. Most people are a little taken aback by my odd behavior. Zoe seems to roll with the punches. Without saying a word this morning she brought me milk, sugar and Cheerios in completely separate containers. She made me some toast but was careful not to have it touch anything else on the table. It was kind of cool. She didn't make a big deal out of everything.

When I reach the receptionist's desk, her brow creases, and she blurts, "You're not supposed to be here."

"I know. Change of plans. I need to speak to Mr. Macklin." I try not to fidget.

"Oh … Okay. Let me see if he's in. Have a seat. I'll be with you in a moment —" She turns away and talks into her headset.

I walk over to the bank of chairs in the waiting room. I'm sure they were very expensive, but they're not as comfortable as the couch at Hope's Haven.

After a few minutes, Tristan comes downstairs and greets me, "Phoenix! I thought you would be across two or three states by now."

I stand up and shake his hand. I try my best to make direct eye contact with him. "That's actually what I came to talk to you about."

"Is there a problem? Let's go talk in my office."

Just his words make my palms sweat. I hate confrontation. Unfortunately, this isn't like junior high school. I can't send my mom in to fight my battles for me. I've worked hard to minimize the effect of my Asperger's Syndrome. It's time for me to step up and act like the man I am.

I've worked for Identity Bank since before I

graduated from high school, but this is the first time I've actually been in Tristan's private office. Usually, he holds meetings in a small conference room. The inner sanctum is much more casual than I expected. There is a framed pen and ink drawing of his wife Rogue and pieces of pottery sitting on his bookshelf. To me, it seems chaotic, but then again nearly everything does.

Tristan opens the mini refrigerator and grabs a bottle of water. He turns to me. "You want one?"

I shake my head. "No thank you, sir."

"You've been a member of the Identity Bank family long enough you can just call me Tristan."

"Thank you sir … I mean Tristan."

"I expected you to be well on your way to Oregon, what happened?"

"Life got in the way. Or at least, saving a life interrupted my plans."

"Wow! What happened?"

"I saw a dog get hit by a car and I took him into Hope's Haven because I thought there would be a vet there."

"That explains how you met Zoe. You didn't know her before, right?"

"Zoe helped me fix up Bruiser," I explain.

"Oh, so this *was* your dog?" Tristan clarifies.

"No, sir! I wouldn't treat a dog like that. I just saw Bruiser get hit."

"Is the dog all right?"

"He was doing much better this morning. Dr. Austin says he'll be fine. It's a miracle he wasn't more seriously injured."

"I appreciate you stepping up to do the right thing. A lot of people wouldn't. So, if you need a couple more days to get to Oregon, just let me know."

"Actually, I'd like to ask you about Oregon," I reply.

Tristan raises an eyebrow. "Shoot."

At first, I am puzzled by his remark, but then I realize it's just a figure of speech and he wants me to talk. "Am I being punished?" I blurt.

"What?" Tristan asks with surprise in his voice. "Why would you think that? I'm offering you a chance for a promotion."

"It's just that I like my job here and you didn't seem too happy with me during my performance evaluation. So, I thought maybe you were punishing me for something."

"As much as I would like you to be more interactive with the staff here at Identity Bank, I know it's probably not within your nature. I understand your dilemma because I am shy and don't like to interface with other people much. It has taken a lot of practice for me to be able to get up and speak in front of people. I would much rather be programming my computer."

"Oh, I thought you were angry with me about something and wanted to send me away."

"No! You are one of my best problem solvers. You relate to computer code like no one I've ever seen before except for Ketki from my beta team. I figured having your own office and private space away from the rest of the staff would be something you would appreciate. The layout of the new building is much more conducive to that kind of working environment. I want you to meet with Jameson to see if it would be a good fit for you. If it's not, it's no a problem. You can keep your job here."

"Thank you. That makes me feel better. Zoe told me about Ketki. I guess Ketki and I have a lot in common."

Tristan's eyebrows raise. "How is it you and Ketki haven't worked together? She is wicked smart on the computer. The two of you would probably get along like two peas in a pod."

"I'm not sure. I'm not close to anybody, but I'd still like to meet her."

"Fair enough. After you get back from Oregon — assuming you're still going — I'll see what I can do."

"Thank you," I respond, unsure what to say next.

"For the record, you're a talented programmer. I want to do whatever I can to make your job easier. Just let me know what you need."

"Well, you could explain what you're doing if you send me away for another job," I quip.

"I thought I did. Unfortunately, it seems like we got our wires crossed."

"Yeah, catastrophic things can happen when wires get crossed."

"I guess I'll have to be more precise the next time."

"I'm a big fan of precision. You know, mathematics is kind of my hobby."

"Okay, I'll keep that in mind. Let me know what your plans are for your trip," Tristan says with a warm smile.

"For now, I'm going to check on Bruiser and Zoe. I'll update you once I make my plans," I respond.

"By the way, what did you think of Zoe?"

"She's nice," I assert.

"Is that all?" Tristan raises an eyebrow as he grins at me.

"She's good with dogs," I add.

"Uh-huh, I'm aware. Anything else?" Tristan asks with a twinkle in his eye.

"She's very pretty and she smells good," I admit awkwardly. "I think she's cool."

"Well, that's something. I was beginning to wonder about your powers of observation."

Little does Tristan know, my powers of observation are in overdrive.

CHAPTER SIX

ZOE

I DON'T KNOW WHAT came over me but I've suddenly been possessed by the spirit of Betty Crocker. Devon came in today and did all the routine chores I would've done to keep my mind off of Phoenix. So, I decided to bake instead. I chose plain sugar cookies and roast beef with mashed potatoes and corn. Those are pretty much universal comfort foods. Maybe Phoenix will feel at ease eating them. When I hear his motorcycle come up the drive, I throw open the door and step out onto the front porch. Bruiser follows me.

"How did it go," I ask as soon as he gets off his bike.

Phoenix walks up to the front porch slowly. It's clear from his expression he is confused by my enthusiastic, happy greeting.

"Okay, I guess. You were right. Tristan wasn't trying to punish me or make me feel bad for having Asperger's syndrome. He was trying to find a better working environment for me."

Phoenix stands in front of me and reaches down to pet Bruiser.

"That's great news. I want you to know Bruiser missed you terribly. He paced the whole time you were gone — even though he's not supposed to be very active. He didn't settle down until he heard your bike coming up the street. I think he was worried about you."

Phoenix starts to stroke Bruiser's ears. "It's nice that he likes me, but I'm afraid it creates a problem."

"Problem? What do you mean? Bonding is usually a good thing."

"It would be if I was going to stay in Gainesville, but I'm headed to Oregon. What is Bruiser going to do once I leave?"

I frown as I ponder Phoenix's question. "It will be a rough transition for sure. Bruiser seems unusually attached to you."

Phoenix looks anguished. "I've got a few days of flexibility in my schedule. Maybe I should stay here until Bruiser is feeling one hundred percent."

"You can if you want to, but I don't know if it'll make it any easier on Bruiser. He seems to have adopted you as his human whether you wanted him to or not."

Phoenix sighs. "Either way I go, it's a bad choice. I don't want to leave Bruiser, but after I talked to Tristan today, I understand why he wants me to go. I can't really disregard that."

"The weather is awful, why don't you stay the night and think about your decision."

Phoenix smirks. "Obviously, you don't know me very well if you believe I won't think about the decision. I over think everything. I obsess over stupid stuff like what I'm going to wear or how much cheese to put in my grilled cheese sandwich. Thoughts spin in my head twenty-four hours a day."

"That must be exhausting. You look like you've had a long day. Do you want something to eat? I made dinner."

Phoenix looks at me in surprise. "You did? Why?"

I chuckle. "Despite my early mistrust of you, I usually treat my guests with kindness — and like it or not — you are my guest. So, I made you roast beef, mashed potatoes, and corn."

Phoenix wrinkles his nose. "Please don't tell me you put all those things in some weird casserole or something."

I take Phoenix's hand and escort him to the dining room. "No, I know better than that. Everything is separate. Come see what I found for you. When I went into a little craft boutique to find a present for a friend, I ran across these." I point to the plates on the table.

"Oh wow! Were they made that way? That's like someone crawled in my head and pulled out my thoughts. Usually, if I find a divided plate, it's the size of a hockey puck. That's fine for kid's plates, but not for someone like me. These are perfect. Look how high those dividers are. My food won't be cross contaminated. That's cool."

"I thought so too. I thought about going back and buying the rest of them. You are not my only friend who doesn't like to have your food mixed together."

"Am I your friend?" Phoenix asks.

"I think so, why?" Before I can finish my question, my phone rings. I look at Phoenix with an apology in my eyes as I whisper, "I have to take this, I'm on call tonight. This is the business line."

"Hope's Haven, this is Zoe. How can I help you?"

My heart drops to my toes as I hear the threatening voice of my brother. "Back off and mind your own business if you know what's good for you and those puppies you claim to love. Obviously they mean more to you than your big brother. You don't know anything about what happened. I didn't do anything to you. Why are you interfering?"

"Vinnie, I don't have a choice. I have to testify."

"No, you don't. You could have a terrible case of the flu, a migraine, or malaria for all I care. Just make sure you're nowhere near me or the courthouse. If you don't, I know where you work and I know how to use a cigarette lighter. Have I made it crystal clear for you? If you testify against me, I *will* ruin you."

The phone goes dead in my hand. I stand there stunned for a few moments. My brother, the man I used to worship as a kid just threatened to burn down my employer's business. That was incredibly cruel of him. He knows all about my phobias.

One time when I was giving him a tour of Hope's Haven, I told him I was afraid to work completely by myself because if I did, I wasn't sure I would ever get the dogs out in time if there was ever a fire. He totally used my deep-seated fear against need to terrorize me. I don't know what to do. I sway as the edges of my vision grow gray.

Phoenix rushes over to me and helps me sit in one of the chairs. He's in such a hurry he still has his fork in his hand.

"What happened?" he asks looking at me with concern.

I rub my eyes with the heels of my hands. "My

brother. My brother freaking happened. I can't believe it. Maybe this is the ugly side of him others have talked about —"

"What did he say to you? Are you okay?"

Phoenix's questions send thoughts ricocheting around in my brain. "Oh my gosh, I need to let the police know what happened. Isn't it a crime to threaten a witness?"

Phoenix nods. "Yeah. That's straight up intimidation or witness tampering."

I look at Phoenix as tears continue to spill out of the corner of my eyes. I can't seem to stop crying even though I am furious with my brother. "You know how to work a computer, right?"

Phoenix gives me a strange, confused look. "Zoe, you know what I do for a living, don't you? I debug computer games. I use a computer for this — sometimes ten hours a day. I can type almost as fast as you blink."

I take a gulp of soda. "I know this is going to sound weird. But, remember I told you I was dyslexic?"

Phoenix nods.

"Honestly, I don't write well either. I mean, I can have the thoughts in my brain, but when I try to put them on paper, nothing seems to come out right and everything ends up sounding like some illiterate kindergartener wrote it. Would you mind taking notes on my computer for me as I talk to you? That would be so much easier for me. I need to get all of this out before I forget what my brother said to me. I can't believe Vinnie would stoop so low."

Phoenix sets down his fork next to the plate. "Do you want to do this now or after dinner?"

I blush. In all the craziness, I completely forgot about dinner. "Do you mind if we do it now? I don't want to forget anything. Right now, his words are still so fresh in my mind my heart is pounding. I think I need to convey that fear while it's still happening."

Phoenix shrugs. "I can wait. Just point me to your computer."

After I finish writing my statement with Phoenix, I feel like a weight has been lifted off my shoulders. Not only was he able to help me put my thoughts in a coherent order, his insistent questions helped me remember more of the conversation. I was still so numb from it, I was afraid I wouldn't be able to remember anything, but Phoenix's methodical approach makes me confident I haven't forgotten anything crucial.

After dinner, as my shock wears off, I realize I have at least one more call to make. Phoenix is taking Bruiser for a walk, so I take the opportunity to change into my pajamas before I make my call.

Jessica is the one who picks up the phone. "Hi Jess, this is Zoe. Is Mitch around?"

"No, he went to the grocery store to buy some diapers for me. Is there anything I can help you with?"

I sigh. "I'm not sure. I don't even know how to explain all this."

"Well, you know I work in a library so you know I'll tell you to explain it like a book. Start at the beginning. Hope's Haven isn't on fire or anything is it? I know my stove is a little touchy."

I know she meant her words as a joke because she couldn't possibly know why I'm calling. Still, they feel like a physical blow.

"No, Hope's Haven isn't on fire. Actually, we're doing pretty well here. I adopted out the last Chihuahua which was dumped on our doorstep. But, that's not why I called."

"Okay, now I'm dying of curiosity. What's going on with you?"

"You were friends with Katie before she moved, right?"

"Yeah, I miss her a lot."

"Before she met Logan she was supposed to get married. Did you know about that?"

"Of course I did. I think half of Florida knows. The story of how she met Logan is pretty legendary. Not every girl can pick up a guy while she's wearing a wedding dress."

"I don't know how much you knew about Katie's life but, my brother was the jerk she was running from. Katie was almost my sister-in-law."

"Oh … I'm so sorry. You can't pick your relatives. If I knew Vinnie the Pooh was your brother, I've long since forgotten."

"Unfortunately, these days I can't seem to forget my brother. He's angry because I have been subpoenaed to testify against him at his trial for kidnapping and rape."

"I'm so sorry. It's tough when legal matters come between family members."

"I'm afraid that's not all. Tonight he called me and

threatened to burn down Hope's Haven if I testify."

Jessica gasps. "What are you going to do? If you have a subpoena, you can't just choose ignore it."

"I don't know. I feel so stuck. But, I don't want to put the dogs at risk. Maybe Vinnie has a point. Maybe I should get a case of the flu during his trial so I don't have to testify."

"I know it's tempting to run. But, what if the information you give at the trial prevents him from being free to kidnap and rape other women?"

"I don't want to believe what they're saying about him. However, his attitude concerns me."

"If I were you, I would call Tristan and ask him to up the number of security patrols in your neighborhood."

I sigh. "I already did that when I invited Phoenix to stay with me."

"Phoenix? What are you talking about?" Jessica asks with surprise in her voice. I don't blame her. I'm not one who is well known for socializing with my friends.

"Yeah, I talked to Mitch about this yesterday. Phoenix is a who, not a what. He rescued a dog and he's been sticking around to check on Bruiser's progress. Phoenix is really sweet. He helped me write down everything about the phone call with my brother. Without him, I wouldn't have remembered so many details."

"Normally, I would be giving you a big sister-type lecture about taking it slow and easy and learning a lot about each other. But, quite frankly I am glad there's someone else there with you. Our facility is pretty isolated. Still, I think you should contact Tristan or Isaac and let them know what's going on. It sounds like the threat level has gone up several hundred notches."

"Okay, I'll call them. Oh, wait I need to tell you something. You know when I told you Phoenix would be staying here a day or two to watch out for Bruiser? It turns out that when he's not riding his motorcycle around, Phoenix Wolf works for Identity Bank."

"Shut the front door! That is just wild. Well, he should be able to pull some strings for you."

"Something tells me that Phoenix won't be much help in that department," I answer with a laugh.

"I guess we'll have to do it the old-fashioned way. Go ahead and send your notes to Mitch. He has a meeting with Tristan when we get back. I'll have him bring it up. After all, we want to make sure that all the critters at Hope's Haven are safe regardless of whether they have two legs or four."

"You're coming home in a couple of days, correct?"

"That's the plan. Gracelyn is not happy in her car seat. I can't wait to get home and be in a regular routine again. Nobody told me how hard it was to travel with a little one."

"Aww, I'm sorry. Tell Mitch I'm sorry my brother is stirring up all this drama."

"Maybe this is all a big bluff. You know, big brothers being tough and all. I bet he's just lashing out because he's hurt. He probably thought you'd be unabashedly on his side regardless of what he did to other people. A lot of people put a ton of stock in family loyalty."

"I'm not trying to be disloyal. I'm just trying to do the right thing."

I hear Jessica sigh through the phone. "I know.

That's the part of this that stinks. You shouldn't have to feel bad for doing the right thing. This is your brother's problem. Don't let him make you feel small."

"Thanks for the advice. I'll try not to. Something tells me his opinion counts with me more than it's actually worth." I respond. "Have a nice trip home. I'll see you tomorrow."

When Jessica hangs up, I sag against my headboard.

Small. That about sums up my entire existence more succinctly than I care to admit.

Phoenix

"Go find Zoe," I issue the command to Bruiser after I unhook his leash. I have no idea whether he understands, but he seems to know a lot of stuff already. I guess it's theoretically possible. He looks at me as if he's puzzled by my words. He takes off running to the kennel room. Fortunately, he doesn't seem to be struggling much although he does seem to be favoring his rear left leg a little.

I struggle to keep up as he scampers down the halls. Finally, we reach the threshold of the door I could not cross the other day.

Zoe is pouring a gargantuan bag of dog food into a large barrel. It's hard for me to tell, but it looks like she's upset. I rush over to help her lift the heavy bag.

When I grab the bag, she jumps as if she wasn't expecting me. "Oh, geez you about gave me a heart attack. My nerves are so on edge these days. I feel like I'm constantly looking over my shoulder and waiting for the other shoe to drop."

"That's understandable after the run-in you had with your brother."

"Hey, I appreciate the help. I thought you couldn't

come into this room."

"All the dogs are sleeping and not having their own barking symphony. The smell is still a little much for me but if I'm only dealing with one overwhelming thing, I generally can work around it. But sometimes, I just get swamped."

"I understand the overwhelmed part. I'm feeling that way right now. I wish I could run away from my whole life."

"Why don't you?"

"Hope's Haven is the best job I've ever had. I can't just leave them in the lurch just because I'm scared of what my brother might do. If I left, it might make the situation worse because he might lash out at them simply because he can't reach me."

"That's a scary thought. Although, I can't say your logic is flawed."

"Isn't it? I've had nothing but terrifying thoughts tumble around in my brain since he called. I'm scared to death. Even so, I can't let those people down. My brother has shown real ugliness I never expected. It just lends credence to the other stories."

"I think you should go to the police station first, but after you're done, I can take you for a spin on my bike."

"I've been thinking about that. Maybe this isn't as serious as I think it is. If I go to the police, they might laugh me right out of the station. What if Jessica is right and he's bluffing?"

"Based on what you told me, I didn't get the impression you thought your brother was simply bluffing. I think you should go to the police and the DA and let them know what's going on. He shouldn't be able to terrorize you like this. I don't care if he is your brother," I insist.

"Vinnie has intruded on my happy little life here and I hate it. It makes my job really hard because the dogs can pick up on my stress and they don't pay as much attention to the training when I'm out of sorts. So, even if he doesn't do all the stuff he threatened, he's still disrupting my life."

"So, let's do what we can to stop him. Maybe I look at things too black and white and don't see enough gray. But, it seems to me he's done destructive things to a lot of people. I just think a guy like that needs to be stopped. If we can help with that, then that's what we should do," I say emphatically.

"Who is we? Do you have a frog in your pocket?"

"No, I'm just doing an awful job of telling you that I can stick around to help you do that tomorrow, if you want."

"That's just it. I have no idea what I want. I wish I could wave a magic wand and justice would be done. I don't know if my brother did any of the things people are charging him with. But, I'm starting to believe it's entirely possible he's guilty. I don't want to think those things about my own brother. But he runs hot and cold like a broken air-conditioner."

Suddenly, Bruiser runs to the front door. Zoe and I follow quickly. Bruiser lays down with his nose against the threshold and growls. I peek out the window, but don't see anything. Bruiser is not deterred. He continues to growl.

I look at Zoe and shrug. "I don't know what has him all riled up. There doesn't seem to be anything out there."

"Where did you park your bike?" Zoe asks.

"I put it in the blue storage shed like you told me to."

"Is it locked? I don't know enough about motorcycles to know if you can even lock them up."

"I've got an axle lock which works like a parking boot."

"Maybe you should take Bruiser and check it out," Zoe suggests with a hopeful look.

This is like a nightmare for me. Although I have taken Bruiser on several walks and am somewhat familiar with Hope's Haven, I'm not sure of my ability to navigate it in the dark.

"Do you have a flashlight?" I ask.

"Let me get it for you," Zoe offers. She quickly returns with some sort of headgear with a huge light. It's kind of like what I've seen coal miners wear.

When she sees my puzzled look, she laughs softly. "I know this isn't a traditional flashlight, but it's what we use to tend to the dog runs and the play yard. It's remarkably effective."

Zoe helps me position the awkwardly shaped light on my head. As she does, she runs her fingers through my long hair. Usually, I don't like it much when people touch me. But, when Zoe does it, my heart beats a little faster, and I feel warm all over.

"Just a moment, I have an idea," Zoe says. She runs away again but quickly returns. This time, she's carrying a small baseball bat. "Maya left this the last time she came here after baseball practice. I know it's not much but, it might help you if you run across whatever it is that made Bruiser growl."

Freedom

I look at the baseball bat skeptically, but I take it from Zoe. I try not to grimace when I feel the weight of the bat in my hand. As far as baseball bats go, this one is pretty light. Still, I don't want to upset Zoe. "Thanks. I guess it's better to be prepared."

"Hopefully, it's nothing outside of our overactive imaginations because we're stressed out." Zoe offers.

Zoe grabs a leash from a rack on the wall beside the front door. "Here you go Bruiser, time to live up to your name. Keep Phoenix safe from whatever bogeymen are out there, okay?"

I take a deep breath and grab Bruiser's leash. As we walk around the perimeter of the yard, the hair on Bruiser's back stands up. I tighten my grip on the baseball bat. Bruiser starts to growl. I look down toward the ground to aim the headlamp. I almost trip on a stack of sticks. I squat down to take a closer look. The sticks look like they were deliberately placed there. They are in the formation of a tee-pee and there is a clump of dry grass under the crude wood structure. Laying in the grass beside it is a half-used book of matches.

I look around to see if I can find anything to protect the objects from the weather. A few feet away I spot some empty flowerpots. Choosing the largest one, I turn it upside down over the pile of sticks. Grabbing Bruiser's leash, I turn and sprint back toward the house. Bruiser barks as he enthusiastically participates in this new game of tag.

Zoe must've heard my boots on the front porch because she opens the door with a panicked look on her face.

"What did you find?" she asks.

Pulling the headlamp off, I set it on a side table before I take off Bruiser's leash.

I look down at the ground to collect myself. "I'm not exactly sure what I found, but I think we need to call the police."

"What do you mean?"

"I left my phone in the house, so I didn't get a picture of it. Basically, it's a tiny campfire with a set of matches beside it. In light of everything else going on, I interpreted it as a threat. I don't know if the police will agree with me. But that's what it felt like."

"Do you think we need to call 911?" Zoe asks as her voice trembles a bit. She pulls out her phone and types something in.

I shrug. "I think if someone had still been there, Bruiser would've had a fit. We need to call though. Maybe we can use the regular line."

Zoe bites her lip as she reads whatever is on her phone. "It looks like they have a non-emergency line. I think I'll call that."

Before Zoe can do anything more, her phone rings.

"Hope's Haven, this is Zoe," she answers, her voice a bit more steady. Her eyebrows raise in surprise as she listens. "Oh, hi Tristan. That was quick." Zoe looks at me and shrugs as her brows furrow. "Did you see something? Were you able to capture anything on surveillance camera?" she asks insistently.

She swallows hard and twists her hair between her fingers. "Who wears a stocking cap and gloves in Florida? I know it's been raining, but it's not that cold outside."

She listens a little longer. "No! I'm sure it wasn't

Phoenix. He was in the house with me and went out to check the yard when Bruiser started growling."

She looks frustrated. "Yes, I plan to call the police — in fact, I was about to dial the number when you called. Okay, I'll tell them you have footage."

"Okay, hanging up now to call them. No, we haven't touched anything," she responds and then looks to me for confirmation.

I put my hands up and back up to indicate I didn't disturb anything. "I put a pot over it to protect it from the rain."

"Phoenix says he didn't mess with it. He covered it with something."

Zoe hangs up the phone. She walks over to the sink and gets herself a glass of water and takes a couple of sips. "I know I have to do this, but I'm afraid of the can of worms it will open. I'm almost afraid to ask where my brother is. Doesn't it seem like he is mentally torturing me because he knows I am deathly afraid of fire?"

"I'm not sure. Any way you slice it, it's pretty messed up."

"I hate to ask this of you, but can you stick around until they figure out what's going on? I don't want to be here by myself."

Zoe looks so shattered; I can't bring myself to say anything except, "I don't see a problem with that. My schedule is flexible."

"Oh, thank goodness. I'm just about as frightened of the dark as I am of fire. I don't know what I would have done if you weren't here."

"I'm just glad I was here. Let's see if we can get some

more help. Do you want me to call, or do you want to?"

"I suppose I probably should since it's my job to take care of the property when Mitch and Jessica are not here."

Zoe reaches out and grabs my hand. She squeezes it tightly as she dials her phone with the thumb of her other hand.

I can hear voices on the other end but I can't make out the conversation. After a few moments, Zoe seems to relax. She hangs up the phone and announces, "They're sending someone out. They told us to just sit and wait."

I groan. "Those happen to be two things I'm terrible at. In case you haven't noticed, I tend to fidget and pace. I hate to wait. It's so bad that I order my groceries online so I don't have to stand in line at the grocery store."

Zoe smiles at me. "I'm glad to hear I'm not the only one. Sometimes, I feel like I am a preschooler in a grown-ups body."

"What should we do to kill time?"

"It's not very exciting, but I was in the middle of filling food and water dishes when Bruiser started growling. I probably need to get back to that. Do you want to help?"

"Sure," I answer with far more confidence than I have. The last time I tried to enter the kennel room, it didn't go so well. I'd rather not embarrass myself again. But I don't know what else to do.

As we enter the room, Zoe whimpers as if she's in pain. She spins around and grabs the front of my shirt. Instinctively, I wrap my arms around her. She draws in a shuddering breath. "Look at this, Phoenix. Not counting

Bruiser, I've got five dogs in here. If something were to happen to Hope's Haven, how would I ever get them all out of here in time?"

I place my chin on the top of her head as I murmur, "Maybe I'll talk to Tristan about whether he could install some sort of sprinkler system."

"That's a good idea. But I don't know if my bosses have that kind of money."

"Yeah, in older buildings like these, something like sprinklers could be tricky. Maybe the police department will have a better idea how to keep you safe."

As I stand to the side and listen to Zoe recount her conversation with her brother and his history with women, I'm surprised when the cop, Cody Erickson just nods. "I'm sorry Ms. Hurlington, I'm much more familiar with Vincent Hurlington than I ever wanted to be. I had to rescue my partner during her wedding."

Zoe's jaw drops in shock. "Partner? You were involved with her when she was dating my brother?"

Officer Erickson grins. "Only in my dreams. Katelyn Ashford was my partner on the police force before she moved to Oregon."

Zoe becomes pale. "Oh my gosh! I was so stressed out that day — I completely forgot you were there. I remember you had to arrest my brother and haul him away from the church."

He shrugs. "Yep, nobody could ever call Katie's wedding boring."

"I hate to break up this little family meeting, but someone is threatening Zoe. Do you want me to show you what I found?"

Officer Erickson nods. "Of course."

"Did I tell you I took notes of the conversation with my brother?" Zoe asks.

"No, you didn't. It would be helpful for me to see those too."

"What are we going to do if this is her brother?" I ask. "What are we going to do if it's not?" I add, as I weigh both possibilities.

"It's too early for me to say. We have to do some investigating before I can make that kind of determination."

"How long will that take?" Zoe cries.

"I know you're scared, Zoe. We'll try to resolve this as quickly as we can." Officer Erickson glances over at me. "I will need a copy of your ID. You are the newcomer to the situation. I need to rule you out."

"Oh for Pete's sake! Phoenix isn't responsible for this. He was standing in front of me when it all unfolded. Even if he weren't, I'd still know it wasn't him. Everything I've seen from him tells me he's the polar opposite of my brother or anyone like him." Zoe asserts. "Besides, he works for Tristan Macklin."

Officer Erickson looks stunned. "Well, I guess that'll make clearing his background a little easier. I know that Tristan runs a comprehensive background check on everyone he hires every few months. We'll compare notes. I'm sorry, I didn't mean anything personal by it, it's just the way I have to work through a case."

Reflexively, I grimace under the officer's scrutiny. "No problem. I am used to the suspicion. It's not as if I look like an insurance salesman or anything."

Chapter Eight

Zoe

I KNOW MY CONVERSATION with Cody should've made me feel better. But, it didn't — if anything, it made me more anxious. His words were just one more tangible reminder of how dangerous my brother can be. Even though during the wedding confrontation Katelyn was able to barricade herself in the restroom until Cody could rescue her and Vincent wasn't able to lay a hand on her, his words were vile and ugly. It doesn't take much of a leap of my imagination to picture circumstances where a situation between them may have escalated into much more than just words.

Cody and Phoenix escorted me outside so I could tell them how things are usually arranged in Jessica and Mitch's yard. When Phoenix removed the flower pot he'd placed over the little miniature campfires to protect them from the rain, I felt like someone had punched me in the stomach. I was literally knocked back by the sight.

About fifteen years ago, our neighbor's house burned down to the ground. I remember watching from my upstairs bedroom as the neighbor's plate glass window bulging out like a soap bubble on a bubble wand. I shrieked in horror when it burst and made a deafening sound. I jumped into Vincent's arms and trembled. I'll never forget the evil sound of his maniacal laugh as he made fun of my terror. Even though I was scared to death, I couldn't pull my eyes away from the mesmerizing flames.

When I learned my friend Lizzie's grandmother was trapped in the fire and could not get away, I began to have nightmares that I'd die in a fire too. Vinnie thought my phobia was hysterical. He started tormenting me by leaving matches all around the house with my initials carved into the matchbooks.

A couple of years later, after I told him boys were not allowed at my slumber party, I woke up to find a tiny campfire outside my Barbie castle. It had been a while since I had played with my dolls, so I wasn't sure exactly when he put it there, but I was pretty sure it wasn't there when my friends and I went to bed. One of my friends, Rebecca, was making fun of me for still having toys and I remember looking directly at the Barbie castle. I didn't want to get rid of it because I saved my allowance to buy it all by myself.

After I discovered Vinnie had been in my room, I wasn't sure what to do. Mom and Dad told my brother specifically not to be in my room. I was afraid if I tattled, they would take away my privilege to have slumber parties. I never told anyone about Vinnie messing with my stuff. Now, as I study the pictures of the tiny campfires in my yard, I wonder if I should have said something years earlier.

The screen door creaks and I jump as I gasp and hold my hand to my chest. Phoenix takes off Bruiser's leash and hangs it on the hook. He walks over to me and looks past me in his odd way. Over the past few days, I've become accustomed to him not looking directly at my face. "Are you all right? I didn't mean to scare you. Bruiser wanted to go out for a walk and you were on a phone call."

I shake my head as I swallow hard. "I'm fine. I'm just a little jumpy these days. Did you find anything new outside?"

Phoenix shrugs. "I didn't. Bruiser might have though. I was throwing a stick for him and it landed in the bushes. You know — the ones over by the fence on the left-hand side of the dog kennels?"

"I hope he didn't get himself into any trouble. A few years back, Lexicon got sprayed by a skunk back there."

Phoenix shakes his head. "That's not the kind of trouble he found. This is human in nature."

A chill goes up my spine and I sit up straight. "Do I need to call Cody?"

Phoenix squats down next to the couch. "It might not hurt. Do you think he'll be on duty?"

"Why? What did you find?" I demand.

Phoenix shrugs. "I don't even know if this is important or even related to what we found the other day. Bruiser just brought it back after he ran after his stick in the bushes. It might be nothing," he answers as he holds out something shiny for me to see.

I lean closer for a better look. When I get a good look at the gold object, the blood rushes from my head and I feel woozy.

I collapse against the back of the chair and rub my temples.

"Zoe! What's wrong?" Phoenix asks as he rests the back of his hand against my forehead.

Freedom

"We definitely need to call Cody right away," I whisper harshly.

Phoenix pulls his hand away and looks at me in surprise. "Why?"

I point to the object in his other hand. "Because of that; it tells me everything I need to know. It's a fourteen-karat gold money clip. I bet if you turn it over, it will have my brother's initials on the back. My dad got it for him when he graduated from high school because he thought Vincent would take the business world by storm."

Phoenix appears somber as he examines the money clip. "We didn't have much doubt before — but this kind of cements it. The money clip is clearly intended to underscore his threat directed at you."

"I don't understand why my brother is doing this. It's not my fault he got into a fight with his fiancée in front of me and a bunch of other people. I didn't ask to be subpoenaed. I can think of a million other places I'd rather be than testifying against my brother. My family will never be the same. I don't know what he's thinking!"

Walking over to Jessica's pantry, he pulls out a sandwich bag and places the money clip in it. He stops to pour me a glass of sweet tea and grabs a couple of cookies we made yesterday. He pulls the Ottoman up next to the couch and sits down directly across from me. He hands me the tea and cookies.

"I know this won't fix everything. I can't even guess what your brother is thinking. I have a hard time figuring out regular people. People who set out to hurt other people are completely beyond my comprehension. I'm sorry, I wish I understood better."

I pat the couch beside me. "Will you sit here? I'm

more freaked out by this than I want to be. I need a hug."

A look of indecision crosses Phoenix's face. He swallows hard. "Zoe, you have no idea how much I want to — but that's just about the hardest thing you could ask me to do. Is it all right if I stay here and just listen?"

I flush hot with embarrassment. I know from being around Ketki that physical touch is hard for some people. What was I thinking? "Umm, I'm sorry —" I reply.

Phoenix holds his hand up to halt my speech. "Just because it's hard for me doesn't mean I'm not willing to try. How about if I start out small? Can I just hold your hand?" he asks in a hesitant voice.

I nod as emotion chokes me. This is so hard for him, so I'm touched by his willingness to try. When I find my voice, I say, "It sounds perfect."

Phoenix reaches across the space between us and tries to hold my hand. His brows furrow with concern. "This feels a little weird. It's like we're shaking hands before a chess match."

I smother a grin at his consternation.

"I'm willing to try anything once, I suppose," I joke as I try to ease the tension.

Phoenix leans on Bruiser as he stands up and joins me on the couch. Not wanting to be left out, Bruiser jumps up on the couch beside Phoenix. He has the typical goofy grin of a lab on his face when his antics knock Phoenix closer to me.

Phoenix clears his throat. "Thanks for making sure I was cozy, buddy. I appreciate it." He smirks and strokes Bruiser's ears. Phoenix reaches out with his right hand and links his fingers with mine. "I guess Bruiser here has more faith in my abilities than I do."

I smile gently. "Seems to me you're doing just fine. Thank you."

Blushing, Phoenix turns toward me. "This doesn't seem like enough." He lifts our clasped hands between us. "What else can I do?"

I brush my hair out of my face with my other hand, then dig my phone out of my pocket. "Honestly, I'm not looking forward to rehashing this all with Cody. Just having you here makes it easier."

Phoenix draws in a sharp breath and freezes in place. "Okay, if you say so. I won't move."

"Umm … Okay … Great. I'm just going to call Cody and ask him what we should do," I stammer awkwardly.

Phoenix leans forward and pulls his wallet out of his back pocket. He digs out a business card. "Here — try this. Cody gave it to me and said if we needed anything to call this number."

I take the card from him and dial the number. "Erickson," I hear Cody yell into his phone. The background noise is drowning out anything he may be saying.

"Cody! I can't hear you," I respond, reflexively removing my hand from Phoenix's and plugging my ear in an effort to hear more clearly.

"Hold on just a sec!" The background noise becomes quieter and I hear the bells on a door ring.

I look at Phoenix and shrug my shoulders. "Cody, are you there?"

"I am now," he answers. "Sorry about that. Palmer and I were watching the game. We stopped to grab some burgers."

"I'm so sorry. I shouldn't have called this number," I hedge.

"Zoe?" Cody guesses.

"Uh… yeah. But how did you know?"

"Zoe, I don't give my private cell number out to just anyone. I happened to give it to your boyfriend. It doesn't take my finest detective work to figure out who's calling."

"Oh, you misunderstand. It's not like that," I protest.

Cody chuckles. "It might not be at this very moment, but it won't take long. I've seen the way that young man looks at you."

"It's complicated," I respond.

Cody laughs out loud. "Isn't it always?"

"Probably — but right now, my life is more complicated than most. That's what I called you about. Things have become more serious."

"Just a second, let me get into my rig where I've got something to write on."

I rest my free hand on my thigh and Phoenix reaches out to grab it again. Gratefully, I lace my fingers through his and hang on tight.

I hear a rustle on the other end of the phone and Cody says, "It took me a bit, but I'm ready now. What's going on?"

"Are you sure you don't want me to call you back when you're back at the office? This might not even be anything."

"It's okay. My team was losing anyway. I'm not missing much. If you have a gut feeling something is important, I won't ignore that. That's why I gave your guy my number."

"His name is Phoenix Wolf," I correct.

"Right. Anyway, I wanted you or Phoenix to call me if anything seemed unusual."

"Unusual. That's one way to put it. Freakin' scary is another."

"Oh boy! I guess you better start at the beginning," Cody encourages.

"While I was ordering supplies for Hope's Haven, Phoenix took Bruiser outside for a walk. I guess they were playing fetch with a stick and Bruiser found something unexpected in the bushes back by the dog kennel."

"If he's anything like the dogs I grew up with, it was probably a snake."

I sigh. "I wish it was that simple. Unfortunately, it's not. Bruiser found a money clip which I believe belongs to my brother."

This time, Cody lets out a groan of frustration. "I guess the forensic team must've missed that when they were out."

"Either that or my brother has been back on my property again. I'm not sure which is the scariest scenario."

"That's a true statement. I'm off for tonight, but you could still take it in to the station, if you'd feel more comfortable. One of the other officers can handle it for you."

I glance over at Phoenix. "I'd rather stick with the same guy," he mutters under his breath.

I let out the breath I didn't realize I was holding as I

respond in a low voice as I hold my hand over my phone, "Me too."

Phoenix nods and squeezes my hand.

Raising my voice I respond to Cody, "We'll wait until you're on duty tomorrow. I don't want to start over with someone else."

"Zoe, do you have someone to stay with you until we get a handle on this?"

Even though Cody cannot see me over the phone, I nod. "Yeah, Phoenix is here."

Phoenix flinches, but before I can sort out the odd reaction, Cody answers, "I think that's good. I'll see you tomorrow. You guys be careful, okay?"

"I don't think I'll sleep a wink. It's a good thing we've got a bunch of dogs around. It would be nice if we still had a dog like Dozer with all of his protection training."

Cody chuckles. "Keep dreaming. I don't think Darya would ever give him up. After all, he saved her life on multiple occasions."

"Oh, I would never take Dozer. I just wish we could clone him."

"I understand. He is one cool dog. Take care of yourself and I'll talk to you tomorrow."

I sigh as I end the call.

"Who is Dozer?" Phoenix asks.

"He was about the best protection dog we've ever had come through Hope's Haven."

"What happened to him?"

Freedom

"At the moment, he is guarding Darya. She happens to be a phenomenal police detective, but sometimes she needs a little backup."

Phoenix winces. "Speaking of backup, I don't know how much longer I can stay. I'm so sorry. I'm supposed to be on my way to Oregon. Tristan says this could be a big break for me. I don't want to let him down."

I draw in a sharp breath and try to speak without my voice shaking. "I don't even know what to say. It's not really fair of me to ask you to stay. You came here because you were doing a good deed for Bruiser. I guess you're not responsible for me. I'll just have to figure out something else."

Phoenix pulls me closer to his side. "I didn't mean to upset you. I just wanted you to know. I'm here — for now. We'll have to sort out the rest of our lives on another day."

CHAPTER NINE

PHOENIX

BRUISER IS STICKING TO me like glue. It's almost as if he's afraid I'll disappear if he lets me out of his sight. I'm trying to help Zoe with her chores this morning, but I keep tripping over the devoted yellow lab at my feet. Feeling frustrated, I grab his favorite dog toy and put him in the dog run with Hope while I fill the dog dishes in the kennel.

It's only been a few days since I found him, but without Bruiser's constant company, Hope's Haven seems unbearably quiet. As I sweep up the training room, my thoughts tumble around in my brain.

Reading other people's emotions has never been a particularly strong talent for me. I would much rather be deciphering computer code. Even so, the look of isolation and sadness on Zoe's face last night was heartbreaking. I'm not used to people relying on me for support, emotional or otherwise. Sure, my parents try their best to treat me as if I don't have Asperger's syndrome. My dad used to spend several hours a day trying to engage me in mundane conversation just so I would develop the skills I need to cope.

When I saw Bruiser on the side of the road, I never anticipated that I would become involved with his rescuer. Whether I like it or not, I *am* involved. I have to figure out how to reconcile that with my plans. I should've been on my way to Oregon days ago. Yet, I don't want to leave Zoe — especially since I don't know the scope of the danger she faces.

I have put off this call long enough. It's time for me to face the music. It seems to take forever for Tristan's executive assistant to transfer my call.

"Hey! I didn't expect to hear from you. How's the open road? Is the weather treating you right?" Tristan asks.

"Yeah … about that," I answer with more nerves evident in my voice than I'm comfortable with. "I'm still just outside of Gainesville at Hope's Haven."

"Why? Is there a problem with the dog you rescued?"

"No, fortunately Bruiser is just fine. He moves a little gingerly sometimes, but the vet says he probably has bruised lungs and he may have pulled some muscles in his hip."

"Oh I see. You must be hanging around for Zoe. I can't say I blame you; she has one of the biggest hearts I've ever seen. She's pretty cute too."

Tristan's comments surprise me. "I didn't realize you knew her so well," I blurt.

"You know how it goes — friends of friends start to hang out and your circle of friends grows exponentially."

"I guess I'll have to take your word for it. However, you're not wrong about Zoe."

Tristan chuckles. "I suppose this might be a good time to remind you that there is a potential promotion waiting for you in Oregon."

I clear my throat. "I haven't forgotten. I'm just stuck here for the moment."

"Stuck? Did your bike break down?"

"I wish it was that simple. If it was, I would know what to do. Unfortunately, in this situation I'm lost."

"What do you mean?" Tristan asks, confusion clear in his voice.

"I'm not sure how much I can share. But, Zoe has a messed-up situation here. Somehow, she has started to count on me to help her. I don't know what to do. I can't be in two places at once."

"Oh, I remember the feeling well. When Rogue and I first started dating, I had a business down in Tampa and she was working at Ink'd Deep in Gainesville."

"How did you figure out how to be in two places at once?"

"I didn't. I decided Rogue was my number one priority. I sold my business to my assistant manager and opened another branch of Identity Bank in Gainesville so I could be close to her."

"Well, I'm not like you. I don't have the luxury of buying a whole new business so I can hang out with Zoe."

"True enough. I would like to see you oversee the IT department at Identity Bank West. However, I can understand why you might want to stay around here."

My heart skips a beat at his suggestion. I'm not sure if it's anticipation or outright fear. I give a startled bark of laughter. "I'm not sure I'm quite at that point yet, but I'll let you know."

"Okay, just keep me informed. I can't postpone the

opening of Identity Bank West for long. Eventually I'll have to put the staff in place. Ideally, I'd like it to be you. You know the ins and outs of computer programming almost as well as I do. I need someone like you on the West Coast because I can't be in two places at once — as you so aptly pointed out."

"At this point, I still plan to travel to Oregon. I'm just a few days behind schedule. I don't know if I'm going to hit the road for a couple more days. Zoe needs me."

"I understand. Sometimes, you just have to follow your heart. So, let me know what you decide."

"I'm not sure this has anything to do with my heart, but I will give you a call when I determine what I'm planning to do."

Just then, Hope and Bruiser begin to bark wildly. "I've gotta go!" I reply quickly as I stuff my phone in my pocket and run toward the sound. I have no idea why the dogs are so worked up. Zoe is at a private training session with a client. I am the only one here.

As I round the corner and open the gate to the dog run, Hope immediately runs to me. Bruiser has been attached to me like Velcro, so I am shocked when he doesn't greet me at the gate.

I enter the dog run and search for Bruiser. Hope noses me in the leg and takes off running. I follow her to a shaded part of the dog run. Bruiser is trying to lick something off his fur. He is so intent, he doesn't even acknowledge my presence. Hope barks at him. When she does, he stands up and turns around. Much to my dismay, there are trails of red dripping down his fur. When I look closer, I discover the red marks on Bruiser's fur resemble a target.

I curse under my breath as I run toward Bruiser. When I touch his fur, I realize that I'm not looking at blood. I can barely catch my breath when I realize someone spray-painted a target on my dog while I was just a few feet away in the training room.

Bruiser tries to reach the paint and lick it off. I attach the leash I have hanging around my neck and escort Bruiser and Hope into the utility room. I quickly scan Hope to see if she has also been painted. Fortunately, she appears to have escaped unscathed.

Bruiser looks up at me and whimpers. "I know. It probably itches, but I can't wash you yet."

I pull my phone out of my pocket and call Officer Erickson.

After we exchange small talk, I take a deep breath and announce. "Cody, I don't know if you're in the middle of something, but I need you to come out to Hope's Haven. It's urgent."

"I'll be right there," Cody answers. He must be able to hear the sheer panic in my voice.

I grab a plastic 'cone-of-shame' collar off the hook in the utility room and place it around Bruiser's neck to prevent him from eating any more paint. I sink into the ground and Bruiser awkwardly lies down beside me as we wait.

Cody has his cell phone out and he's taking pictures as he whistles softly through his teeth. "So, do I understand this correctly? You didn't hear anything?"

Embarrassed, I shake my head and frown.

"No, Bruiser was really clingy today. I put him in the dog run so I could get some work done. Zoe is really tired because she hasn't been sleeping well since the threat from her brother. I thought I'd surprise her and get some of her routine chores done so she wouldn't have to mess with it when she finishes her class."

"You were inside?" Cody clarifies.

I nod. "I was on the phone with my boss. I was just about to hang up when the dogs went ballistic. They were barking more ferociously than I've ever heard. It surprised me because I don't usually hear Hope bark. In fact, most of the time I forget she's around because she's so mellow."

"Yeah, I'm a little surprised Mitch and Jessica left her behind. She usually travels with them."

"Zoe told me they have Hope in retirement mode. I guess her hip has been bothering her a little." I shrug. "Anyway, Zoe says they are traveling with one of the service dogs in training."

Cody grimaces. "Boy, I sure wish Mitch and Jessica were here. On the other hand, maybe it's better that their little family is somewhere else."

"I suppose so," I concede.

"Whoever this is seems to be escalating. Although this round wasn't particularly detrimental to the dogs, there's nothing to say the next round may not be."

"That's a horrifying thought. They got close enough to paint the dog with an identifiable pattern. I'd hate to think what they could do. I guess I should've done a better job watching out for the dogs."

Cody shakes his head. "Don't be silly. Mitch and Jessica let the dogs run in the exercise yard all the time.

You didn't have any reason to think something would happen to them right under your nose."

I roll my shoulder. "I don't know. I guess maybe I should have figured that things would get worse before they got better. The threat with the matches was pretty explicit."

"True enough. I am glad you are here to watch out for Zoe. Have you checked in with her during the last few minutes?"

I look down at the ground and shuffle my feet. "No. I totally suck at this protector gig."

Cody claps his hand on my shoulder. "Don't worry about it. You did lots of stuff right. You got me here right away and you didn't mess with the evidence. So, that's something."

I feel my face heat up as I blush. "I don't know if it's enough."

"To be honest, I don't know if it's enough either. I know Zoe doesn't want to leave town because she doesn't want her tormentor to win. But in this case, the threats are getting awfully close. I think maybe you should talk to her about that and see if you can encourage her to change her mind."

I slump down on one of the step stools in the training room. "I wish it was that easy. If it was, I would pull out my extra helmet and plop her on the back of my bike in a heartbeat. Oregon is a good place to go on vacation. But, she still has to deal with whatever garbage is coming up with her brother."

Cody frowns. "I forgot about her subpoena. That certainly complicates things."

I swallow hard. "Yeah, I suppose it does. But, if this

idiot is capable of getting so close to something that Zoe loves, who's to say he won't try to harm her too?"

"I wish I had an answer for you, I really do. Unfortunately, I don't. This case is just going to have to run its course."

"What am I going to do?" I ask. "I wasn't even planning to stay this long. But, I can't leave her alone."

"I think the bigger question will be what Zoe allows you to. She is independent and wants to make her own decisions."

"I think that choice was taken out of our hands the first night we received a threat." I comment as I stroke Bruiser's head for comfort.

I groan in frustration when my hair escapes from the leather band at the base of my neck and falls into my face. Bruiser takes advantage of my distraction and tries to get out of the tub. "Hold still. Wait! Don't cram yourself up against the side of the tub. I still have to wash that side."

Bruiser whimpers and lies down in the water. I try to blow my hair out of my eyes. "Well, I suppose that's better than smashing your side up against the wall of the tub."

He wags his tail and splashes me with water. He looks quite smug even though he is soaking wet and shaking.

"What are you doing?" Zoe asks. "Why are you giving Bruiser a bath in Jessica's whirlpool tub?"

When Bruiser hears Zoe's voice, he tries to climb out of the tub again. Zoe comes in and stands beside me as she commands, "Stay!" Bruiser freezes in place and looks up at Zoe with sad, pathetic eyes.

"Oh my gosh! What is that red stuff in the water? Is he bleeding again?"

"He's fine. Somebody tagged him with spray paint." I help Bruiser turn around so Zoe can see the side with the paint remnants.

Disregarding the water, Zoe throws her arms around Bruiser's neck as she cries, "Who would do that to you? What happened?"

"I put the dogs in the exercise yard while I did some work. I was on the phone with Tristan when the dogs went crazy. When I went out to the yard, someone had painted a bull's-eye target on Bruiser."

"Who was out there with him? Did they hurt that dog too?"

I shake my head. "No, fortunately they left Hope alone."

"I can imagine. Hope looks a little more formidable than this friendly guy. Still, I can't figure out why someone would paint on him. That's just cruel."

"I agree. I don't know if it was just teenagers causing mischief or if it's related to the other threats you've received. It's odd that kids would target one dog and not the other. To me, this feels a little more personal."

Zoe blanches. "I can't tell you how much I want you to be wrong. But, I suppose we should call Cody and let him know. It's too bad you washed away the evidence." Zoe wipes away tears with the back of her hand.

"Already did. It was the first thing I did after I got the dogs inside. Cody had an evidence person come out and take pictures in case it's related to the other case."

Zoe examines the tub area. "I wish you would've done this in the grooming tub we have in the red shed."

"I haven't been in the red shed — only the blue one. I didn't know you had a special dog tub. I apologize." I grab a towel off the counter. "I'm pretty sure we have bigger concerns than that," I reply, trying to keep the frustration out of my voice.

"I know. Focusing on the small stuff helps me not freak out over what happened. I don't even understand what all of this means." She wraps her arms around herself. "Come to think of it, I'm not even sure I want to know what it means. I don't know if I should hope that it's the same person stalking me or if I hope it's someone else. Both prospects are terrifying."

"Terrifying is an understatement. You know, Cody suggested that maybe you should leave and keep a low profile for a while."

Zoe's spine straightens. "Do you really think that's necessary? I feel like it'll send the wrong message if I leave. I don't want my brother to think I am turning my tail and running away because I'm scared of him."

As I am washing Bruiser for the fourth time, I admit, "I understand why you feel that way, but I don't think I could handle it if something happened to you."

Zoe's eyes tear up. "For a guy who says he doesn't communicate well, you say the sweetest things."

I don't know what to say to something like that, so I just turn around and continue washing Bruiser.

Chapter Ten

Zoe

I TRY NOT TO throw up as I sit in front of Tori Clarksfield, the attorney prosecuting the case against my brother.

She is examining a file and shaking her head. "I'm sorry Zoe, the trial is due to start in a matter of days. I don't think it would be a good time for you to leave town. I understand things are scary — but if we don't get your brother off the street, they're not likely to get any better. I know you don't know the full extent of it, but your brother is a dangerous man."

I swallow hard. "You don't have to tell me. I've kind of figured it out on my own. But I don't know if my voice will be enough to stop him. There were lots of people at that wedding. Do I have to be the one to testify?"

Phoenix squeezes my hand. "Zoe has a point. Is her testimony really necessary?"

The prosecutor nods. "I'm afraid it is."

Phoenix glares at her. "I haven't known Zoe for long but I know she was absolutely petrified when the first threat came in. I was there. It was disturbing. I'm worried this crazy person is going to hurt her."

Tori leans back in her chair as she studies me. "I understand your concerns. I'll do what I can. Still, I can't make any promises this close to trial."

She stands up and reaches out to shake my hand. When she tries to shake Phoenix's hand, he stuffs them in his pocket. I know this move isn't personal — I've seen him do it a hundred times. From the frown on her face, I can tell the prosecutor doesn't understand Phoenix's issues.

She scowls at Phoenix. "Is there a problem here? I told you I would do my best to protect your girlfriend, but I am not the miracle worker. I'm sorry if that upsets you."

His shoulders slump dejectedly. "I'm not upset. Wait, that's not true. I'm angry, but I'm not upset at you. I'm totally ticked off at the person who thinks he can disrupt Zoe's life. Nothing personal against you, I just don't shake hands very often.

Tori retracts her hand and wipes it on her skirt. "Alrighty then. I'll just call you if I have news. In the meantime, sit tight."

It's a good thing Phoenix is driving us home. My nerves are too frazzled to even think about concentrating on traffic. I'm in full-on rant mode and I refuse to apologize. "Sit tight? Is she serious? What the heck does she expect me to do? I guess if I'm burned to death in my sleep, it'll be on her."

Phoenix's jaw tightens and his knuckles turn white as he grips the steering wheel. "Hopefully, it won't come anywhere close to that. The good news is the trial is soon, so this should all be over quickly."

I slump back against the seat with a quiet moan. "But

what if it's not? What then? How do I go on with my life if my brother gets away with this? Am I going to have to look over my shoulder for the rest of my life?"

We pull to a stop at a light. Phoenix reaches out and grabs my hand. "Zoe, you need to stop torturing yourself like that. It won't solve anything and it makes you feel bad."

"Don't you think I have the right to feel bad? My brother is threatening me — at work! Not only that, he made threats against the animals. What kind of monster has Vinnie become?"

Phoenix clears his throat. "I don't know. However, you have the right to feel whatever you feel."

"Thank God that Mitch and Jessica are back now. Maybe they can figure something out to keep the animals safe."

"I didn't realize they were back. Have you talked to them?"

I nod. "Yeah, they were so nice about it too. If I were in their shoes, I'd be ticked off if one of my employees had a relative who made threats. I'm lucky I still have a job, although maybe not for long. Even Jess told me my stress level is off the charts and I need to take 'a mental health break'. I don't even know what to say to that. She's not wrong."

Phoenix pulls the work truck up into the driveway. After he turns it off, he turns to me. "Ms. Clarksfield said you couldn't leave town for an extended period because of the trial. She didn't say you couldn't be gone for a few hours. What do you say we put all this stress behind us for a little while?"

"How in the world are we going to do that? I'm stuck

here. My car doesn't even work all that well."

Phoenix shrugs. "Not a problem. I've got a perfectly good bike. I haven't ridden tandem on it yet. Now, would be a great time to break it in."

I struggle not to bite my nails as I consider his proposal. "I don't know. Mitch might need me at Hope's Haven."

"…and he may not. Devon is working, right?" Phoenix challenges.

A slow grin teases my lips. "He is. Between you and Devon, most of my routine tasks are finished."

"Great! Why don't you call Mitch and ask him if you can have the rest of the afternoon off?"

"I think I will. It's been a rough morning."

I stuff my hands in the pockets of my jean jacket as I watch Phoenix check out his bike. He opens a compartment behind the seat and pulls out an extra helmet.

"I'm sorry, I don't want to be rude — but why do you have an extra helmet lying around?" I ask as Phoenix places the helmet on my head and adjusts the strap.

After he moves my head around to determine if it's on tight enough, he answers, "I meant to take this out before my trip. I have an extra helmet because my mom likes to ride. She hasn't ridden this bike because I recently traded my old one in for it."

I laugh out loud. "Your mom seriously rides motorcycles? I can't imagine my mom doing anything like that."

"My mom used to have a bike when she was in college. But she sold it so she'd have money for my therapy when I was little. I think when my mom and dad retire, they'll probably buy an RV and tow bikes behind them. They like to travel a lot."

Phoenix grabs my hand and pulls me closer to the bike. It's a little intimidating when I'm standing right beside it. "I'm not sure I'm tall enough to swing my leg over. How should I do this?"

Phoenix squats down and points at his bike. "See these pegs? These are what you rest your feet on. Use them to give you a boost. I'll be in front of you to steady the bike. After you get on the bike, wrap your arms around my waist. The gas tank will be in front of me. When I break, slow down or turn, you can brace yourself against it. Whatever you do, try to keep your head in line with mine so your weight doesn't throw us off balance."

Phoenix stands up and pulls a pair of leather gloves out of his back pocket. He reaches out and pulls my hands out of my pockets and brings them toward his chest as he helps me into the stiff gloves. "Safety first."

I hold up my hands in front of me as I examine the gloves. "You do realize it's hot as blazes outside today, right? The rain was last week."

Phoenix zips up his leather jacket. "It'll be cooler once we're on the road. It's better to be a little warm than get a bad case of road rash."

"Are you saying you're planning to crash?" I tease.

"No, definitely not. Still, it's better to be safe."

He walks toward the front of the bike and straddles it, bracing its weight with his legs.

I watch him skeptically. "There's not much room

there for me. Are you going to be okay with me touching you? I don't see any way I can avoid it."

I can't see Phoenix's face, but even from behind I can see his customary shrug. "I guess we'll find out. I think it will be okay though. I've gotten used to your touch."

In my mind, I throw down a virtual cartwheel. That small admission means the world to me. I step up on the metal peg and throw my leg over the bike. After I get seated, I realize I need to scoot even closer to Phoenix so I can reach all the way around him. When I find a comfortable position, I rest my cheek against the back of his leather jacket. "You're right. This is very relaxing."

"Speak for yourself," he replies with a self-deprecating laugh. "I'm anything but relaxed."

Whenever I saw motorcycle riders on the road, I always envied their sense of freedom. I longed to be in their shoes. Riding one is everything I ever imagined it'd be and more. Even though I've driven on this road countless times, doing it from the vantage point of a motorcycle makes it seem new and challenging. I was always the kid who loved roller coasters and scary rides at the fair. Of course, my ever-so-proper family never understood my obsession.

Phoenix is a careful, methodical driver. He keeps checking in with me to make sure I'm not scared. I'm sure he can tell from the wide grin on my face that this is the most fun I've had in forever.

We pull into Ichetucknee Springs State Park to rest. After Phoenix stops the bike, he issues instructions.

"Okay, you can get off now. Be careful. We've been on the road for a while. Your legs are going to take a moment to get used to being on the ground."

I thought maybe he was exaggerating. I spend a lot of time at Hope's Haven doing manual chores which require lots of lifting. I always thought my legs were pretty strong. Yet, as soon as I hop off the bike, my legs feel like I am a newborn colt.

Phoenix kicks down the kick stand and hops off the bike. When I sway, he turns to steady me. He guides me over to a small retaining wall and helps me sit.

"Wow! You were right. That took a lot out of me."

"Sit tight for just a minute. I'll be right back."

When he returns, he is carrying the small bag he asked me to pack.

"What are you doing?" I ask.

"You said you were afraid of being overheated. I have a plan to keep that from happening. When was the last time you went for a swim?"

My brow furrows as I try to remember. "I'm embarrassed to admit I probably haven't been swimming since high school."

Phoenix smiles at me as he throws the bag over his shoulder and reaches out to help me up. "I guess I won't be the only person stretching my boundaries today. Last one in is a rotten egg!"

"Hey! That's not fair," I protest. "I have to go change into my bathing suit. You already have yours on under your jeans."

Phoenix flashes a smug grin. "Nobody said life is fair."

I shrug. "I suppose not. Still, I bet I swim better than you."

Giving me a startled look, Phoenix asks, "How would you know?"

I brush my fingertips on the front of my shirt in a gesture of pride. "I spent two years on the swim team in junior high. I don't think I've forgotten *everything*."

"So, what you're telling me is I will never keep up with your awesomeness, right?"

I wink at him. "Just remember, you said that — I didn't," I tease as I grab my bag from him and take off at a dead sprint toward the public restrooms.

CHAPTER ELEVEN

PHOENIX

WHEN ZOE COMES OUT of the restroom wearing a red bikini top with tiny blue stars and cutoff jeans, one thought comes to my mind — awesome is not a big enough word to describe Zoe.

It's not just that I think she's sexy — because I totally do. Everything else about her is remarkable too. She has challenged me to do things I never thought I was capable of. If you'd told me a few weeks ago that I would be voluntarily holding someone's hand and letting them hug me, I would've called you certifiably insane. Yet, with Zoe it doesn't seem so hard. Maybe it's different with her because she understands what it's like to feel like the outsider.

Zoe waves her hand in front of my face to draw my attention. She looks around self-consciously. "I know I rarely dress this way, but do I really look so bad? Why aren't you saying anything?"

I blush. "Sorry, I was just thinking how lucky I am that we met. You look beautiful. I can't believe someone like you is hanging out with me."

"Thank you — I think." She looks at my swim trunks which feature Mario brothers. "You don't look so bad yourself. I approve of your wardrobe."

"My grandma got these for me. I think she forgets I'm not a kid anymore."

Zoe shrugs. "I think everyone is a kid once they hit the water. Are we going swimming, or what?" she asks as she walks toward the water.

I adjust my pace so I can walk next to her. I reach out toward her and she takes my hand and gives it a squeeze. I'm amazed every time this happens. I'm so used to being alone and isolated, the simple move makes my heart flutter in a good way. What I used to be afraid of, I now find comforting.

"I guess that depends on how brave you're feeling. Tubing sounds like it might be fun."

Zoe grins. "It does! I haven't been for years. I went once with one of my friends when I was about twelve."

"Then it's time for you to go again." I smile. "Let the fun and relaxation begin!"

I thought I was making progress with my comfort level around Zoe. However, I may have spoken too soon. Things were going well until the outfitter from the inter-tube rental place crams four customers into his super-cab truck.

Somehow in the middle of all the chaos I end up sitting in the middle between Zoe and an another woman. Lara and her husband Brent seem to be in some sort of fight. This is making the short treck to the river awkward.

Lara runs her fingers through my hair and there isn't any room to get away. "You look so sexy. I love men with long hair but Brent says he can't grow his hair because of his job. I wish he looked like you."

Zoe scowls at Lara. "Rude much? Get your hands off my guy."

My guy? My chest puffs up a bit in response to her possessive words.

Lara pulls her hands back as if my hair suddenly caught fire. "Well, excuse me! It's not like it's not crowded in here."

Zoe crams herself tighter against the truck door. I immediately move to occupy the additional space. I release a grateful sigh.

"Well, if he's your guy, then you know all about how great it feels to run your fingers through his hair — give a girl a chance."

"Lar — do you have to do that here? You're embarrassing me. These poor people didn't do anything to you. Knock it off," Brent reprimands sharply.

Lara's bottom lip pops out. "You never let me have any fun. I wasn't hurting anybody. I'll probably never see this dude again."

She reaches up in tries to stroke my hair again. I pull my head away abruptly. I want to stay calm, but my panic level is rising. Finally I bring my gaze to hers. "Please don't!"

"Some vacation this is," Lara complains. "Nobody lets me do anything I want to do."

Zoe looks down her nose at Lara. "What are you? Twelve? You don't put your hands on another person without permission. That's just beyond rude."

Before Lara can respond, the truck pulls to a stop in

front of a little ramp that goes down to the water. Without even having to speak, Zoe and I exit the truck. I rub the golf ball in my pocket and try to calm my nerves. I can't let some weird stranger derail our day. I take a deep breath and let it out.

We pick up our inner-tubes and follow the tour operator down to the water. The guy checks our lifejackets to make sure we are using them correctly. After that, he salutes us and says, "Have fun! Don't let those gators bite you."

"Gators?" Zoe eyes grow wide. "I didn't think about those."

"I am pretty sure they're more afraid of us than we are of them. Besides, I'm certain they have a way of managing them here. Otherwise, no one would ever go in the water."

"Is he right?" Zoe asks as she looks at the guy arranging the inner-tubes.

"I wouldn't try feeding them or anything. We try to keep them away from here — you know, small kids and all? Anyway, gators be bad for business. I was just kidding. Go have yourself some fun."

When I take Zoe's hands to help her in to her inter-tube, I can feel her trembling. "Are you okay?"

"Yeah, I'm fine. I'm just a little weirded out by the thought of swimming outside. Usually, I'm in the pool with nice clean tiles and straight lines painted on the bottom. This will be new to me."

"I'll be right beside you. We can do this together" I assure her. But, then I wonder if I misread her cues. Hedging my bets, I add, "Unless you would rather not. I don't want to make you feel uncomfortable. There's lots of things to do at this park which don't involve getting wet."

Zoe shakes her head. "No, this is exactly what I want to do. I got a little freaked out that's all."

She looks so lost and vulnerable for a moment, I feel an urge to hug her. Unfortunately, I'm trying to hang onto my inner-tube while helping her into hers. I'm stuck and I'm not sure how to help.

The guy releases the anchor rope. For a moment, our inner-tubes are touching so I reach out and squeeze her hand before I grab the handles. "Are you ready for this?" I ask as I feel my excitement grow.

Zoe gives me a tight grin. "I guess it's a little too late if I'm not ready. I keep telling myself I'll like this because I love roller coasters."

I laugh out loud. "Zoe, we're going to float down the river in big rubber doughnuts. We're not going white water rafting or anything."

"I know that," she comments, as her inner tube makes a sudden move to the right. "Whoa!"

As I hit the same small current, my tube splashes water on her back. She shrieks in surprise. I can see her shaking her head at me. "You know what they say about payback, right?"

"It was totally an accident! I swear!" I say as my inter-tube picks up speed.

This time, Zoe shrieks with joy. "This is so much fun!"

For a moment were separated when the current takes me a different direction. I glance over at Zoe to see where she went. To my surprise, I am quickly gaining on her because she isn't moving.

She appears to be stuck. She is rocking her inner tube to try to work it loose. Before I can say anything to stop her, she rocks the tube a little too hard, and it flips over. I try not to panic when I see her disappear underwater. She said she was an excellent swimmer. I hope she wasn't just bluffing.

Pulling on some limbs, I bring my tube closer to Zoe. Finally I'm near the spot where she went underwater. I take a deep breath and try to slow my breathing. That's when I notice the water isn't particularly deep in this spot. I grab the rope from my inner tube and tie it to a low hanging branch. Once I secure it, I jump into the water.

All sorts of scary thoughts are running through my brain. Maybe she hit her head on something or she's caught underwater. I dive under the water to see if I can find her. When I have to surface for air, I'm startled when I feel her tap me on the shoulder.

She looks soggy, but she has an amused smile on her face. "Looking for something?"

Without thinking, I spin around and pull her toward my chest. She looks up at me with wide eyes. I lean down and brush a kiss across her lips. Suddenly, I remember we are standing in the middle of the water. I move away abruptly. She places her hands on my cheeks and pulls me back for another kiss.

"Oh wow! Being dumped in the freezing water totally sucks, but that may have made up for it."

I ring out my hair and tie it in a knot at the base of my neck while I collect my thoughts. "I'm definitely not as cold as I was. I didn't really plan on that, but I guess sometimes the best things in life can't be planned."

I pick up a piece of pineapple from one of the many small dishes around my dinner plate. "How did you even come up with a place like this?"

"I understand you need to be in control of your food. So, when I saw on Google that this Mongolian restaurant specializes in cooking food at your table, I figured it would be perfect for us."

"Perfect is an understatement. The chef who helped us was amazing. He didn't even mind cooking my food separately or leaving the sauce off."

Zoe picks up a clump of jasmine rice and sticks it in her mouth. "Mmm. The food is delicious."

Drawing on the skills my dad tried so hard to teach me, I gamely ask, "So, are you having fun?"

Zoe nods. "The water was much colder than I remember it being. But, the freedom of going wherever the water takes you is worth it. I'm lucky you were able to catch me when I slipped on the wet rock. That could have been ugly."

"We did a good job of watching out for each other today. You totally helped me keep my crap together when the sawgrass wrapped around my ankle. If you hadn't been here, I would've had a complete meltdown. That stuff is so slimy and gross. It's almost as if my brain was ready to short-circuit."

"Hey, it was nothing. You're not the only person to think underwater plants are gross. That's why I prefer swimming inside. At least I know the pool is relatively clean. If it's not clean, at least there's a bunch of chemicals in it to keep the germs under control."

Freedom

"So, does that mean you don't want to do this again?"

The corner of Zoe's mouth hitches up. "I didn't exactly say that. There were parts of today I liked very much."

"I'll probably regret asking this. I guess it's because I am a debugger. I have to know what didn't work so I can fix it."

Zoe reaches out and pats my hand. "Relax, we're supposed to be having fun, remember? You don't have to analyze this."

"I have news for you. I will be analyzing it — whether I ask you for information or not. So, you might as well tell me," I insist.

"Okay. That's honest, I guess. Umm… Let's see — the parts of the date I could do without include getting a mouthful of water, getting tangled up in sawgrass, stubbing my toe on the bottom and being so cold I thought my teeth would never stop chattering."

I scrub my hand down my face in dismay. "Was there anything you liked?"

A secretive grin appears on Zoe's face. "Umm … there were plenty of things I liked very much on this date. Things I would like to do again.

"Really?" I ask skeptically.

"Really. I've never seen so many turtles and the only place I've ever seen cranes so close is on National Geographic. I loved cuddling up to you and feeling the wind through my hair and the sun on my back while we rode. Even though we were doing something inherently dangerous, I still felt safe and secure."

"I'm glad you liked it," I respond, feeling unusually emotional.

"But you want to know what my favorite parts of the day were?"

I shrug because I can't find any words.

"My favorite parts of the day were when you held me in your arms and kept me safe." Zoe blushes and plays with the end of her ponytail. "I would feel dishonest if I didn't tell you the rest."

"That doesn't sound so promising."

"Actually, I loved it when you kissed me. It's the single best thing which happened all day."

Chapter Twelve

Zoe

PHOENIX'S LOOK OF DISCOMFORT makes me want to curse my smart mouth. Sometimes, I'm just too darn honest. Why did I have to say something like that?

After several moments, Phoenix lets out a deep breath. "Oh, thank you. I thought it was just me. I was nervous I'd moved too quickly. I didn't know what to expect, but I liked it too."

"Well, at least we're on the same page," I suggest.

Phoenix slumps back in his chair. "Part of me feels guilty though. I don't want to make you any promises because I have to leave soon."

"There's so much up in the air, I'm trying to forget about that part. I wish you could stay for my brother's trial."

Phoenix frowns. "I wish I could too. But, Tristan said he needs to make staffing decisions quickly. So, I should get there as soon as I can."

I take a drink of my soda. "I know you said you don't fly. But, what if I flew to Oregon with you after Vinnie's trial is over?"

Phoenix appears stunned by my suggestion. "I don't

think you understand. I don't know if I *can* fly. I've never done it before."

"Really? I kinda got the impression from Mitch and Jessica that Tristan flies his friends everywhere on his private jet."

"Yeah. Maybe he does that for his friends, but I haven't ever gone."

"But what if you could? I mean, you're doing lots of things now that you weren't doing before you met me. What if flying on a plane is one of those things?"

"I don't know. Flying from Florida to Oregon is a really long flight for my very first one. What if I have a meltdown in the middle of the flight? I don't know for sure that I won't."

"You don't know that you will either. I'd be right beside you. I would fly with you."

"Zoe, that's incredibly sweet — but I still don't know if it would make a difference. You saw how I was when that chick got into my personal space this morning."

"I don't think that's a fair comparison. Anyone in their right mind would've been upset about that. She was crossing boundaries left and right. If someone would've done that to me, I couldn't tell you what I would do — but it wouldn't have been pretty."

"I can't give you an answer right now. I have to think about it. Still, I would love to be able to help you with your brother's trial. Besides, now that Jessica and Mitch are back. I probably shouldn't be staying at Hope's Haven. I probably need to go back home."

"I'm sure Jess wouldn't mind if you wanted to stick around and work with Bruiser."

Freedom

Phoenix's phone rings. When he sees the number, he holds up his finger to his lips to indicate he needs to take the phone call.

I look down at my plate and start eating in order to give him some privacy.

"Hi, Mom," he greets. "Mom! Why are you crying? What happened?"

He listens for a few moments. "What do you mean they threw something over the fence? Who is they? Did you take Gizmo to the vet?"

I hold my breath as he holds his phone up to his ear with a shocked expression on his face. "What do you mean the vet couldn't save her? Don't they have antidotes or something?"

At this point, Phoenix's mom starts to cry loud enough I can hear her sobs through the phone, even though it's held up to Phoenix's ear.

"I'm sorry mom I didn't mean to make you upset. I'm just trying to figure out what happened. Why would anyone want to poison Gizmo? I mean, she's not the brightest dog, but she's never hurt anybody!" Phoenix insists.

His mom explains something else. Phoenix reaches in his pocket for his golf ball as he listens. "I know, Mom. I'm sure you did your best. Have you talked to the police?"

His mom replies.

"Mom, I know she's just a dog. But there's been some weird stuff happening in my life recently and I think you ought to get the authorities involved. Whoever did this might be doing the same thing to other dogs. They need to be stopped."

Phoenix wipes away tears.

"Okay, Mom. I'll talk to you later. I'm so sorry, I know you guys loved Gizmo too. I apologize if I made it sound like I'm blaming you. I'm not. I'm just trying to figure out what happened."

Phoenix hangs up the phone and buries his face in his hands. I see his shoulders shake as he silently weeps. "I don't know why all this crap is happening!" he exclaims as he wipes his face with a napkin. "First, someone just dumped Bruiser out on the freeway. Then, you got all those strange threats and now someone killed my dog. Out and out murdered my dog! Why would they do that?"

I get up from my seat and place my arm around Phoenix's shoulders. "I don't know. I've never figured out why people hurt animals."

Phoenix shrugs away from me and closes in on himself. "I don't even know what to do or say. This is just surreal. I mean, I've seen this kind of stuff happen on television, but I never dreamed it would happen to my family."

"Maybe the police will come up with an answer. Do you need to go home to be with your family?"

"No! That's the insane thing. If the jerks had waited one more day, Gizmo would have been at doggy daycare for a week. My parents are going to go to some sort of retreat with my dad's job. They were looking forward to the trip because they haven't traveled in a while. My dad has been looking at golf clubs for six months. My mom finally got him the one he's always dreamed of for his birthday."

"I wish I could do something to fix it. Is there

anything I can do to help?"

Phoenix looks around the restaurant which is beginning to get crowded. "I need to get out of here." He picks up the check and signs it. He stuffs his credit card back in his pocket. "Come on, let's go home."

"Are you okay to drive? I don't know how to operate the motorcycle."

"I'm fine. I just want to go someplace where I'm comfortable."

"Do you mean Hope's Haven or your house? I can get a ride from someone if you need to take me to your home."

Phoenix shakes his head. "As strange as this seems, Hope's Haven has become like my home. I'll be okay there."

"Are you sure? It might be difficult for you to see the dogs —" I warn.

"You're right. It won't be easy, but Gizmo was a one-of-a-kind type of dog. I'll always miss her. But, I think being around Bruiser will help. He seems to always know what I'm thinking."

Phoenix stands up and puts my jacket around my shoulders.

"Thank you," I murmur as I thread my arm around his waist. "I'm here no matter what you need."

"I know that. I don't know what I need right now. I'm still in a state of shock."

"I don't blame you. But, I can't help but wonder if this happened because you're associated with me? What if my brother is taking his threats beyond just me?"

"When we get home, I'll call my mom again and

encourage her to go to the police. After I have the name of the investigator, I will call them and let them know about what's going on up here."

"I'm so sorry if I caused this. All you did was rescue Bruiser, you didn't ask for any of this."

We stop in front of his bike. He turns me toward him. "You didn't cause any of this. Whoever the wacko or wackos are, they are the ones responsible. Not you."

"In my head, I know you're right. But in my heart, I wonder if you're suffering because you and I crossed paths."

"Never think that. Your presence in my life has made more difference than you can even imagine," Phoenix replies. He takes the helmet and gently places it on my head.

"I can imagine many things, but I'm not sure I've had such a positive impact. I think maybe I've just made your life more complicated."

Phoenix kisses my forehead. "Maybe a little, but you've also complicated my life in wonderful ways I could have never predicted."

I hug Phoenix a little closer on the way home as I tried to impart some comfort to his soul. Losing an animal is devastating — but losing one to a senseless, random crime is tragic. The ride home definitely had a cloud of sadness over it.

I can't help but wonder if any of this has to do with my brother and his threats against the animals at Hope's Haven. I never thought my brother would be capable of something like this, but I never expected him to threaten to burn me alive either. The only part of the scenario which doesn't make any sense is how my brother figured out that Phoenix is staying at Hope's Haven. Even if he figured that out, how in the world could he figure out where Phoenix lives?

I look at my cell phone. Crap! I'm running late. I'm never late. I don't know where my head is at. Actually I do, but it's nowhere good. I need to find my focus quickly because Mitch has a training class tonight and I've agreed to help out. The dogs are really attuned to my emotions. If I'm stressed out, they don't comply with my commands as well.

I go to the kennel to retrieve Jolie, a hearing assistance dog in training. The sheltie is wicked smart but also a little on the mischievous side. I attach her lead and escort her toward the training room. I was hoping Phoenix would work with Bruiser tonight. Given what just happened, I understand why he disappeared into his room as soon as he put his motorcycle in the shed. If something like that would've happened to my dog, you probably wouldn't be able to get me out of bed for days and it would be a long time before I could look at another dog.

I place Jolie in a down-stay in the hallway near Phoenix's room. I lightly knock on his door. After a few moments, he pokes his head out. "I wanted to let you know I'll be in a training class for about an hour. You're welcome to join me with Bruiser if you're feeling up to it."

Phoenix rubs his eyes with the heels of his hands. "I might as well. It's not doing me any good to sit in this room and think about what happened. I feel crazy thinking about all possibilities."

"Okay, but if it gets to be too much, please let me know. Bruiser is in his kennel. I've got to go help Mitch set up the class. I'll meet you there."

By the time Jolie and I reached the classroom, Mitch is already setting up with one of his favorite students, Maya. Maya and her dog Atlas don't need this beginning class. Even though Maya is only nine, they are already competing in agility meets statewide. Even so, Maya likes to come help Mitch run his classes. Mostly, I think she likes to show off what the tiny Chihuahua can do.

When Maya sees us, she runs up to Jolie and me. "Can I pet her or is she working?"

"Jolie doesn't have her service vest on, so you can pet her."

"She's pretty small, but she's still bigger than Atlas. What are you teaching her to do?"

"Jolie is learning to be a hearing dog. That means if someone's doorbell rings, alarm clock goes off or smoke alarm beeps, she will let her owner know."

"That's cool. Who else is coming to class? My mom can't come. She just had a baby."

"How is Chahani doing?"

"She makes more noise than I thought she would. But, she's a pretty good baby. My mom is really tired because she doesn't sleep much."

"Your sister will get more interesting as she gets older."

"Yeah, I know. I can't wait until I can teach her how to play baseball."

I look up when I hear the door to the classroom

open. Phoenix appears a little shell shocked, but Bruiser just wants to come in and make friends.

Maya looks up at me with wide eyes. "Who is that? Why does he look like he wants to run away?"

"That's my friend, Phoenix. He is having a rough day. He's new to dog training. He probably does feel a little overwhelmed."

"Like he's the new kid at school?" Maya asks.

"Exactly like that," I respond with a smile.

"That's okay — I'll sit next to him and teach him how to do things. He looks like he has a nice dog."

"Bruiser is really nice. Phoenix rescued him, so we're not sure if Bruiser has any training."

Maya carefully watches Bruiser for a couple of minutes. "I think that dog is really smart. This is going to be fun."

"Be gentle, Maya. Phoenix is shy. It's hard for him to make new friends."

Maya places her hands on her hips and scowls at me. "I help Mitch all the time. I know better than to be mean to people."

"I know you do. Just try to be patient with Phoenix."

CHAPTER THIRTEEN

PHOENIX

As I stand in the doorway, Bruiser leans against my leg. It's almost as if he can feel the anxiety rolling off me. At this point, I'm wondering why I'm here. Not just at this class, but why am I still in Florida? I should be gone — long gone and halfway across the United States by now. Yet, I can't seem to bring myself to leave.

I'm trying not to obsess over the idea Zoe presented this afternoon. But, I keep turning it in over my head. She's right, if I could just muster up the courage to fly, I could spend three more weeks with her. I just don't know if I can. Never have three weeks seems so important.

Lost in my thoughts, I jump when a little girl with long dark hair and deep brown eyes pulls on my hand. "Hey Mister, are you gonna come in? Class is starting soon. I saved us seats."

"Why would you do that?"

"'Cause you look scared. This is a fun class. Really! I was scared at first too. I used to be afraid of dogs, but I'm not no more. Your dog looks really nice. What's his name?"

The little girl takes my hand and pulls me into a circle of chairs. "Wait! Slow down. I wasn't going to sit with everyone else. I was just going to watch and see what happens."

"That's just silly. You need to see Mitch and Zoe. They make animals do really great stuff. My name is Maya. Atlas and me help teach the class."

"Why?"

"Because. When I first started learning, I didn't know anything about dogs. Now, Atlas wins agility competitions. I'm here to help other people learn what I know. I'm even better at dog training than I am at baseball — and I'm pretty good at baseball."

I can't help but smile at Maya's enthusiasm. Still, it's a bit much for me to process. "That's great. But, I don't know if Bruiser has ever been in a class like this. We might not do so well."

Maya pulls on my arm as she tries to lead me to the circle of chairs. "Come on, you can do this. You might even be great at it. You gotta try."

Reluctantly, I follow her. This is the last thing I want to do today. Across the circle from me is a dog that looks remarkably like Gizmo. Sadness hits me like a ton of bricks and my knees buckle slightly before I sit in the chair. Bruiser knows something is up. He rests his head in my lap and leans against my leg. Even though my heart hurts, his calm, steady presence is the anchor I need.

Maya grins at me. "Look at that! See? He's already a good dog. I bet this'll be easy for you guys."

Zoe walks Jolie up the stairs of the training structure they built to simulate real-world situations. Mitch introduces her and Jolie to the class and then takes a seat as Zoe puts Jolie through her paces. He is providing real-time commentary and training insights as Zoe and Jolie complete several tasks.

Maya puts Atlas in a down-stay and runs up to ring the doorbell. Jolie finds Zoe and paws at her pants leg while she runs back and forth between the door and Zoe. Jolie's focus is impressive considering several of the dogs in the class are barking like crazy.

Next, Zoe lays down on a little loveseat and pretends to sleep. An alarm goes off on her phone. Jolie jumps up, lies beside her and starts to poke Zoe with her nose. When Zoe doesn't respond, Jolie licks her in the ear. Zoe gives a startled yelp of surprise. She turns to the audience and says, "Obviously, we have a little work to do. I don't know about everyone else, but that would not be my favorite way of being woken up."

Mitch chuckles. "You are such a stickler for details. But, I'm sure Jolie's future owner will appreciate your efforts." He turns back to us. "Aren't Zoe and Jolie impressive? You may think you may never get there with your dog. But, just a few months ago Jolie was found eating garbage out of the dumpster behind a restaurant. In the beginning, she didn't even know how to sit or lay down. When she completes her service training here, she will be able to alert to a knock on the door, and alarm clock, a smoke alarm or other people talking."

Someone from the class comments, "That's great. It really is. But I just wanna stop my dog from jumping on everyone that comes to my door."

"We can do that too. It just takes a bit of time, patience, and consistency. We'll teach Maverick to have great manners. Thank you, Zoe and Jolie for such a great demonstration."

Zoe chews on her bottom lip. I can tell from her

body language she isn't comfortable being the center of attention. She gives a little curtsy and leads Jolie off to the corner of the room. As she passes me, she smiles and gives me a thumbs up. Her small gesture of support helps more than she can imagine.

Maya and Atlas are standing in front of the class next to Mitch. "If you need some help, just ask Maya. She is my junior dog trainer. She might be small, but she's mighty. She's proof you can do anything you set your mind to."

I rest my head against the edge of the couch as I wait for Zoe to finish setting up our picnic. This has become a ritual of sorts for us. Whenever we have to deal with something challenging, we retreat to this room.

"You look wiped out. Maybe I shouldn't have invited you to class," Zoe offers with a sympathetic look.

"It was exhausting, but I'm glad I went. Maya is a riot. You can't be sad around her. It's impossible."

"Maya and Atlas have been one of Mitch's success stories, for sure."

"I thought I knew a little about dog training because I watch a bunch of shows about it. Still, Maya gave me some pointers I've never heard."

"She's a natural born teacher, because you and Bruiser did a great job today. I would never guess that this is the first time you've ever been to class."

I sigh. "I'm still not sure it was a good idea for me to work with him. Won't that just make him more attached to me? What happens when I have to leave? I hate that I have to give him up."

Zoe bites the corner of her lip. "Who says you have to? I mean, I haven't run this by Mitch yet. I haven't had a chance. But, what if I could expand on Bruiser's natural tendencies to protect you and teach him to help you with your autism?"

I rub the back of my neck as I think. "I'm not sure my parents are ready for another dog. They loved Gizmo."

"Phoenix, I'm not talking about placing a stray from the pound with you. I'm talking about preparing Bruiser to be a service dog. He'd be with you twenty-four hours a day."

"How long will that take?"

"I don't know. I can't give you an honest assessment of that until I've worked with Bruiser a little more. He has good basic manners. It seems to me he's had some training before. I don't know how that will translate into service dog training." Zoe shrugs.

"Are we talking years?" I ask with a frown.

"No, I don't think so. If things go well, it might be a month or two. I have to do behavioral screenings on him and test him in many different environments to see if he has any triggers."

I glance up at her with alarm. "Do you think he has problems?"

Zoe takes a bite of her peanut butter sandwich before she answers, "Not necessarily. But, it's something we always have to check for. When I first started this job, I worked with a dog I thought would be spectacular. It wasn't until several weeks into training that I realized she was terrified of people wearing coats. We don't wear coats much around here, especially in the summer. So, it never occurred to me something like that might happen."

"What did you do with the dog?"

"Mitch worked with her. He has more experience than I do. After that, he placed her at a nursing facility where she serves as a comfort dog for the residents."

"That's good, I guess," I concede. "But I don't know how it's all going to work. I need to go to Oregon, remember?"

Zoe turns away for a moment. When she turns back, I notice there are tear tracks on her face. "Trust me, I know. I can't forget. I guess I shouldn't be surprised that it's working out like this. If I didn't have bad luck, I wouldn't have any luck at all. I finally found someone who I can relate to and you're planning to leave."

I move to sit beside Zoe as I gather her in a one-armed hug. "I'm sorry. I wish there was another way."

Zoe leans into my side. "I think there might be. What if you told Tristan about our plan to train Bruiser to be your service dog? Do you think he would give you a couple weeks of leeway?"

"Probably. But that's not my only issue. Remember, I've never flown before. How in the world could I ever fly with a dog?" I ask, my breath coming in short pants as my anxiety level rises.

Bruiser jumps down from the couch and shoves his head into my lap. As I rub his ears, I find it easier to breathe.

Zoe whispers to Bruiser, "Good boy!" She catches my eye and looks at me directly. "Obviously, Bruiser has an innate connection to you. So, the ball is in your court. Are you even interested in having a service dog?"

I nod slowly. "Yes. If Bruiser can do all the things you say he can do for me, I'd be stupid to turn down your offer."

Zoe places her arm around my waist and squeezes. "Then don't. I'll work with Bruiser as much as I can. I don't know how much time the trial will eat up, but I'll do my best to work around it. If I can't handle it, I'm sure Mitch would be happy to step in and help with the training duties."

"You make it sound so easy. This is going to change my whole life."

Zoe shakes her head. "No, I don't mean to seem like it's going to be easy. I need to put you in situations which stress you out so I can reinforce Bruiser's natural tendencies to protect you."

"I can't say I like that part of the plan," I say wryly.

"The process isn't always fun, but I think in your case any price you pay now will be worth it in the end."

"I hope so," I start to answer as my phone beeps. I dig it out of my pocket and realize it was my mom. My heart sinks to my toes when I read my messages.

Zoe lays her hand on my forearm. "Are you all right?"

"Honestly, I don't know. My mom wants me to come home. I don't know if it's because she wants to check in on me or if my dad is having more chest pain. She wants me to come right after they get back from their business conference."

"Oh no! Is there anything I can do to help?"

"Yeah, actually there is. Coping with my life seems easier when you're around. Would you mind coming with me?"

I've had many homecomings in my life, but I've never been so nervous. This is the first time I've brought anyone with me. I hope my parents don't make a huge deal out of it and embarrass me. I'm not a kid anymore, but I think sometimes my parents forget that.

When we stop at the front door, Bruiser immediately sits and waits quietly. Zoe was right, he is a natural in harness. I take advantage of the peaceful moment and bend down to brush a kiss across Zoe's lips.

"It's gonna be okay," Zoe whispers. "It's a good thing you're coming home to fill everyone in on what's been happening."

I smile and run the back of my fingers down Zoe's cheek. I quickly drop my hand when my mom opens the door and gasps when she sees Bruiser. "Phoenix Sky Wolf, what have I told you about bringing stray dogs into our home? I thought you knew better than to do that."

I hold up my hand to stop the barrage of questions. "No mom, you don't understand. Please wait before you decide."

"Why should I wait?" my mom challenges. "You didn't even wait until Gizmo's body was cold in the ground before you moved on to another dog. I'm disappointed in you."

"Mom! Stop please. Bruiser isn't just any dog. He is a dog being trained to help me with my autism. He's a service dog you know, like the guide dogs for the blind only he is for my autism."

Bruiser leans into my thigh and noses my hand. As the tone of my voice raises toward my mother, his alerts become more intense. Finally, I reach down and stroke his ears. His presence gives me enough time to slow down and catch my breath.

"Oh … do you really think that'll help? I've read stories, but I really don't know anyone who has a service dog like that."

"Yeah, he does really help. I am tackling things now that I was too scared to try before. He seems to make things easier for me. Strangers don't focus as much on my weird body language and ticks with him around. He is a good way to start conversations. I just feel much more relaxed when he's around."

My mom steps aside and ushers us in the house. I go toward the couches in the living room. While we are on our way, my dad steps in front of me. "Good looking dog there, son. How did you find him?"

"He was hit by a car and no one knows who owns him. I found him and helped nurse him back to health."

"Well, all that's well and good. But what if the old owners come back to get him after you've made him your working dog?"

Zoe steps forward and offers an explanation. "Hi, I'm Zoe. I work at Hope's Haven. We have made every effort humanly possible to find Bruiser's owners. He's such a nice dog I can't imagine anyone giving him up. But, then again I've seen all sorts of strange things in my job. So, I guess nothing should surprise me anymore."

My dad reaches out to shake Zoe's hand. "I guess that's true enough, my name is Clarence. I'm Phoenix's dad."

Freedom

"I'm Phoenix's mother, Moon Water. Most folks just call me Moon these days," my mom announces as she pulls Zoe in for a hug. Much to Zoe's credit, she doesn't cringe and pull away. Honestly, a lot of people think my mom is on the strange side.

My mom works as a discharge coordinator for a large hospital and my dad is a CPA. My mom is a child of the 60s. My grandparents were bona fide hippies — back when hippies were the "in thing".

My father squats down and starts to pet Bruiser. I flinch. "Dad … can't you see Bruiser's working? It's better if you don't pet him."

My dad pulls away and stands up. "Sorry son. He doesn't look like he's doing much he's just sitting there."

"It's hard to explain exactly what Bruiser does for me. But, just having him around has made a world of difference. Zoe is training him to be a service dog for me," I reply.

My mom's eyebrows lift as she looks at Zoe. "Isn't this the dog that Phoenix found?"

Zoe nods. "Yes, Bruiser is alive because of Phoenix's fast action. He also seems to be incredibly in tune with your son. Hope's Haven is a rescue organization. Phoenix did the right thing in bringing Bruiser to us. We place several dozen dogs a year in new homes. In this case, I think that the best match for Bruiser happens to be Phoenix. If I didn't, he would be placed somewhere else."

My mom seems reassured by Zoe's words. "Oh, thank heavens! You know, Phoenix just lost his dog Gizmo and I would hate for him to lose something else he was attached to just because someone came to get him."

"Mom, did you guys contact anyone about what happened to Gizmo?" Phoenix asks as he walks into the living room and sits on the couch. He pats a spot beside him and then places his arm around my back as I sit close to him.

My dad looks so surprised it's almost comical. He narrows his gaze as he drills me with questions, "I thought you said you met Zoe when she was helping you rescue Bruiser. It looks to me like there's a lot more than just dog rescuing going on here. Are you sure you're ready for all that?"

I practically growl. "Dad! Way to embarrass me. I'm not a kid. I graduated from college and I have a stable, steady job. I'm up for a promotion."

My mom walks behind the couch and pats me on the shoulder. "We know, honey. But you have to admit, relationships are not your strong point. Does she know what she's getting into?"

CHAPTER FOURTEEN

ZOE

PHOENIX GRIPS MY HAND tightly as I sit beside him totally stupefied. I just blink and shake my head in disbelief. Finally, I clear my throat and try to formulate a response which doesn't get me kicked out of Phoenix's home.

"Yes, 'she' understands what's going on. Phoenix is not the only person I know with Asperger's."

"Well, just because you know one person doesn't mean you know autism," Moon counters.

I lean forward and look directly at Phoenix's mom who is sitting on the armrest of Clarence's chair. "Yes, I'm aware of that too. Phoenix has been very open about himself. I'm going into whatever this is between us with my eyes wide open."

"You need to know loving Phoenix is not easy work."

"Perhaps not, but maybe it's not easy to like me either. I'm shy, terribly awkward and can barely read. I've only known Phoenix for about three weeks. But, he has been incredibly supportive of me — even in situations where I know he is not the most comfortable."

Phoenix abruptly stands up and addresses his family. "Did you even bother to look at how things are between

Zoe and me? I was holding her hand. I've taken her on a long motorcycle ride and we've gone tubing at the Springs. She has encouraged me to do things I've never been able to do. Why are you trying to ruin all that?"

"We're not trying to ruin anything. We just want you to be realistic about your … expectations." Clarence replies.

"Look Mr. and Mrs. Wolf, I don't know how things are going to go with your son. I don't think anybody knows. But, I do know he is one of the most compassionate, trustworthy and straightforward people I know. Right now, I need that in my life. Doesn't he have the right to the same expectations as everyone else? He's bright, funny, and more supportive than he needs to be."

"What about Oregon? I thought you were headed there to get a big promotion?"

Phoenix shrugs. "We're still figuring that out. For right now, I'm here. Bruiser and Zoe need me."

"Are you sure Zoe is good for you? Usually, you have all the stuff figured out months in advance. She's getting in the way of your plans."

"Mom! That's not fair," Phoenix yells, unable to keep the anger out of his voice. "Zoe got in the way of nothing. Life got in the way. You should be happy. For once I'm making decisions outside of myself. Isn't that what you always told me? I had to care about other people and get out of my bubble? Well, that's what I'm doing! I'm sorry if that upsets you." Phoenix stalks back over to the couch and sits next to me. He grasps my hand again.

"Oh dear, I didn't mean to make you angry. The two of you need to make smart decisions together. Son, I know you try — but you're not exactly normal."

"Oh good God!" I spit. "When did you ever hear me say I was looking for normal? I wasn't looking for anyone at all when Phoenix came into my life. I've had it with men in general."

"Then what are you doing with our son?" Moon presses.

"For now, I'm being his friend. We've got a lot of things to figure out before we move forward in our relationship. But, make no mistake. I like your son. I'll admit he's quirky, unusual and sometimes baffling. But, aren't most people?"

My dad frowns. "Phoenix, are you willing to give up everything for a 'maybe'?"

"Dad, you're not listening to what I said. I'm not giving up anything. Zoe has made things so much easier for me. You cannot even imagine. I didn't say I wouldn't take the job in Oregon. Sure, this time I won't be able to make the trek across the country on my bike. But it's not the end of the world. I'll get there somehow. Tristan and I have talked about it. He allowed me to have a few more weeks here before I have to interview with the new Identity Bank West."

Bruiser gets up from where he was sitting By Phoenix's feet. He places his front paws in Phoenix's lap and rests his head against Phoenix's chest. Phoenix reaches out and starts to stroke Bruiser's ears. I watch as he takes a deep breath and lets it out. I can feel a sense of calm come over Phoenix as he takes a few moments to gather himself.

"I can't tell you how things are going to go between us, because I don't know. I like Zoe a lot. She has accepted my faults and quirks without making me feel bad. If you give our relationship a chance, I think you'd like her too."

"Son —" Clarence interrupts.

Phoenix holds his hand up to stop his dad from speaking. "See what Bruiser is doing? He knows I'm upset and on the verge of a meltdown. So, he is interrupting my spiral of thoughts and keeping me calm. I wouldn't have even known anything about service dogs for people with autism if it weren't for Zoe. She has poured her heart and soul into training Bruiser to make it so I'm more functional. I'm here today because of Zoe's help. If it were not for her, I don't know that I would've been able to deal with Gizmo's death. We came here today to check in on you to make sure everything was okay and that you were able to get help from the police department."

"Why do you care so much about whether we turn this incident into the Sheriff's office? They probably won't do anything anyway," Clarence snaps at Phoenix.

Phoenix sighs. He runs his hand across Bruiser's head. "There are so many reasons I care. I can't just isolate it to one. But let's start with the fact that people shouldn't be allowed to poison dogs. Whoever did this should be caught. Secondly, someone is making threats against Zoe and I want to make sure the incidents are not related. I've been working with animals every day since I rescued Bruiser. I would be heartbroken if anything happens to any of them."

"Why didn't you make that clear before?" Clarence asks. "We would've handled it differently if we would've known there were other things going on. We talked to a Detective Palmer. But we told him that it was probably nothing important. Maybe we should call him back and let him know about what's going on with you."

I look over at Phoenix. "That name sounds familiar. Isn't that who Cody works with?"

"Who's Cody?" Moon asks me.

"He is the officer who has been responding to the threats against me," I reply. "I think I'll give him a heads up. I'd be devastated if something happened to your dog because of all the crap that's going on with me."

Moon frowns at me. "What exactly is going on with you?"

I press a little closer to Phoenix for support as I attempt to explain the chaos that is my life. "When I introduced myself, I didn't tell you my full name. My name is Zoe Hurlington."

Clarence shoots a confused glance at Moon. "Isn't that the fella's name who's been all over the news? Is he your husband or something?"

I can't help myself as I give a full body shudder. "Thank heavens, no!" I exclaim emphatically. "It's bad enough to be Vincent Hurlington's little sister. I can imagine what it would be like to be married to him."

"What does your brother have to do with the reason why Phoenix isn't going to Oregon?" Moon asks with a befuddled expression.

I grip Phoenix's hand a little tighter. "Do you remember the story of the runaway bride a while back?"

"Yeah, I saw that in the paper. They did an update not too long ago. She saved the life of that guy she met in the bar while she was wearing her wedding dress. I never understood her. What kind of floozy goes running from the arms of one man into another?"

I shake my head vigorously. "No! You don't understand. Katie is amazing. She didn't do anything wrong. It's a good thing she didn't marry that guy."

"How do you know that? She could have left that poor guy at the altar —" Moon asserts.

"I know because I was there. The guy she was supposed to be marrying is my brother, Vincent."

Moon gasps and places her hand over her mouth. "The guy who was charged with kidnapping that teenager?"

I nod and wipe away a tear with the back of my hand. "The very same. That guy is my big brother. I was at the wedding and I saw what went down between him and his fiancée. My brother was downright abusive toward Katie. I completely understand why she ran away. I probably would've done the same thing. But, now since I was there I have to testify against my brother."

"Oh you poor thing," Moon whispers.

"You don't know the half of it, Mom," Phoenix interjects. "Her brother is not very happy with her. In fact, he has been leaving threatening items at her place of work."

"Don't forget the lovely phone calls I've been receiving," I add.

"I don't think I'll ever forget those phone calls. He threatened to kill you and all the dogs you work with. That's not something I could easily forget."

"I hope someone is watching out for you, young lady," Clarence says gruffly.

I squeeze Phoenix's hand and lean my head against his arm for a moment before I answer, "Someone is watching out for me. Your son is doing a phenomenal job. He is what is keeping me sane throughout this whole process. Sometimes, I'm so scared, it's hard to breathe. Yet, Phoenix has been by my side every step of the way since we met."

Clarence looks at Phoenix with the new admiration. "Keep it up son — it's an important responsibility. Let us know if you need any help."

"What are you going to do about the job in Oregon?" Moon asks again. "That job has been so good to you. I don't want her to be messing with your success."

Phoenix's nostrils flare with frustration. "Mom, it's not really any of your business. I like the job I have now. So if I don't get promoted, it's not a big deal. But, Zoe isn't going to let me off the hook that easy. She and Bruiser are going to help me learn to fly. We just have to get through the trial first."

"Okay. Like you said, you're a grown up. I'm going to trust you know what you're doing. That doesn't mean I won't worry though."

"That's understandable," I concede. "Even if we muck up the whole relationship thing, I will always cherish Phoenix. He has been a great friend."

"Take good care of our son. This is all very new to him and I don't want to see him get hurt."

"Believe me, I don't want to see him hurt either," I say as I brush some hair out of Phoenix's face.

I fidget as I pull down the mirror on the visor. I check my teeth for lipstick stains. "You have no idea how much

I wish we could just take off on your bike somewhere. The last place I want to be this morning is testifying in front of a room full of people and the jury who will decide my brother's fate. I don't really want to have to choose sides. This is so hard."

Phoenix takes a moment to study me while we're stopped at a stop sign. "I don't think your suit would've faired too well on my bike. Besides, you look too beautiful today to be picking bugs out of your teeth."

I wrinkle my nose. "Eww! That's disgusting! I thought that's what the face shield was for."

"It is. But, inevitably some of those little suckers get through."

"That's gross! You know the next time I go on your bike, bugs are going to be the only thing I think about, right?"

"Probably. I'll have to come up with something else to distract you when that time comes."

"Oh, so none of this was really true. You were just trying to distract me from my nerves?"

"I can neither confirm nor deny the truth of your statement," Phoenix smirks.

I'm startled when we pull into the parking lot at the courthouse. "Well, apparently you did a really good job of distracting me because I have no idea where all the time went."

"Seriously, don't worry about it. All you have to do is tell those people what really happened and how you discovered your brother's true nature. Don't hold anything back to protect his reputation. If something happens to your brother, it's his fault not yours. He is the one who did all those things. You are not responsible for what happens to him. Your only job is to tell the story the best way you know how."

I reach out and squeeze his hand one more time before I enter the courthouse. "Thank you. Thank you for being here for me. I know I can't change what my brother did, but I still feel slimy going up against him. But, I know what he did to Katie and whoever this new girl is, she's totally wrong. He can't be allowed to continue. So, I have to do this even if it tears my family apart."

"Your bravery is so impressive. I am so proud of you for doing the right thing even though it's hard. That's why the jury is going to believe what you say. You don't try to sugarcoat the tough stuff, you just deal with it. The jury's gonna see your honesty and respond."

"Do you really think so?" I ask as my heart pounds. "I'm not really good in social situations. In fact, I'm kind of terrible. I would rather be at home drawing or playing with the animals. This stuff entirely freaks me out."

"You can do this. Just tell the story the same way you told it to me and to Cody or anyone else you've spoken with. It's just another conversation. Sure, there are more people there. But all you're doing is answering questions."

"Do you think his defense attorney will tear me apart on cross examination?"

Phoenix shrugs. "I don't know what their strategy is, or who they're planning to discredit. It might be tough, but stand your ground. You know what happened that day. You saw it all go down with your own two eyes. So, all you have to do is tell everyone in court what really happened."

"What if it's not enough to make him pay for what he did? If he is free after this trial, I'm as good as dead. You know that, right? He probably will burn down Hope's Haven and everything or everyone in it."

"Well, let's do everything in our power to stop that from happening. You will be amazing. If every witness is as good as you, your brother is toast."

CHAPTER FIFTEEN

PHOENIX

I THOUGHT I KNEW what to expect. After all, I watch legal dramas on television all the time. However, the experience of sitting in the courtroom and watching someone I care about be torn to pieces on cross-examination is unlike anything I've ever experienced before.

Then again, Zoe's brother isn't anything like I expected him to be either. I had built him up to look like some fictional monster. After all the horrible things he has said to Zoe and the threats he has made against Hope's Haven, I expected him to appear like some nasty troll from a child's book. Instead, he looks like he could have walked off an ad for a bank. Speaking of money, it's clear Vinnie the Pooh, as Zoe calls him, has some. His attorneys clearly have a bigger budget than the prosecutors.

At least to me, it seems as if the judge is siding with them more often. I guess this is the side you don't see on television. It seems like all the evidence which would help the prosecutors win their case has been ruled against. I never anticipated so much of this would be done outside of the presence of the jury. The attorneys seem to be fighting over whether i's are dotted and t's are crossed.

After one particularly long and contentious sidebar, Zoe was sworn in again. She looks calm and composed. Privately I know she's not. Her nerves have been making her throw up for days. The longer she has been on the stand, the more confident she is becoming. At first, she couldn't even bring herself to look at Vincent and her parents. Now, she is staring them down. After yesterday's testimony, her parents won't even acknowledge her presence in the courtroom. Today, the defense attorney is trying his best to demoralize Zoe and undermine her testimony.

When the defense attorney basically calls her a drifter without any direction in life, it's all I can do to stay in my seat. I want to stand up and shout at them to leave her alone because she's not the bad guy in this situation. But, I can't do that. It's a good thing Bruiser is here with me otherwise I might just lose it. I try to focus on stroking his belly with my foot as I ground myself against the hard, wooden benches in the courtroom. As angry as I am, I have to remember I'm here to support Zoe. If I have a meltdown, it would just make things worse.

After I take a few calming breaths, I focus back in on the proceedings.

"Ms. Hurlington, isn't it true that you've separated yourself from your family because you hate your brother and have something against him?"

"No!" she answers emphatically. "I'm really disappointed in the person that my brother has become, but I could never hate him. I'm just here because I was subpoenaed. I'm not here to destroy him. I'm here to tell what happened the last time I saw him interact with another woman."

"Don't you think he had the right to be upset when

he was ditched at his wedding?"

"Well … of course. Anyone would've been, but not everybody would've threatened the life of their bride. When I came to see if I could help, he was trying to kick in the door. Sane people don't that."

"Objection! Assumes facts not in evidence and Miss Hurlington is not qualified to render an opinion on the defendant's mental state."

"Overruled." The judge looks down her nose at the defense attorney. "It's your cross. If you don't want the witness's opinion, perhaps you should structure your questions differently."

"Yes, your honor," the attorney replies reflexively. Still, you can tell from his expression he's not happy with the ruling.

The attorney doing the questioning is undaunted. "Just to be clear, you did not see your brother physically harm Katelyn Ashford, did you? In fact, isn't it true that you've never seen your brother raise his hand toward a woman?"

A wave of pain crosses Zoe's face as she struggles to stay composed. "Honestly, I knew nothing about Vinnie's online activities and I don't even know the victim in this case. But, it's not true he's never raised his hand toward a woman."

"Ms. Hurlington, I think you need to clarify that answer. After all, you don't want the jury to think you're making things up just to get your brother in trouble."

"Objection!" The prosecutor says as she shoots to her feet. "Counsel is badgering the witness and putting words in her mouth."

"Sustained," The judge replies. She looks at the

defense and says, "Re-ask the question appropriately or drop the matter, counsel." She turns to the jury. "Please disregard that question."

The defense attorney takes a deep breath and let it out. He slams his legal notebook on the table before he asks, "I'll ask again — what did you mean by your statement?"

"It's been a long time since I've thought about this, but when Vincent was a teenager, my mom told him he couldn't drive because he had gotten a speeding ticket. When my mom tried to take the keys away from him, he backhanded her. It was hard enough to make her mouth bleed."

"Zoelle Dominique Hurlington!" her mom hisses from the gallery. "You were told never to speak of that moment again."

The judge pins Zoe's mom with a withering look. "This is your last warning. If there is another outburst, you will be held in contempt of court and removed from this courtroom. Do you understand?"

"Yes ma'am," Zoe's mother says contritely.

The judge looks back at Zoe. "Were you finished?"

Zoe shrugs. "I guess so."

The attorney looks at the prosecutor. "We're finished here. Your witness, Counsel."

Tory Clarksfield walks up to the stand and smiles at Zoe.

"Ms. Hurlington, this testimony has been very hard on your family, correct?"

"You could say that. These days, I'm the least favorite person on the planet to my family."

"So, it wasn't an easy decision for you to come here and testify?"

"No!" Zoe reflexively answers. Then she appears to reconsider. "Well, in some ways yes. I knew I had to do the right thing. He couldn't keep on hurting women just because he felt like it."

"Speaking of women, the defense asked a good question. Are you aware of the defendant hurting any other woman or child?"

Zoe looks frozen in place for a moment. "I don't know. I'm not sure if this is even important to the case, but Vinnie used to twist my arm behind me and yank it up toward my neck until I screamed in pain if I did something he didn't like. So, I don't know if that's the same, but it was painful and scary when it happened."

Tori Clarksfield gives Zoe a small bow. "That'll be all, thank you."

The judge looks at the defense table. "Any recross?"

The attorney barely looks up from the tablet he is writing on. "No, Your Honor."

"Ms. Hurlington, you are dismissed from the stand. Thank you for your testimony. Please do not discuss your testimony outside the courtroom until this trial is complete and a verdict is rendered."

Zoe visibly relaxes and lets out a deep breath. She stands up and sways a little. Instinctively, I stand up, call Bruiser to me and walk up to the front of the court room. I offer my arm for her to lean on as we walk back toward our seats.

"Phoenix I need to leave. I can't breathe very well."

"Just a moment, let me grab my things and we can

go," I reassure her.

By some implicit agreement, we do not speak until we reach a small, out-of-the-way coffee shop. I order Zoe hot chocolate with extra marshmallows and a black coffee for myself.

When I sit down at the table with the drinks, Zoe sobs. "I can't believe that's over — or at least I hope it is. I don't want to ever do that again. Did you see the hate in my parent's eyes? Things will never be the same — especially if Vinnie is convicted of all the horrible things they say he did to that teenager."

"I hope you don't have to testify either. It was excruciating to watch them tear you down."

"Tell me about it. I was the one they were saying those things to. For the record, just because I work with animals doesn't mean my job is not important or that I'm a bimbo. That was just stupid. So, I didn't go to some Ivy League college like my brother, but that doesn't mean I'm garbage!"

I reach down and stroke Bruiser's ears. "I can tell you without a doubt that those attorneys are wrong. What you do is very important. You have changed my life in just a few weeks. I never thought it would be possible for me to do the things I'm doing these days — including sitting in that stupid, stuffy courtroom. They were simply being mean to try to make a point."

Zoe sighs. "Welcome to my world. All this junk being thrown at me is kind of my new normal now. I don't know if my family will ever recover."

"You did your best. You couldn't have done

anything more. It's up to the jury to figure out who they believe."

"I don't know if what I said will make any difference. It seemed like every time I tried to say something against Vinnie, they squished me like a bug."

"I might be biased. I think you helped Ms. Clarksfield a lot. I hope the jury was paying attention to your brother's body language. He was deliberately menacing you."

"I know. But the court ruled that I couldn't tell the jury about the threats against me or Hope's Haven. She said it was too prejudicial. But, that doesn't make any sense. It seems like the more people he threatens; the more credible the accusations are against him. I wish I could've told my whole story."

"Well, hopefully they got a sense of things through your testimony. I understand Katelyn will be called too."

"Really? Katelyn is coming from Oregon to testify?" Zoe asks after she squeaks with happiness.

"I heard the court personnel talking about it when I went to the restroom. I guess she works for Aidan O'Brien. People seemed really hyped up. Maybe they thought Aidan would be coming too."

"Katelyn says Aidan is a really nice guy. But I'm not sure about her move across the country. I hope I get a chance to see her when she's in town. I always thought she was really cool."

"Zoe, I know this has been tough on you, but you did a great job. Anyone who's been watching closely will understand that you are the one doing the right thing here. The rest of your family seems to have lost their way."

Zoe slumps back in her chair. "I know. I'm not sure how we're going to find our way back. Honestly, I'm terrified my brother is going to get off and he'll come after me."

"We can only hope and pray that doesn't occur. You did what you can do, the rest of it's up to the jury."

"If he is let go, can I run away to Oregon with you? I don't think it'd be safe for me to stick around here."

"Zoe, I would love for you to be by my side anywhere I go, but I don't want you to be running away from something when it happens. Call me crazy, but I would prefer it if you run into my arms because you want to, not because you have to."

As I return from taking Bruiser for an exercise session, I walk past the break room. Zoe is on the phone. I take a moment to watch her simple beauty since her back is to me. Abruptly, she turns slightly and slams her phone on the table.

"I can't freakin' believe this!" she grouses as she picks her phone up again.

I take Bruiser's leash off, but he follows me anyway as I enter the room.

"Everything okay?" I lay a hand on her shoulder.

Tears are flowing down her face and I don't know what to do—I don't know how to fix it because I'm not sure what's wrong. I hate this feeling of helplessness.

I walk over to the sink and get a couple of paper towels. I put water on one and give the other one to her dry. After I hand her the towels, she finally looks up at me.

She looks devastated. She wipes her face with a wet towel and dries it. "Thank you," she mumbles. Louder, she says, "No, I'm not all right. I may never be all right. That was Tori Clarksfield on the phone. She says there has been a brief delay in the case while they wait for an expert witness to arrive. Apparently, the witness is stranded in Atlanta."

I hold my arms out and gather her to my chest for a hug. "I'm sorry. I wish I could fix all of this for you."

Zoe sighs. "I'm not sure anyone can fix this. Heck, I don't know if my brother is convicted of all of this mess it will go away. It's like someone turned my whole life upside down and I don't know how to make it right itself."

I stroke her hair. "I promise that your life won't be this way forever."

"Yeah? It sure feels that way. Now, we have to wait even longer to figure out whether I'll have to watch my back for the rest of my life. I can't handle this stress. I'll go crazy."

"Hopefully, this is just a bump in the road and everything will go back to normal soon."

"I used to like my normal. Now, even work isn't enough to keep my mind off of things. I don't know what I'm going to do. I've got three days off. I'll be climbing the walls before long."

I stick my hand in my pocket and clutch my golf ball as I gather my thoughts. "Do you think Mitch will allow us to borrow the truck tomorrow?"

"Which one, his personal truck or the work truck?"

"Does one of them have a tow package?"

"His personal truck does. Why?"

"I think it's time for us to schedule some fun."

"Sounds like a plan. What are we going to do?"

"I'm going to keep that a secret. It's about time you anticipated something good for a change."

"I'm not sure I like that part of the plan," Zoe says as she takes a drink of the soda sitting on the table.

"Are you going to be okay? I need to go make some phone calls. After I'm done, we'll watch a movie or something. You can choose."

"Oh, I don't think so. The last time I chose our movie, you flinched every time there was a kissing scene."

I turned her around in my arms and brush a light kiss across her lips. "I have a feeling I would do better this time because I decided I like kissing."

Zoe pulls my head back down toward hers. She kisses me thoroughly and then cuddles against my chest for a moment. "You know what? I like kissing too. That's a pretty big admission for me to make since before we met I had completely sworn off guys for the rest of my life."

I clear my throat nervously before I hit the connect button. Tristan prefers to do videoconferencing rather than speaking over the phone. So I prop my phone up between two books I've been reading.

"Hey, Phoenix! I see you're still at Hope's Haven. I've been in that room. How are things going?"

"Well, Mr. Macklin, that's what I called to talk about."

"How many times have I told you to call me Tristan?"

"A bunch, but it still feels awkward."

"Okay, call me whatever makes you feel comfortable. So, I hope you're not calling me to tell me that you're not going to go to Oregon."

I cringe because if I'm honest with myself and Tristan, I am not sure if I'll end up in Oregon. But he doesn't need to know about that right now.

"I don't know how to do this without just flat out asking you. Zoe has had a tough time with this trial. Who am I kidding? It's been awful for all of us."

"I'd be shocked if it was a pleasant experience. Trials rarely are."

"True enough. But, this one has been an especially tough one because it has torn her family apart. She's feeling trapped and helpless."

"That's too bad. Zoe is a great person. What can I do to help?"

"That's the reason I called. I remember a while ago you let one of the guys borrow your ATVs for his graduation party. Could I borrow them too?"

"It depends. Are you planning to take them all the way to Oregon?"

The expression on Tristan's face makes me laugh. "No! I was just going to plan a trip to the Ocala National Forest. They have some trails there. I thought maybe Zoe would enjoy being in control of something for a change. Besides, getting away from town seems like a really good idea."

"The trails there are great. Rogue and I have been several times. Sure, when do you need them?"

"I thought we would leave in the morning. Is it all right with you if she wants to stay overnight?"

"Not a problem. It sounds like you both could use a true vacation."

"Thank you so much."

"I know you have a lot on your mind right now, so this conversation can wait. Eventually, we will have to talk about Identity Bank West and whether you plan to work there."

"I understand, but I don't think I can leave Zoe while she's still waiting for a verdict in her brother's trial."

"You're one of the good guys. I appreciate you watching out for Zoe. I'll pick up the ATVs from Isaac and Rosa. The trailer will be parked in the driveway beside my house. Do you need to borrow a truck too?"

I have to swallow hard before I answer. I didn't expect to get a complement. Even though I should know better, I'm always surprised at Tristan's generosity. "No, I think Zoe is going to borrow Mitch's truck. But I'll let you know if that changes."

"Good enough. Have a great time," he answers before he hangs up.

I let out the breath I've been holding. That conversation was easier than I expected. Hopefully, it's a good omen for what is coming tomorrow.

CHAPTER SIXTEEN

ZOE

A FLOORBOARD CREAKS AS I tiptoe through Mitch and Jessica's house. I cringe. The last thing I want to do is wake up the baby. When they discovered my parents were giving me grief about my apartment, they offered me their mother-in-law apartment. It's tiny, but it has everything I need.

It is hard not to resent all my family has taken away from me. I haven't even shown Phoenix the eviction papers I found when I went over to check my mail. He doesn't need one more thing to stress about. I don't want him to treat me as just an annoying responsibility.

Even though the sun is barely up, I walk over to Hope's Haven to feed the dogs. Devon says he doesn't mind working on my days off, but I hate to leave him with things undone. Besides, keeping busy helps keep my mind from wandering places it shouldn't.

One of the Newfoundland pups we recently took in is so excited to see me, he knocks a bowl of food out of my hands and it crashes to the cement floor.

Phoenix races around the corner wearing only board shorts. "Are you okay?" He asks me as he inspects me for signs of trauma. It appears he thinks I've been attacked.

Before I reach for the broom, I stop to give Phoenix a reassuring hug. "I'm fine. I just had an enthusiastic customer this morning. We made a bit of a mess. I'm sorry we woke you up."

When the scattered dog food finally catches Phoenix's eye, he chuckles. "It looks like Smoke here is going to clean it up before you can get to it. He is like an enormous vacuum cleaner."

"It seems so." I watch Smoke stretch to reach every last kibble.

Phoenix looks down at himself as he holds his hand over his chest. "I guess I should go get dressed. I'm awake now! My heart is beating a million miles an hour."

"I didn't plan it this way, I swear. Still, I can't say I'm sad that we're getting an early start today. I'm curious about where you are planning for us to go."

Phoenix's stomach growls. "I'm still not going to tell you. But, I guess we'll start with breakfast wherever we end up."

"You want cereal?"

Phoenix shakes his head. "I'm feeling adventurous today. Let's go out to eat."

I give Phoenix a high-five when we get back in Mitch's truck. "I wonder what your mom would say if she knew you tried a few bites of my eggs Benedict. That's a lot of food intermingled. You were incredible!"

"Thank you. I surprised myself. But it looked so good. I couldn't resist."

"So, what do you think?"

"The texture thing was a little hard, but it was delicious."

"It was fantastic. Do you think you'll ever order it again?"

Phoenix sighs. "Honestly, I don't know. Some days I cope with things better than others. Today is a great day, probably because you're here with me. I don't know if I would've been brave enough if I'd been alone. You notice I tend to eat the same thing over and over."

"Why? Is it because you don't like other foods?" I ask.

"I guess I just like to know what to expect. But, today showed me I may be missing out on a bunch of phenomenal food."

"Is there anything you would like to try?"

"You're going to think this is totally stupid. When I was a kid, I went to this birthday party. The kid had a giant ice cream sundae. All the kids—except me—helped him eat it. Everyone was having such a great time. But … I just couldn't bring myself to touch it. There was ice cream, whipped cream, all sorts of sauces and bananas mixed together. I wanted to join in the fun, yet I just couldn't. That's when I started figuring out that something was very different about me. I didn't know what to do. So, I pretended I had a stomach ache and asked Brock's mom if she would call my parents and have them pick me up. I was so angry at myself for not being like a normal kid."

I can't help myself. I reach out and stroke my hand down his arm. Much to his credit, he doesn't flinch anymore when I touch him. I guess he trusts me now. "I'm so sorry. It makes me sad for the kid you once were."

Phoenix shrugs. "It's all right. I survived. But, it took me years to summon the courage to attend another party. I guess that's why I got so good at figuring out computers. I had nothing else to do."

"It was like that with me too. When I was in junior high, Harry Potter books and Twilight were popular. A lot of my friends loved reading them. Since I can't read well, I felt excluded. It was just easier for me to get along with animals. Lucky for me, I found a vet who was willing to allow me to shadow his veterinary technician. It was as if I'd found my calling."

"Did you decide not to become a vet tech?"

I slump back against the truck seat. "I really wanted to but my parents didn't think it would be a good idea for someone of my social standing to do such a menial job."

"Why? Taking care of animals is not menial!" Phoenix exclaims.

"Oh, I know. There's nothing like the feeling when you're able to save an animal. Unfortunately, my parents feel like they have the right to tell me how to live my life if I accept money from them. Besides, I don't know if I'd be able to handle college. From what I understand, you're expected to read there."

"There are things you can use to help with dyslexia," he suggests.

"I suppose. My life went in a different direction than all of my friends. I began working at a pet store. Jessica came in to buy supplies. She told me what she and Mitch were doing at Hope's Haven. I asked to volunteer. They liked my work so much they offered me a job." I sigh. "No, that's not giving them enough credit. These days, they're providing almost everything for me because of my parents."

"I'm glad you found someone to believe in you. It's wrong of your parents to withhold money just because they don't agree with what you major."

I reach out and squeeze his hand. "I'm glad you think so too — but it doesn't change what they're doing. So, I'll just have to figure out a way to cope."

"I guess I was lucky. Despite what you saw the last time we went to my parent's house, for the most part, they've been supportive of whatever I wanted to do."

"It's okay. I'd like to think your parents were under stress. Maybe the next time will be better." I look out the window and notice where we're at. "Oh my gosh! You didn't tell me we were coming to see Tristan."

"We won't be here too long. I just came by to pick up a trailer for our activities today. Tristan's like the best boss ever."

I nod. "I'm sure he is. He's probably one of the nicest people I know. There's a reason he's friends with Mitch and Jessica."

Phoenix drives the truck around Tristan's circular drive. I hop out. "I'm gonna go see if Rogue has any coffee," I commented as I hold up my thermal bottle.

"Go ahead, it'll take Mitch and I a bit to hook this up."

Just as I am about to step onto their porch, my phone rings. I don't even look down at my phone before I answer it. "Hi … You've reached Zoe," I answer

"Zoe, I just want to give you a heads-up about something," Tori Clarksfield replies before I say anything more.

"Oh, please don't tell me we're going to have to wait even longer for the verdict."

Tori clears her throat. "I'm afraid that's exactly what I'm calling to say. Somehow, your brother has escaped from his guards. I don't really know all the details because I just got the news today."

"What do you mean he escaped? When I saw him in court, he had handcuffs and leg shackles on."

Tori made a humming sound in agreement. "They should have been taking those precautions. Yet somehow he still is on the run."

I let out a loud groan of frustration before I respond, "I bet he bribed somebody. He used to bribe his classmates and the staff during high school to cover for him so he didn't get in trouble. As the little sister, I heard all about it."

"I don't know. Like I said, I wasn't officially briefed or anything. I got a call from the bailiff. Since Vincent's been threatening you, I wanted to let you know as quickly as possible."

"Now what do I do?" I ask, tears coloring my voice.

"Now, it's the ultimate game of hide and seek," she responds.

"What do I do in the meantime?"

"Obviously, the trial has been put in recess for the time being. The only person who still needs to testify is the defense expert. If I were you, I would think about leaving town. I know it would be cathartic for you to see the verdict, but I've seen the psychological evaluations of your brother. I wouldn't want him anywhere near me. By the way, that's my personal opinion, not my professional opinion," she adds with a dry chuckle.

My hands are shaking as I reply. "Okay, I have to figure out what to do. I'll let you know if I leave town." After a few beats, I moan, "What am I going to do? I've got a job to worry about."

"Perhaps your employer will be sympathetic to your exigent circumstances. This wasn't something we could predict. With any luck, your brother will be quickly found and new charges will be added."

"I hope so too," I whisper as I tearfully hang up the phone.

My knees are shaking so much I have to sit on the front stoop to avoid falling. I stick my phone in my pocket and bury my head in my hands as I start to sob. Phoenix and Tristan must have heard me because they are running toward me at a dead sprint.

Phoenix comes skidding to a stop right in front of me. He reaches down to grab my hand and pulls me up toward him. When I'm standing, he studies me for a moment before he asks, "Zoe, what happened?"

"It's my brother," I wheeze between sobs.

"What about your brother? Don't tell me those high-powered lawyers of his got him off! Weren't they supposed to call you before the verdict?"

I shake my head. "It's not that. It's worse. He disappeared!"

Tristan's spine stiffens. "What do you mean — disappeared?"

"I don't know anything. The prosecutor isn't sure either. It seems like somehow he escaped from the guards. No one knows where he's at" I choke back a sob.

"He must have had help," Tristan asserts. "I've testified in that courtroom. It's secure and their guards are top-notch."

"So, you're telling me the man who threatened to burn you alive is free as a bird and no one knows where he is?" Phoenix asks me. His face is contorted with disbelief.

I nod as more tears flow down my face. "Yeah, that's exactly what I'm saying. It's my every nightmare come to life. Only, it's worse because this time the police can't really help me."

Phoenix looks over at Tristan. I can tell his mind is working a million miles an hour as he contemplates my dilemma. "Let's hurry up and get the trailer attached. I need to get Zoe out of town quickly."

Tristan lays a hand on Phoenix's shoulder. "I think your instincts are good, but I'm not sure the Ocala National Forest is far enough away." He pivots toward me. "Zoe, how do you feel about taking an impromptu vacation in Oregon?"

I hold up my hands in a T symbol for timeout. "As much as I'd love that, I can't leave Mitch and Jessica without notice. They are even more at risk with Vincent being on the loose."

Phoenix addresses Tristan. "You are the security expert here, I just fix games. But, can't you beef up your presence at Hope's Haven?"

Tristan nods. "Consider it done. If Jessica and Mitch need help, I can help cover the cost of temporary staff to cover for you while you're gone."

"That's so generous of you. I hate to put you out

over what essentially is my own little family drama." I respond.

Tristan shrugs. "It's what we do around here. Isaac and I have had to intercede in many family dramas and domestic violence situations. They are among the most volatile things we deal with. I don't think we can overstate how important it is for you to stay vigilant and avoid contact with your brother."

Abruptly, I sink down to the steps as I think about the ramifications. "Okay, let's just say for arguments sake, I decide that ditching everything I care about is the smartest strategy, how can we make it happen?"

"I'm going to put the two of you on a plane and send you West. Phoenix was planning to go there anyway. I'm sure that Jameson will be flexible about his timing. Especially if I tell him what's happening."

Phoenix turns a little grey. "This isn't exactly how I planned for things to go. I thought I would have more time to gradually work myself up to the challenge of flying."

Tristan shrugs. "I'm sorry. Sometimes things don't go the way we planned. But I am confident you'll be able to adjust."

Phoenix breathes deeply causing his nostrils to flare. "I'm glad you have so much confidence in me, I just wish I could be as optimistic."

He looks so lost as he tries to save face in front of Tristan. My heart swells at his bravery. I know the only reason he's doing this is because of me.

I jump to my feet and place my arm around Phoenix's waist. "I know you can do this. Besides, I'll be right beside you every step of the way."

Chapter Seventeen

Phoenix

I SLIDE FORWARD ON the vinyl chair as I try to concentrate on the texts Zoe is sending. It's pretty funny because she is sitting right next to me. If I wasn't wearing noise canceling headphones, we would be able to have a normal conversation.

As awkward as it is, these noise canceling headphones are keeping me relatively sane. It helps that it's crazy early and there aren't a lot of people at the airport. My heart is racing a little and my hands are sweaty, but I'm coping pretty well considering this is the first time I've set foot in an airport.

A message from Zoe pops up. "You okay? You're falling behind. If you keep this up, I'll be the undisputed champion of Candy Crush."

"I'm fine, just a little nervous."

"You want to go to the gift store and get a book?"

"No, I'll be okay."

"Are you sure? We've got a while to wait. Besides, you should buy some gum."

"Why?" I type.

"You know when you drive in the mountains and

your ears pop? It's worse on a plane."

I nod as I put my tablet in my backpack. As I stand up, I hold my hand out for her. She takes it and we walk down the airport concourse as if we're a normal couple. I guess from the outside people can't see my stress level. To me, it feels like I'm wearing a neon sign.

We walk by a store and Zoe looks in the window. She pulls my headphone can off my right ear and says, "Look! Hand dipped caramel apples! Ooh … they have some with chocolate and nuts. Let's go in!"

Reluctantly, I follow her in to the crowded store. She stops by the candy aisle and picks up a pack of gum and then leads me to a glass case with several kinds of apples on sticks. I see one covered in cinnamon candy and I smile. I haven't seen one of those since I was a kid.

"You're right. These look great. What kind do you want?"

"Today seems like a dark chocolate and pecan day," she replies as she points to a tray of apples.

The lady behind the counter smiles at me as she asks, "What kind do you want, son?"

"We would like a cinnamon covered apple and one with nuts and dark chocolate, please."

She hands the apples over the counter. As she rings up our purchases, she says to Zoe, "Make sure you grab plenty of napkins, honey. These are delicious but messy. The two of you are so cute I'd hate to see you get all sticky."

Zoe blushes. "Thanks, I'll be sure to get some."

After we leave the store, Zoe motions me to follow her. We walked to an empty gate where there are no passengers.

I remove my headphones since it's relatively quiet here. "Are you lost? This isn't our gate," I warn.

Zoe shrugs. "I know. I figured you'd enjoy the peace. The food court can be noisy." She reaches in her jacket pocket and pulls out a stack of napkins. "Okay, let the party begin. In my mind, these are even better than an ice cream sundae. I didn't think I would find anything to smile about today. I was wrong. Caramel apples always make me smile. They remind me of when I was a kid and used to go over to my neighbor's house. My mom has never been much of a cook. Usually, she hires other people to do that for us. So, it was a real treat for me when my neighbor lady would help me make caramel apples for Halloween. I looked forward to it every year."

"What happened? Did she move away?"

I watch as Zoe fights back tears. "No, unfortunately, she was killed in a house fire when I was younger."

"I'm sorry." I wipe away a tear rolling down her cheek.

"It was a long time ago. Even so, I can't stop thinking about fire. What if my brother is as crazy as everyone seems to think he is? What if he sets Hope's Haven on fire while Tristan sends me on 'vacation'? I could never live with myself if something happened to Jessica, Mitch and their daughter."

"I work on the software side of Identity Bank — but, I worked on some projects with Tristan for the security side of the business. The man is meticulous. If he said he will step up protection for Hope's Haven, he will. In spades. In fact, he and Isaac are probably planning to take turns personally watching your facility. That's just the kind of guys they are."

Zoe hangs her head. "I know you meant for that to be a comforting thought, but in some ways it makes it worse because it puts even more friends at risk. I shouldn't be the one who gets to escape all this."

"I know how Tristan would view this. He would say that if you're not here, it's one less thing he has to keep an eye on."

"I know that in my head, but my heart says I should stay behind and protect my friends."

"You said you were friends with your brother's ex fiancé, right?" I ask.

Zoe looks a little puzzled by my question. "Yeah, I think Katelyn is awesome."

"I know you felt bad when she was here to testify and you guys couldn't meet up. So, why don't you get together when we arrive in Oregon? Maybe you guys could go out to lunch or something."

Zoe smiles wistfully. "That would be fun. I hope she's not angry at me for all the stuff Vinnie has put her through."

I raise an eyebrow. "I don't see any reason why she should be. Your brother treated her like dirt ... you didn't."

"I guess you're right. But, I still feel awful about the whole thing. I think it's bizarre that I'm taking responsibility for what Vinnie did, but he's not. There's something really wrong with that picture."

"Zoe, listen to me. There *is* something wrong about that. You don't need to feel guilty for what he did. I bet Katelyn doesn't hold you responsible for the fact that your brother is a jerk."

A staticky voice comes over the intercom and pages passengers for our flight. I draw in a deep breath. Zoe tosses what's left of her apple into a nearby garbage can. When she comes back to my seat, she pulls me up to a standing position by grabbing both of my hands. She squeezes them and asks, "Are you ready for your next adventure Mr. Wolf?"

I take the package of gum out of the sack and place it in my pocket. "I guess I'm as ready as I will ever be." I try not to sound fatalistic.

I startle awake and glance down to see Zoe curled up against my side. True to her word, she hasn't let go of my hand, even in her sleep. Never in a million years did I think it would be possible for me to fall asleep on the plane. Zoe downloaded some "brain calming" music as she calls it.

Between the music, my noise canceling headphones and my chronic sleeplessness since the trial started, I didn't stand a chance. Of course, it didn't hurt anything that Tristan purchased us first-class tickets. I check on Bruiser and find him sprawled half under the airline seats. He seems totally unfazed by his first plane ride. Then again, I seem pretty unscathed as well. I could get used to this kind of travel. No wonder Tristan gushes about his private plane. I get it now.

Zoe wakes up and stretches. She bops me in the nose mid-stretch. "Oh sorry, how long have we been flying? I'm sorry I didn't stay awake to entertain you. I didn't realize how exhausted I was until I got into these comfy seats. I feel like I could sleep for a week."

I kiss the hand which hit my nose. "It's okay. I fell asleep too." I pull my cell phone out of my jacket pocket and took the time. "Wow! We've been flying for about five hours since we left and stopped for the layover in Atlanta."

"Really? We're not very far from Portland. That's amazing! I'm so proud of you."

"Don't be. I was a nervous wreck when we landed in Atlanta."

"I think everyone is a little unnerved on takeoff and landing. It just makes you normal. You are handling all of this remarkably well. I wasn't nearly as calm as you've been on my first flight."

"I don't know how much credit I can take for that. Most of the things which are making this easier for me were your ideas. I don't know what I would've done if you weren't with me. You are a great travel companion."

Zoe picks up her glass of 7-Up and toasts me. "Here's to a lifetime of successful travel. Where should we go next?"

I grab my bottle of water and toast her. "Here's to having a phenomenal travel partner." I lean in and drop a kiss on her surprised lips. I never understood public displays of affection before Zoe. She makes it easy for me to forget my surroundings.

"Aww. You're so sweet." She smiles at me. "Are you being serious? Where would you want to go if you could travel anywhere?"

"I honestly don't know. I haven't thought about it much because it just wasn't an option. I'll let you know when I figure something out, okay?"

My fingernails have left crescent shaped impressions in my palms. Unfortunately, the landing was not as smooth when we arrived in Portland. I hesitate to think about the damage I've done to Zoe's hand and arm. If I hurt her when we landed, she hasn't said anything. Mercifully, Bruiser slept through the whole experience.

As we stand in front of the baggage carousel, all I can think about is leaving the airport. There was a mechanical failure of the device so, now people are crowding around me as we wait for the luggage to finally show up. I shove my paperwork in Zoe's direction as people start to swarm in my personal space. "I'm sorry. I know I should stay to carry the bags, but I have to get out of here," I croak in a panicked voice.

"It's all right. I've flown alone many times. Bruiser probably needs to take care of his business anyway. I'll meet you by the benches located near the front door." She holds up her cell phone. "If you get lost, just send me a text. I'll find you guys."

I nodded tightly. "Okay." Bruiser can sense my distress. I don't know if Zoe taught him this, but he has taken to placing his foot over mine when I'm stressed out and I am on the verge of a meltdown. I roll my shoulders to relieve the tension and reach down to stroke Bruiser's ears.

Someone who smells strongly of cigarette smoke and cheap cologne backs into us as he muscles a huge case off the baggage carousel. My knees buckle for second as I'm overwhelmed by the sensory affront. The guy turns around and gives me a dirty look. I'm about to say something to him when Bruiser leans his body weight against my leg. I take a deep breath and blow it out as I try to focus on my dog rather than my panic. I have more important things to do right now.

Zoe notices my unease. "It's all right. Bruiser has you covered. I'll be right behind you as soon as our luggage appears."

I feel like I did when I was a kid and my dad lost sight of me in a corn maze at Halloween. My palms are sweaty and my heart is racing.

Bruiser noses my hand as if to remind me of what's important. "All right, buddy. Let's go for a walk." As soon as I say the word, Bruiser perks up and starts to wag his tail. I swear he just smiled at me.

Zoe skillfully pulls the Lexus into a parking spot in front of the hotel. I have to give Tristan credit, he rented a far nicer car for us than I would've chosen. Much to the rental agent's credit, she didn't even bat an eyelash when she saw Bruiser's service vest. She just wished us a pleasant trip.

"You know, when we got up in the middle of the night to take off today, I didn't understand why we needed to leave so early. I figured Tristan was just trying to accommodate my autism. Now I see there was a reason for it."

Zoe rolls her neck and stretches. "Yeah, it's a long flight. I'm so proud of you and Bruiser. You did a great job."

I scoff at her. "Yeah … right. Did you not notice I practically passed out at the airport?"

"I did — but the point is you didn't. You and Bruiser handled it like you guys have been partnered for years," she counters.

I flash her a wide grin. "True. We did survive it with flying colors. I'll be honest, when you first told me that you could train Bruiser to help with my Asperger's syndrome, I thought you were a little nuts. I'd never seen anything like that. But, having him around really does make a world of difference."

Zoe winks at me. "I noticed you were downright chatty with the flight attendant."

I shrug. "Who knew I would run into anyone who has the female version of Bruiser?"

Zoe smirks. "It's not like yellow labs are popular or anything," she teases.

"*Touché*. Even you have to admit Bruiser could be twins with her dog — right down to their crooked teeth.

"Did you have a good time exchanging stories with her?" Zoe asks.

I nod. "Surprisingly, I did. If you would've told me a couple months ago that I would be easily conversing with a person I'd never met without feeling like I need to crawl out of my skin, I would've thought you were crazy."

Zoe takes the keys out of the ignition and reaches over the back of our seats to pet Bruiser. "I'm so glad this has worked out for both of you."

This time, I am better equipped to handle the luggage as Zoe checks us in. For this solid-middle-classer, the opulence of the hotel is enough to take my breath away. After Zoe handles the paperwork, she walks up beside me and reaches for my hand. "Are you ready for another adventure?"

Freedom

I slide my arm around her waist and pull her closer to my side. "Bring it on — within reason of course," I add with a chuckle.

Chapter Eighteen

Zoe

I sigh as I unpack my bags on one of the queen-size beds. It's been an incredibly long day — but it's been more successful than I could've ever dreamed. I usually don't get to see the dogs I place in their natural working environment. Even though Bruiser and Phoenix are pretty green as a team, they've exceeded my every expectation.

I glance over at Phoenix. He is pouring food into Bruiser's dish. "I'm kind of hungry too. Do you want to go out to eat or do you want to binge on food we can find in the little market downstairs?"

Phoenix looks toward me but his gaze doesn't quite meet mine. "You mind if we skip the whole going out to eat thing? I've had about all I can handle today." He appears vaguely guilty and disappointed.

I shrug. "That sounds perfect to me. I'm exhausted too. Let me check — a hotel as nice as this must have room service."

"Okay. I hope they have hamburgers. You'll probably laugh, but I eat my hamburgers dry. I don't like anything on them."

"I'm not surprised. Would you like them to put your

hamburger patty on a different plate?"

Phoenix freezes in place for a moment. "That's really what I'd like, but everyone will think I'm strange."

"No worries. I'll just tell the kitchen I have dietary needs. They don't need to know why. It's none of their business."

Phoenix sinks down on the other queen-size bed. He looks like all of his bones have dissolved. I wasn't closely watching him earlier because I was too busy messing with my stuff and getting it organized. I feel awful that I haven't noticed he looks positively wrecked. Bruiser leaves his bowl and hops up on the bed beside Phoenix.

Phoenix scrubs his hands down his face and then shakes out his hands as if he's trying to relieve stress. "You don't have to do that for me. We'll be staying here for a while. They don't need to think we're both strange."

I pull my hair up and tie it in a loose knot on my head, exposing the purple stripe on the underside of my hair. "Does it really look like I care what people think about me. I simply don't. Besides, who's to say these people haven't seen the news coverage. One of my friends called to say she saw me on a network news station. Of course, they had to be filming on the day I was being cross-examined. I looked like death warmed over. Anyway, people will say whatever they want. I can't stop them. Eating your hamburger the way you like it is not a big deal."

Phoenix sinks back against the pillows. "Do whatever you want. I can't deal with life today. I'm done."

"How about if we're both weird? I'll order yours plated separately and mine on lettuce instead of bread. Money is money and if they don't want to customize burgers, they shouldn't have the option on their menu."

Phoenix yawns. "Go for it," he mumbles before he shuts his eyes. Bruiser licks his hand and gives me an odd look before he places his head on Phoenix's chest.

I resume hanging my clothes up in the closet and putting them away in the dresser. The next time I look over at Phoenix, he is sound asleep. I guess not everything happens the way it does in romance movies.

I stop what I'm doing and place my hands on Phoenix's shoulders as I instruct, "I know you're anxious, but hold still or I'll never get this right."

"You really think it's a good idea for me to wear a suit? I mean I don't know how Jameson plans to run this branch of Identity Bank, but the Florida office is downright casual — especially for those of us who are in the programming division. Of course, the guys on the security side of the business dress nicer than us. Still, don't you think this is overkill?"

I have to fight to hide my smile. I think that's the most words I've ever heard Phoenix utter in a row. "Relax, you'll be fine. You look amazing and smell even better."

I finish tying a knot in his tie. I stand up on my tiptoes and brush a kiss across his lips. "You'll do great. Tristan wants you here, remember?"

"I know. Do you think it looks like I'm trying too hard? What do I do with this?" he asks running his fingers through his long hair.

"What do you *want* to do with it?"

He looks at me with pleading eyes. "I don't know. I've spent so much time thinking about how to present myself that I'm not even sure."

"As much as I like it down, it might look more corporate if we did something else to it."

"I don't want to get it cut," Phoenix says with an edge of panic in his voice. "I'm growing it out for little kids who need wigs."

I run my fingers through his hair. "I'll miss it when it's gone, but it's for such a great cause — so I guess that'll be okay. I wasn't expecting you to cut your hair today, I just need to know how you wanted me to get it out of your face for the interview?"

Phoenix throws his arms up in the air. "I don't really know."

I hug him lightly before I ask, "Trust me?"

He looks at me as if I've lost my marbles. "Of course I trust you. We got on the plane together. Do you understand what that means?"

"I do. If you trust me, let me decide what to do with your hair. I promise I won't make you look funny. Read a book on your phone or something. I'll take care of this."

Phoenix shrugs. "It's not like I have a better plan."

I grab a brush off the dresser and urge him to sit on the bed. I kneel behind him and work with his hair. It is shiny and soft. I just want to bury my nose in it but unfortunately, we have places to be and people to see.

I take a couple of hairbands off my wrist. One day, Devon noticed I always carry hair ties around, so he made me a copper bracelet which holds them when I'm not using them. After I finish running a brush through his hair, I gather it all up in a large ponytail at the base of his skull. I take a long critical look and decide that maybe in Phoenix's case a long ponytail isn't his best look. I pull the rubber band out and start again.

"What are you doing?" Phoenix asks with annoyance in his voice.

"I'm making an already gorgeous guy looking even better. I thought you said you trusted me?" I tease.

Phoenix turns around and looks at me for a moment. "I do — more than you can imagine."

On our way to the interview, Phoenix accidentally grabs the wrong cup of coffee from the drink holder. After he takes a long sip, he wrinkles his nose. "I don't know how you drink this; it's kinda like melted ice cream."

I shrug and grin. "So what? I like my sugar and cream with a tiny bit of coffee. What's your point?" I pick up his cup of coffee and trade him. "That's okay; I don't understand how you can take it black. It tastes worse than nasty cold medicine."

"To each his own," Phoenix adds philosophically.

"Exactly!" I say as I study the big log cabin being built in front of us. The word log cabin doesn't seem to do it justice because it's absolutely huge — but it looks like a traditional log cabin. "Remember, they're not only interviewing you, you're interviewing them too. After all, they want you to move across the United States and away from your family. If they want to keep you, they're gonna have to work for it, right?"

Bruiser licks Phoenix's hand as he reaches his long

arm into the back seat and grabs a leather portfolio with his paperwork. Last night as he was putting it all together, I was surprised to see he graduated at the top of his class. I was under the impression college was extremely tough for him. When I asked him about it, he told me, "People are hard, computers aren't."

He messes with the latch of his portfolio. I put my hand over his to still them. "It's okay. You've got this."

"I hope so," he replies in a broken whisper. "Come with me please. I don't know if I'm ready to face this on my own."

"Okay, I guess they won't care if I sit in the lobby. Besides, don't forget you're not alone. You've got Bruiser here with you."

I try not to look at my watch as Phoenix and I cool our heels in what is functioning as a waiting room. In reality, it's just a very large room. It doesn't even have carpet yet. Every sound echoes across the empty room and bounces off the cement floor. This isn't even my job interview and my heart is pounding as if I've run a marathon.

Just then a blonde woman comes rushing through the front door. "Oh my gosh, I'm sorry you guys have been waiting for so long. Jameson has a thing about breaking phones. He broke another one today. Otherwise, he would've been able to tell you he's running late. One of our contractors substituted some lower quality material without authorization. So, Jameson has his military hat on and he is reaming the guy a new one." She takes a moment to take a breath since she ran out of steam in the rush of words. "Anyway, he should be here in a few minutes. Great man-bun, by the way. You'll fit right in here in Oregon."

Phoenix self-consciously touches his hair and then stands to introduce himself. When he does, Bruiser hops to his feet and sits in a heel position. Apparently, the woman didn't notice the dog before. Her face softens as she takes in his goofy expression. She leans toward him as if she's planning to pet him.

Phoenix clears his throat. "Please don't. Bruiser is still in training and if I allow people to pet him, he gets distracted."

The woman pulls her hand back as if she's been burned. "Oh, I don't even know what I was thinking. I know better than to pet a service dog. Jameson was just telling me one of his former coworkers has a guide dog for the blind."

"I've heard about John, but I haven't worked with him yet. We've haven't been assigned to the same project yet."

"I think Zoe had a role in training his dog," Phoenix announces as he pulls me up to my feet. He turns back toward the woman and sticks his hand out. It's hard to tell he doesn't do this all the time. "Hi, I'm Phoenix Wolf. This is Bruiser's trainer — and my girlfriend, Zoe Hurlington."

"Nice to meet you, I'm Kendall Kordes. I don't officially work here, but I might as well. I'm here so much, Jameson threatens to give me my own office," she answers as she shakes our hands.

"What do you do?" Phoenix asks politely.

"You mean when I'm not covering for my fiancé,

Jameson when he is running late?" Kendall asks with a twinkle in her eyes.

Phoenix seems a bit puzzled by the joke, but nods.

"I am the director of Locate My Heart."

Phoenix's face lights up with the recognition. "Oh, it's an honor to meet you. My boss, Tristan, thinks you're all kinds of cool. Word around our shop was he wanted to recruit you away and have you work for Identity Bank."

Kendall looks around. "As much time as Jameson and I spend worrying about this place, I might as well be working for Identity Bank."

A fierce looking guy with a beard and no hair enters through the front door. "Sorry … I got hung up."

"I know you — or at least I've heard of you," Phoenix blurts. "I'm glad your brother was found alive. I tried to reconstruct his online activities for Tristan, but so many of the sites were shut down I wasn't very effective. So, I'm glad it worked out anyway."

"Yeah, me too. If you decide to come on board at Identity Bank West, one decision you'll have to make is whether you think my little brother is bright enough to be on your team."

Kendall playfully slaps Jameson on the arm. "Way to go, honey, as if Phoenix didn't have enough pressure on him just being here for a job interview."

Jameson cringes slightly. "She's right. I don't want to influence your decision one way or the other because I want us to build the best team. Toby may not be the best match because he still young."

Phoenix lets out a small breath. "That's okay, I was

young when I got hooked up with Identity Bank. Tristan recruited me when I was still in high school. He gave me a job and supported my education while I finished my degree in Computer Science."

Before I remember Phoenix is in the middle of a job interview, I remark, "Really? I knew Tristan was a good guy. He's helped Hope's Haven with some fundraisers, but that's extraordinary."

Jameson shrugs. "Yeah, Tristan is one of the nicest guys I know. It took me a long time to get used to his generosity."

Kendall smiles fondly at Jameson. "That might be true, but I notice you're still planning to take him up on his offer of a private flight on his plane when we go on our honeymoon."

Jameson grins back. "No one has ever accused me of being stupid. It's first class all the way for you, Kendall." He pivots toward Phoenix. "You ready to show me your programming skills? Tristan says you're worth your weight in gold. Let's see if he still remembers what he's talking about."

CHAPTER NINETEEN

PHOENIX

I SHIFT MY LEGS around on the blanket Zoe has laid out on the hotel room floor so I can lean up against the side of the dresser. I guess old traditions die hard. We are having a picnic dinner with steak and baked potatoes from room service. After I take another bite and wash it down with fancy sparkling water, I continue my story, "You wouldn't believe how he's planning to deck the place out. I thought I had a powerful system, but it's nothing compared to what Jameson is installing at Identity Bank West. I wish you would have been back there with me. The room Tristan wants me to work from is probably bigger than this hotel room. I'd have it all to myself. Jameson promised. He said I won't need to have anyone in the room with me. It would be like my own little wing of the building where I can figure out code glitches in total silence if I want to."

"That sounds cool. Although when you showed me your office before we left Florida, I thought it was pretty nice," Zoe replies with a shrug.

"It's a great place to work if noise doesn't bother you. But, it was designed to be like a traditional business space with cubicles. Unfortunately, cubicles don't do a great job of filtering out sound and people's movements in their office. So, I always found myself focusing on the ambient noise rather than what I was doing on the computer. Some days I just about went nuts. This would be so much better."

Zoe looks dejected. "So … that's it? Are you moving to Oregon? What does your move mean for us?"

"I don't know. Jameson is offering me the chance to hire my team and supervise them. He wants me to develop training materials so our games at Identity Bank have less intrinsic errors."

Zoe glances over at me with tears in her eyes. "I was afraid this would happen, I knew you were too good. That's the reason Tristan was willing to let you take a whole month off to get across the country — you are just that valuable to him."

I drop my head for a moment as I admit, "I know. It's crazy! I thought I was going to get fired — but this is like the promotion of a lifetime. I don't think I can afford to turn it down. I may never get another opportunity like this."

"So, what's next?" She wipes away a tear with the sleeve of her sweater. I don't think she wants me to notice her shattered demeanor.

"I haven't made any commitments to anyone. Jameson is introducing me to some people he's considering as new hires. I'll have a voice in the final decision … that is, if I decide to stay."

"Why wouldn't you?" Zoe asks. "This job is everything you thought it would be in your wildest dreams. You have everything here you could ever need."

"No, actually I don't. Because if I am here and you are in Florida, part of me will be missing. I don't know when you became the other half of my heart. Still, that's how it is. I don't know what the right answer is. I worked darn hard to become good at programming. It's taken me years and a mountain and a half of student loan debt to achieve."

Zoe turns away for a moment. When she glances back, she's sporting a weird smile which doesn't go all the way up to her eyes. She looks like she's posing for a picture at DMV. "I'm happy for you, I'm just sad for us," she admits.

I gather her close and tuck her next to me. "I am too. I have never felt this way in my whole life. I've never had a girlfriend — or even a friend who accepts me for who I am. You don't make me pretend to be someone else. I have a sense of freedom around you I've never had. Even with my parents. My parents are always pushing me to be someone different — as in someone less autistic and more normal."

Zoe looks up at me. "Are you sure that's not what I'm doing with you too? After all, I got you to try new food and bake a cake with me. We have gone swimming and hiking in environments I know are not your favorite. If that wasn't enough, you gave up your motorcycle trip of a lifetime to stay with me when I needed you. You got on a freakin' plane for me. What if I've been pushing you too hard like your parents?"

I place my arms around Zoe's waist and I kiss the back of her neck. "You're wrong. There's a huge difference. You make me want to do the things which are hard. But, you never make me feel like a failure if things don't go the way we planned."

"Plan? I can't make plans — my crazy brother might still be after me."

"That's the beauty of our plan, if you stay here with me, there's a whole continent between you and your brother. I can't imagine so much distance is a bad idea."

"You're right. What do I do about Hope's Haven?"

I rest my chin on the top of Zoe's head. "I wish I knew. Maybe we'll have more answers tomorrow. For now, this is supposed to be a celebration. We are alone together with only tomorrow's meeting on our schedule. Jameson won't be in until after two thirty in the afternoon. So, we're on our own. We can watch anything we want on TV or do something outside — I don't know."

Zoe looks up at me with a tearful smile. "I guess you'll have to find a way to distract me from the bad news."

I hop up and grab my iPad off the dresser. "I've got just the thing. Jameson gave me a game he and his brother developed. Since I've never seen it before, he wants me to pretend I'm a typical first-time user to see if they need to change the interface."

Zoe chokes back a snort of laughter. "Okay, that wasn't exactly what I had in mind. It does sound fun though."

I point to myself. "Am I not the very picture of fun?"

Zoe pops a chocolate covered strawberry in her mouth before she answers, "Surprisingly, you are incredibly fun to be around. I'm going to miss you when you move to Oregon."

"Who said I was moving to Oregon for sure? I have lots of things to consider."

"All I know is what I see. Although you said you like your job in Florida, you're not completely jazzed by it.

You are more than ready to take on Identity Bank West and make it your own."

The way she says it practically makes my heart stop. "I don't know if I'm ready to take on so much responsibility. Tristan knows I'm not great at interacting with people. Maybe I'm not even qualified to do this job. I should probably turn it down, shouldn't I? I don't want to disappoint Tristan."

"You've worked for Tristan for years now, right?" she asks gently.

"Yeah, since before I graduated from high school."

"So, he probably knows you better than any other person in your life right now —" Zoe lets her speech trail off.

"Yeah, so?" I ask.

"If he knows you so well, he has a good idea of what you can and cannot do. If he thought you weren't capable of handling the tasks at Identity Bank West, he would've never put you up for the promotion. Tristan believes in you and so do I. The next step is to make Jameson a fan."

Yesterday, I noticed things are even more casual at Identity Bank West than the East Coast branch. Today, I've decided to wear clothes which make me feel comfortable. I'm relieved when I see Jameson wearing the same type of outfit.

"You wanna come back and see what our project list looks like for the next couple of years? It's pretty exciting. At Identity Bank West, I hope to integrate our services a little more. When Tristan put together Identity Bank, he did it one piece of the puzzle at a time. We have the benefit of seeing how Tristan's services complement each other."

I nod. "That makes perfect sense. Sometimes, when I'm fixing errors in code, I think it would be great to be able to work with the graphic artists to make sure we don't introduce errors into our work along the way."

"That is a great idea. I'm curious to see how you'll structure your department."

I hold my hands up in front of me as I protest. "I don't want to mislead you, although what you're doing is phenomenal, my life is back in Florida. I don't even know if I'm qualified to a whole department. I'm talented when it comes to computers — when I have to interact with other people, I'm not so great. I'm not even sure why Tristan thinks I'm ready for this."

Jameson grins at me. "About a year ago, I was saying those same words. I lived in Florida, but the woman I loved lived here. I had worked for Tristan for a few years before he tapped me for this position. I was reluctant to say the least."

"How is it working out for you?" I ask with open curiosity.

Jameson laughs out loud. "It's a fair question. If I'm going to be your boss, you probably want to know if I know my stuff."

"I didn't mean it like that, honestly. I'm simply trying to figure out what to do. My parents still live in Florida and so does Zoe. I like working for Tristan, but recently Zoe has shown me that pushing my own boundaries a bit has some great rewards. So, I'm trying to figure out whether this is one of those situations."

"I hear you. Those were the same things I struggled with but I can tell you that I haven't been sorry I picked up the challenge Tristan issued. Had he not pushed me, I would probably still be fixing security systems, computers and networks for him. He basically dared me to make myself better. It was probably one of the best things to ever happen to me."

I try to absorb what he says, but my brain is spinning with ideas. Finally, I decide the fair thing to do is to be brutally honest.

"This may not be the best place to tell you this, but I feel like you need to know some things about me. Remember when I said computers were easy, but relating to people is harder for me? Well, there's a reason for that — I have Asperger's syndrome."

"Okay … Does it affect your ability to program computers?"

I chuckle softly. "In some ways, it probably makes me better at what I do. As a kid, toys I could sort and put in order were my favorite things. I love patterns — especially patterns which repeat. Computer programming has always come very easily to me because everything is orderly and it's easy to see when something doesn't fit a pattern."

"I understand. Computers are much more predictable than human beings."

"Yeah, that's exactly what I'm saying. If this job was merely programming or debugging, I'd be all over it. But, you want me to supervise. Honestly, some people have a hard time relating to me. I do things which make them feel uncomfortable. I'm working on all that stuff, but I don't know if you want me in charge of others."

"Thank you, I appreciate your honesty. I haven't worked with you directly before, but I've heard good things about your skills. If Tristan thinks there's a way we can make this work, I'm willing to work with him to make it possible. I guess the way I see it is that we're all different; you're just different in an unusual way. I think we can work around your unique challenges and strengths," Jameson says as he stands up to shake my hand. "Take some time to think about it."

"Okay, I will put some serious thought into your offer."

As we're headed out the door, he turns to me and asks, "What are you guys doing tonight? You met Kendall yesterday, she's my fiancée. Aidan O'Brien is putting on a small benefit concert for Locate My Heart. Do you and Zoe want to come?"

"Aidan O'Brien? Doesn't Zoe's friend Katelyn work for him?"

"She does," Jameson answers, "although she most often protects Tasha and Mindy."

"Do you know if she's coming tonight?"

"As far as I know, Logan and Katie are planning to be there."

I smile widely. "This will be a fun surprise to pull on Zoe. Just text me the details and I'll see you tonight."

I grip Zoe's hand tightly as I try to find us a back table out of the way of all the enthusiastic fans.

"What is this place?" Zoe asks.

"I'm not really sure, Jameson just said we should

come," I answer, trying not to give anything away.

For a brief second the curtain opens up and Aidan O'Brien is visible as he straps on his guitar.

"Oh my gosh! How in the world did you score tickets to something like this? Do you know how many years I've been trying to get Aidan O'Brien tickets?"

"You didn't know Aidan and Tristan are friends?"

"I guess I should've figured it out. Katie went to go work for him instead of Identity Bank. I know I went to a birthday party at Rogue's house and Tristan was trying very hard to recruit Katie away from the local police department—but this was before she moved to Oregon. Although I was happy for her, I still miss her. She was cool. It would've been great to have her as a sister-in-law."

Someone clears their throat behind Zoe. "Yeah, I was bummed too. I was looking forward to having you as a sister. John is cool, but he's still only my brother."

She turns around, leaps to her feet, and shrieks, "Katie! I can't believe you're here. Well, I guess I can believe it. Are you working tonight?"

Katie shakes her head. "No, Nick has Aidan's back tonight. I told Kendall I would help with organizing the auction—but I'm done now."

Zoe pulls out a chair. "Have a seat!" Her excitement bubbles over.

Katie shrugs. "Okay, I'll just text Logan and tell him where we are."

"Can you believe what Vinnie the Pooh did?" Zoe presses.

I shake my head slightly. "Remember the judge's

instructions? You're not supposed to talk about the trial until after it's all over," I caution.

Zoe sinks back into her chair. "I know you're right. Tori Clarksfield didn't seem to think I would be called to testify again, but you never know."

Katie glances over at me and smiles. "Whoever this is, he's one smart cookie. I don't want to get in trouble with our judge. She already seems to hate our side."

I nod. "Thanks, I was just paying attention to the small details. My name is Phoenix, obviously you already know Zoe."

Katie's eyebrows furrow, "I'm sorry, I don't remember seeing you at the trial."

"That's okay, you were probably distracted by everything. I like to make myself as invisible as possible. I guess maybe I was more invisible than I thought," I say.

"I guess so," Katie concedes. "Obviously, we have way more important things to talk about than my ex-fiancé. What's up with you?"

Zoe points down to Bruiser at my feet. "Well, it turns out I met this great guy with gorgeous hair and a very cool motorcycle when he called Hope's Haven for help to rescue Bruiser here after he was hit by a truck on the freeway. He decided to stick around to see how well Bruiser's health improved."

A peal of laughter escapes from Katie. "I can tell by looking at the two of you, he was interested in checking out more than just the dog — although kudos to that. Not everyone can be a rescuer."

I flush and I can feel my face heating with embarrassment. "I can't deny what you're saying. Zoe was good incentive to stick around even when I had other places to be."

"Hey, you work with my brother, don't you? I knew your name sounded familiar," Katie responds as her face lights up.

Again I blush as I admit, "I am not great at meeting my coworkers. I've seen your brother around but I've haven't met him yet."

"You sound just like my niece, Ketki."

I raise my eyebrows in surprise. "You're not the first person to tell me about Ketki. I guess when I get back to Florida I'll have to look her up."

"Are you going back to Florida or are you staying here to work for Jameson?" Katie asks pointedly.

"I don't know yet. I haven't decided. There's a lot of stuff up in the air. My life is in Florida."

"I completely understand. It was a tough decision. Of course, it was made easier by the fact that I had a couple of crazy men stalking me," Katie says with a smirk.

"Did I hear from Darya that you shot one of your stalkers?"

"I did. He was going after people I was responsible for protecting. So, I had to kill him," Katie admits with shrug and a sad expression on her face.

I have to remember to close my mouth. Katie doesn't really look like a lethal law enforcement officer. "Everything work out with that?" I can't help but ask.

She rolls her shoulder and her eyes. "As well as something like that can work out. I mean, a guy's dead. But, at least he was the bad guy. It could have been much worse because Logan, Mindy, Tasha, and Jude were all in the car with us."

"Are you sorry you ever left Florida?"

Katie laughs out loud and tilts her head toward where Logan is talking with a woman in a wheelchair. "At first, I was homesick a lot. But I definitely got the best end of the deal. After I fled my wedding, I never believed I would ever fall in love again. Now, despite all that's happened to get us here I am happier than I've ever been. Logan is my rock."

"What does your family think of all this?" I probe.

"At first, my parents were a little worried and sad, of course. They came out here when Aidan threw a surprise engagement party for us and ended up buying a quaint vacation place up here on the edge of the forest. Sometimes they stay here and sometimes they're with John in Florida. It works out great for everyone."

"What about your friends? Don't you miss us?" Zoe asks.

"I do, very much. Fortunately for Logan and me, Aidan travels a fair amount. Whenever we tour on the East Coast, I try to go home for a visit and see as many friends as I can."

I squeeze Zoe's hand. "I didn't consider that possibility. But, I bet if I take the position here, Tristan will want to bring the staff of both branches of Identity Bank together for training. So, even if we moved to Oregon you would still be able to see your family a few times a year."

"What about the whole plane thing?" Zoe asks me with a raised eyebrow. The skepticism on her face is clear.

"I don't know," I shrug. "I did far better than I ever thought I would. I suppose it probably gets easier the more you fly. Who knows? I might even become a frequent flyer or something."

"What about me?" Zoe asks in a small, timid voice as a tear slides down her face.

Katie puts her arm around Zoe's shoulders. "Try not to worry about it, Zoe. I heard Phoenix say he wasn't planning to make the move without you. It's all going to work out. It's only hard while you're figuring it out. Once you guys are on the same page, it'll get easier. Come on Zoe let's go get freshened up before the concert starts." Katie comments as she walks around and pulls Zoe out of her seat.

Zoe looks at me with a startled look. "Oh ... okay I guess we'll be back."

I try to make myself invisible as I watch people mill around and greet old friends. I stick in my earbuds and play music while I scroll through my messages. I take a deep breath and try to shake out my hands. I've been clenching them tightly and they are numb.

I am about to open an email from Tristan when someone taps me on the shoulder. I jump about four inches in the air at the intrusion. When I turn around and see Jameson, I quickly remove my headphones and mumble, "Sorry about that."

Jameson looks around with a concerned expression "Where's Zoe?"

I point in the direction I saw her go when she left our table. "She and Katie went off to the restroom to do whatever girl stuff they do in there."

Jameson pulls out a chair and sits on it backwards. "Awesome, that's probably the best place for her."

"What do you mean?" I ask as a knot of anxiety forms in my stomach.

"I just got off the phone with Isaac. He was monitoring the security feeds from Hope's Haven. Someone was messing with the gates to the dog runs. I guess Tristan told them to start locking the runs since someone was tampering with the yard."

My eyes widen as I process his words. "Do they think it was Vincent?"

Jameson shakes his head. "Isaac says it could not have been him because he would've had to shrink about 5 inches and grow a full head of blonde hair to fit the description of the perp."

"Maybe it's just random teenagers messing around —" I suggest.

"Isaac doesn't think so. I guess their actions were quite deliberate. Besides, Isaac has some contacts over at the jail and it seems that Vincent was caught trying to recruit someone over the phone to do Zoe harm. Apparently, he's trying to eliminate all the witnesses against him."

"Man! That's scary. Do they have any idea where Vincent disappeared to?" I try to quiet my racing heart.

Jameson shakes his head. "I wish someone knew. Zoe's brother seems to have vaporized into thin air. This doesn't have anything to do with your job offer at Identity Bank West, but I think it's a good idea if Zoe considers leaving the state of Florida. After she does, she shouldn't tell anyone in her family where she's at. I suspect her parents are feeding Vincent information about her.”

“I’m not in a position to tell Zoe what to do. I’ll make a few suggestions and hope for the best.”

CHAPTER TWENTY

ZOE

I'VE FORGOTTEN HOW MUCH I enjoy Katie's company. We joke about it, but I really am sad she won't be my sister-in-law. While we were in the bathroom, she announced she would like me to be one of her bridesmaids even though we're not blood relatives. I almost cried when she said she'll always consider me the sister who got away.

After a while, we decide we should probably rejoin the party before Logan and Phoenix begin to wonder where we are. We're walking hand-in-hand back to the table and laughing about the upcoming wedding. "Wouldn't it be funny if we could set it up so I was the opposite of a runaway bride? I could sprint toward Logan wearing my obnoxious florescent orange running shoes," Katie whispers as she breaks out into another round of giggles.

"Don't forget, you'll need to wear the darkest of dark ivory dresses. After all, didn't my brother call you trashy because you were wearing ivory instead of white?"

"Yeah, a spat over the color of my wedding dress is what started the whole debacle. I'll never be more grateful for an argument over clothes as long as I live. I can't believe I was ever so stupid, but the fight showed me Vinnie's true colors and they weren't pretty."

I sigh. "I've learned a bunch of stuff about my brother I never wanted to know."

"I can imagine. He was doing a good job of disguising everything until the wedding day." Katie looks over at our table and I follow her gaze. Phoenix, Jameson and Logan are in the middle of some intense conversation. The mood has clearly changed. I didn't think Katie and I were gone long, but maybe we were longer than we thought.

I walk up behind Phoenix and lay my hand on his shoulder. "What are you guys doing?"

Phoenix flinches slightly at my touch. He pales when he realizes it's me. His reaction is so odd it makes the hair on the back of my neck stand up. Apparently, I'm not the only one. Katie looks at Logan with a narrowed gaze. "What's going on? You have your work face on. I thought we were here to have fun."

Jameson takes off his ever-present baseball cap and fiddles with the brim. "That's what we all thought too, but there's been a development." He frowns.

Before I can ask any of the million questions which flood my brain, Katie straightens her spine and takes a chair from a nearby table and places it next to Logan. She sinks into it gracefully and takes a sip of Logan's drink. "Okay. Spill what you know. We can't deal with it unless we know what's going on."

"I got a call from Tristan," Jameson answers. "Apparently someone tried to enter the dog runs at Hope's Haven."

Katie rolls her eyes. "Please tell me it wasn't my scum bucket of an ex." As soon as she blurts it, her gaze darts to mine. "Sorry, I always forget there are people in this world who still love Vincent."

I shrug. "If even a fraction of the things I've heard about my brother recently are true, I'm not a fan either." I turn to Jameson. "Well, was it Vinnie? Did they nail his butt?"

Jameson shakes his head. "Sadly, that's a negative on both accounts. The perp did not fit your brother's physical description and he got away before the police could get there."

"Stuart says there are a ring of people who steal cute pets from peoples' yards and sell them on the Internet. Could it be that?" I suggest.

Jameson places his baseball cap back on his head. "Could be — it's hard to know. The way I understand it, your brother was caught on tape trying to arrange someone to go after you to stop you and everyone else from testifying against him."

Katie runs her fingers through her thick brown hair. "Why can't that guy get a clue and disappear from our lives?" Her disgust is plain.

"I think that's part of our current problem. He did disappear. It's hard to punish a guy you can't find," Phoenix adds.

Before I can formulate a response, the band on stage starts to play and Aidan begins to sing one of his latest hits. Phoenix looks as if somebody sucker-punched him. His hands are trembling as he takes a drink. Last time I saw him like this it was outside the doorway of the dog kennel. As the situation becomes clear to me, I dig around in my purse and hand Phoenix a box.

He turns the box over in his hands several times before he sets it down and texts me a message.

"What is this?"

It takes me a while because I usually dictate my text messages — but that's not possible in this noisy environment.

"I knew your big headphones bugged you. I got you these. It should help with the sound."

Phoenix concentrates on opening the box. When he sees what's inside, he gratefully sticks them in his ears. His eyes widen and he shoots me a thumbs up sign. He appears much more relaxed as he leans back against the chair and rests his arm around my shoulders.

I rest my head against Phoenix's shoulder as we walk side-by-side into the hotel. After the elevator door shuts, I face him. He cups my face with his hands as he leans down and brushes a kiss across my lips. "Thank you," he whispers.

"Thank you for what?" I ask puzzled by his sudden intensity.

Phoenix shrugs. "For everything. Thank you for making it possible for me to fly out here. Thank you for being by my side and guessing everything I might need. If it weren't for you and Bruiser, I would've lost it tonight when the music started. I didn't even consider earplugs. I was so focused on making sure I didn't mess up in front of Jameson, I forgot how loud concerts can be."

I stand on my tiptoes and return his kiss as the elevator door opens.

After he unlocks our room, I walk over and sink down on the luxurious bed. I pat the spot beside me to invite him to sit down. Bruiser doesn't think twice, he jumps up on the bed and stretches out across the pillows. I don't know what his life was like before, but he is definitely a spoiled boy now. Phoenix shrugs out of his jacket and his shirt. He sits down on the bed, unlaces and kicks off his motorcycle boots.

I scoot back on the bed and sit cross-legged as I face him. "Seriously, it was no big deal. I was happy to do it. I was at the mall today while you were meeting with Jameson. I was bored, so I checked out an electronics store. When I saw the earplugs, I knew they would be the perfect solution. The noise canceling headphones are okay sometimes, but sometimes I need to talk to you. These seem like the perfect compromise. I had no idea we were going to go to a concert tonight though. The timing was perfect."

"You're right, it was. They work exceptionally well too. I was able to listen to Aidan and Tasha sing without feeling like I wanted to crawl out of my skin. I can't remember the last time I enjoyed a concert. In fact, I don't know if I ever have. Usually, they make me feel tense and uncomfortable."

"Did you have fun tonight?" I ask, feeling curious about his experience.

"I did. I was having a great time until Jameson dropped his bombshell on us. After that, my brain was a little scattered. Your friends didn't make me feel weird or anything — even when I asked for my burger to come disassembled."

"It's like Katie said, they're used to special orders because they have to make them to accommodate Logan's diabetes."

Freedom

"Still, it was a refreshing change not to have people stare at me when I do odd things. I'm just sad your brother cast a dark shadow over our night."

"Relax, Phoenix. You didn't come across as odd at all. You fit right in with everyone. But, I'm with you about Vincent. I can't believe we're clear across the United States and he can still frighten me. He has so much power and I hate how helpless I feel. I can't imagine what it's like for Katie."

Phoenix reaches out and grabs my hands as he rests them between us on the bed. We look like we are about to play some elaborate game of patty cake or cats in the cradle.

"If this was a computer glitch, I'd know how to fix it. I'm frustrated because I don't know what the right answer is. I feel like driving over to Eastern Oregon and hiding you in the middle of nowhere so your brother can't locate us. The idea that no one knows where he's at keeps me awake at night."

My lips curl up in a grim smile. "Welcome to the club. I don't think I've had a great night sleep since before Katie and Vincent were supposed to get married."

"So what are you going to do?" Phoenix asks as he reaches out to brush some hair out of my eyes.

I sigh. "I don't have any great ideas. If I run away from my job, he wins. I love working at Hope's Haven. It's always felt like home — even before it literally became my home."

Emotion clouds Phoenix's face. He swallows hard. "So, do you mean you don't want me to take the promotion?"

"No! I didn't mean —" I interrupt.

Phoenix holds up his hand to stop me from talking. "I didn't have a chance to tell you — I told Jameson."

"Told Jameson what?" I ask with trepidation.

"I leveled with him about my concerns regarding my Asperger's syndrome."

I squeeze Phoenix's hands as I ask, "Yeah? Good for you. So … what did he say?"

"He basically said he would work around my issues. The conversation went far better than I could have ever expected. I never figured he would make me feel so normal after I told him about all the things I struggle with."

I shrug. "I know how you feel. I felt the same way when I started working for Jessica and Mitch. The difference was night and day."

Phoenix rakes his hand through his hair. "This is so messed up."

"Messed up?" I ask feeling stung by his response.

"Yeah, it seems that way to me. The best thing to ever happen to my career might cost me you. I'm not sure if I'm willing to pay such a high price — even if the job is tailor-made for me."

"I don't want you to sacrifice your promotion to make me happy," I protest.

"If I don't, I would be asking you to give up your job for me. You told me over and over how working for Mitch and Jess has changed your life. Is it fair for me to drag you away from your home and friends?"

"Life is rarely fair. I learned that lesson a long time ago."

"I wish we could come up with a solution which

would make everyone happy."

"I don't think those kind of endings ever happen in real life. I think people just deal the best they can with what they've been given," I comment as I lean forward and put my arms around his neck. "I wish there were easy answers. I like having you in my life."

Phoenix places his arms around me and gives me a tight hug. I marvel about how far we've come in a few weeks. When I met him, he didn't feel comfortable shaking my hand. Now we are like two pieces of a very complicated puzzle.

Breaking off the hug, Phoenix pushes Bruiser off the pillow as he shimmies up the bed and rests against the headboard. He pats the bed beside him. I join him and rest my head against his bare chest. "Just so you know, I like having you in my life. It's becoming harder to imagine my life without you in it."

"I'm glad," I whisper into his chest. "I hereby give up swearing off of men. You are the best man I know. I'm glad we were able to rescue each other while you were rescuing Bruiser."

Chapter Twenty-One

Phoenix

I HEAR A SIGH of contentment and then realize it came from me. Bruiser lifts his head off my lap to see if I need something. I stroke his ears and he drifts off to sleep as I continue to work on the crossword puzzle and eat my Cheerios.

Zoe is sketching us on a pad using a pencil and charcoal. I didn't know she likes to draw — but she's great at it. I glance up and smile at her.

She grins. "I gotta tell you, Mr. Wolf you are gorgeous when you let loose with a smile."

I blush. "I hope I'm still smiling after I meet with Jameson today. I don't know what I'm going to tell him. I want the job, but I don't want to lose you in the process."

Zoe looks crestfallen. "I know. I thought about this all night. I'm still not sure what the right answer is."

"I do know if it's a question of right or wrong —" I say as my phone rings interrupting the quiet atmosphere of our hotel room.

I answer the phone, "Phoenix Wolf, can I help you?"

"Hey Phoenix, this is Jameson. Sorry to interrupt you

so early, but I need you to come into Identity Bank West as soon as possible. Bring your luggage and the rest of your belongings."

"Can you tell me why?" I ask.

"There's been a development in Vincent Hurlington's case."

"Please tell me they found the jerk —"

"Sorry. As far as I know, there's nothing new there. But, the news filtered down to us. I guess other people have known for a while — but we just got the message. I'll tell you more when you get here." My phone goes dead in my hand.

I'm still holding it as I try to figure out what the development means. Zoe and Bruiser notice my distress at about the same time. Zoe puts away her tablet and charcoals, brushes off her hands and comes over to me. She climbs in bed and joins me. She is careful not to spill what's left of the milk in my Cheerios.

"You gonna tell me what your call was about?"

"We need to pack up and leave ASAP."

"Why? I thought we weren't leaving for a couple more days."

"All I know is that it has something to do with your brother — but not about his escape — and we need to get back to Identity Bank West as soon as possible with all of our stuff."

"Oh No! I wonder what it could be?" Zoe scrambles off the bed and starts to throw things in the suitcase. "You know, I'm really pissed at him. He seems to intrude every time you and I are having a great time."

"I know. But hopefully this means it'll be over soon.

Maybe they're hot on his trail."

When we reach the offices of Identity Bank West, Kendall greets us there and takes the bags from our hands. She loads them in Jameson's rig.

"What are you doing?" I ask, a little put off by her presumptive move.

"I'm taking you guys to the airport. Jameson will return your rental car. Trust me you don't have time to mess with all that."

Jameson comes out the door with his keys in his hand. "Sorry about this, but there was a lapse in communication. We need to get you to the airport or you're going to miss your flight."

"Why do we need to take a flight today?" Zoe asks insistently.

Jameson starts the car up and waits for us to get in. After we have our seatbelts on, he backed out of the driveway. "I'm sorry to have to tell you this on the run, but the judge has ordered a trial in absentia. I guess the case will continue whether your brother is there or not. It starts back up again bright and early tomorrow morning."

"Why wouldn't the prosecutor tell us this?" I ask.

Jameson shrugs. "If I were to guess, I'd say they probably sent you a letter via snail mail which is likely piling up in your mailbox. Someone obviously forgot to call you. Isaac only found out because he was playing chess with the judge. She mentioned the unusual procedure and Isaac put two and two together. I checked the docket online and your brother is definitely on the schedule for tomorrow morning."

"No one knows where he's at?" I press again.

Jameson shakes his head. "He seems to have performed a vanishing act worthy of a magician headlining in Vegas."

"Knowing my parents, they're probably helping him. For some reason, even with all the evidence to the contrary, they believe he can do no wrong."

Jameson flips on his blinker to merge into the traffic on the freeway headed toward Portland. "I wish I could say you're wrong, but I've seen it happen. Even when faced with insurmountable evidence, some family members refused to see the obvious."

Zoe slumps back against her seat. "It's weird. None of this was obvious to me until recently. I thought my brother was a normal, conscientious guy."

I laced my fingers through hers. "Sometimes, we don't know the people behind the facade. The important thing is that once you figured it out, you didn't put blinders on."

"Phoenix is right," Jameson asserts. "You've done everything in your power to make sure he doesn't harm anyone else. There's not much more you can do. We'll have to wait and see how all this plays out."

"Waiting is not my thing," Zoe replies. "What if he hurts someone while he's on the run? It could be somebody I know. He might go after Katie or her parents. They testified too. What if he goes after the poor teenager who started this whole thing?"

"I worked with law enforcement types for years. Trust me. They've played out all these scenarios and have plans in place."

"I hope the plans are more comprehensive than what we were told," I comment bitterly. "We basically came up with our own plan — the police couldn't do much."

"Sadly, there just aren't enough resources to go around. I wish there were. Hopefully, whatever is happening with the trial will help bring an end to the drama."

"One can only hope. Still, I don't think I'll hold my breath."

Right before we hit the secure area of the airport, Jameson reaches out to shake my hand. "I'm sorry we didn't get to talk about things more. But, make no mistake I'd like to have you on my team. I hope you'll at least think about it. I know it's complicated. I just did the same move. In my case, it was so worth it and I think it'd be beneficial for you guys too."

Zoe throws her arms around Jameson's neck. "Thank you so much for supporting us through all this craziness. Thank you for believing in Phoenix. It means the world to me."

Jameson shoots her an amused smile. "Not a problem. I hope this is not the last time I see you guys in my neck of the woods."

Zoe winks at him. "You never know. Oregon is growing on me."

Jameson looks over at me. "Regardless of what happens, please let us know how things turn out."

"Will do." I promise solemnly.

Freedom

As nearly as I can tell, Vincent Hurlington's attorneys are making one last frantic effort to prevent the trial from continuing. Most of this legal mumble jumble is over my head but to me it seems like the judge is not overly sympathetic to their plight. If I was a juror, Vincent's absence is like a red blinking neon sign. Apparently, that's what his defense team is worried about. One of his defense attorneys actually leaves the courtroom in a huff after their motion was overruled.

The judge calls for a recess. When we return she pointedly asks the one remaining defense attorney whether they would like to resume presenting their case. He explains the expert witness is no longer available, so the defense rests.

The judge looks at Tori Clarksfield, "Do you have a rebuttal case?"

The prosecutor shakes her head. "No, Your Honor. In light of the current circumstances, the prosecution has elected to rest as well.

The judge smiles and addresses the jury, "We need to adjust some paperwork, but closing arguments will start after lunch."

As the courtroom empties out, I take a moment to text Zoe. "Good news! It will all be over soon."

"Hope so," she replies. "With Vincent, you never know."

Zoe grips my hand tightly as we wait for the attorneys

and the judge to enter the courtroom. Frankly, I'm a little surprised she elected to join me in the gallery today. When we had to sit through closing arguments and she heard the case against her brother summarized so succinctly, she was heartbroken. I can't imagine how she feels right now. While she would like her brother to face the appropriate punishment, she still can't believe he did the things he's been accused of. It's an impossible place to be.

Tori Clarksfield enters the courtroom. When she sees us sitting behind the victim, she smiles. I suspect she intends her expression to be encouraging, but it doesn't quiet the flock of butterflies in my stomach.

A tear slides down Zoe's face when the defense attorney enters the room and the bailiff asks everyone to stand for the judge. "Oh crap! This is it," Zoe whispers.

The judge enters the room and calls the courtroom to order. She turns to the foreperson of the jury. "I understand you've reached a verdict?"

The older lady with a serious expression nods. "We have."

"Please give your verdict form to the bailiff," the judge instructs. After the bailiff hands her a piece of paper, she takes a moment to study it. "Everything seems to be in order. "She hands the piece of paper to the court clerk. "Mr. Richmond, please read the verdict of the jury into the record."

A slender man with an ill-fitting suit opens the piece of paper. Even from here, I can see his hands shaking.

"We the jury in the above entitled case find Vincent Garland Hurlington guilty of kidnapping in the first-degree, one count of sexual battery in the first-degree and two counts of sexual battery in the second degree and traveling to meet a minor."

Zoe sags against me. "I can't believe it. I knew it was coming, but still —" she whispers under her breath.

Bruiser whines softly and places his head on Zoe's lap.

"What have you done to my little boy?" Zoe's mother shrieks as she points her finger at the jury.

"There will be order in my court. If you cannot contain yourself, you need to leave," the judge snaps as she bangs her gavel on the bench.

She turns to the jury. "Is this your unanimous verdict?"

The foreperson nods. "It is, Your Honor."

The judge looks at Vincent's attorneys. "At this point I would usually order a case evaluation, however, it will be difficult without Mr. Hurlington present. Nonetheless, sentencing will begin a month from today."

Chapter Twenty-Two

Zoe

I TRY NOT TO squirm in my seat as Phoenix and I drive down my parents' driveway. I'm almost as anxious about this meeting as I was about the trial. I've had several days to stew about it. Coming here without Phoenix was out of the question. But since he's been busy completing his work at Identity Bank East, today is the first day we've had a chance to do this.

I'd like to say we have everything settled between Phoenix and I, and that we have made some decisions about what to do. Sadly, I can't. I'm not sure what to do. I can't leave Mitch and Jessica in the lurch after all they've done for me. I don't know how well a long-distance relationship would work between us. His aversion to talking on the phone is legendary. I'm afraid if he goes to Oregon, our relationship will die a slow, painful death. If I can't see him in person or talk to him on the phone, I don't see how there's any hope.

I jump when Phoenix cups my face and wipes away a tear with the pad of his thumb. "Why so sad?"

"I think it's a bit of everything. I don't know what to do. I'd rather not even face my parents today because I don't have any answers."

"I know. But, you can't find answers until you do this."

I lean my face into his hand. "True. Even so, it doesn't mean I'm not scared out of my wits."

"I understand. But look on the bright side. After this is done we get to go to Jessica's birthday party."

I straighten up and take my seatbelt off as I dab my tears off my face with a stray napkin from our last date at Starbucks. "You're right. Let's go face this. I have to warn you, it'll probably be even uglier than the last time we were at your parent's house."

Phoenix walks around the truck and helps me out. He takes a moment to grip my hands between his. "One thing I've learned is the two of us can handle the ugliest of ugly and still come out in one piece."

"You have a point. We certainly have faced a bunch of challenges together. I guess I should consider this just one more."

Phoenix pauses to give me a sweet, lingering kiss before he opens the door to the cab in the truck and calls Bruiser to his side. He bends down to attach Bruiser's lead. I smile as Bruiser licks the end of Phoenix's nose.

"How dare you have the nerve to show up on our doorstep? Do you know what you have done to this family? Are you stupid?"

I stiffen my spine and level a gaze in the direction of the offensive speech. Before I can speak, Phoenix draws himself up to his full height and confronts my mother, "I'm sorry, I must have misunderstood. Don't you mean what your son has done to your family? Your daughter did nothing except tell the truth."

"What good is the truth if it destroys a good man?

She should've known better," my mom counters.

"Mom, the jury has spoken. If Vincent had any good in him, what he did to that poor young woman should convince you it's gone."

"The whole trial was a sham. If they had been fair to Vinnie, they would have allowed him to tell his side of the story," my mom huffs.

"Blythe let it go. Zoelle has clearly chosen someone else over her family," my father says as he walks up behind my mother and places his hands on her shoulders. He scowls at Phoenix.

"Sterling, our children have abysmal taste. First, it was Vincent and that Katelyn woman who set out to destroy his reputation." My mother looks down her nose at Phoenix. "I don't even know what to make of Zoelle's judgement. This man looks like he's homeless or some deranged serial killer."

"Mother!" I exclaim with disgust. "You have no idea what you're talking about! If the last few months have taught us anything, it's that people with the darkest hearts can look like Ivy League prep boys. Unlike the rest of you, Phoenix's never asked me to do something against my moral fiber. I'm sorry you're angry with me for telling the truth, but I didn't have a choice. I'm as disappointed as everyone else that my brother turned out to be a felon. But, it's the way it goes. It's not Phoenix's fault. He has been nothing less than honorable."

My dad looks down at Bruiser. "You've always been fond of bringing home strays. This poor excuse for a human being is probably just another one of your rescue projects. I bet he doesn't even have a job," my father snaps. "Besides, he has shifty eyes."

Freedom

"He does not have shifty eyes!" I protest. "For the record, he has a job which pays more than yours. Not only that, he has a job promotion waiting in the wings."

Phoenix kisses my temple and puts his arm around my shoulder. "Zoe, you don't have to take this. You can get your paperwork elsewhere. This isn't worth it to you."

My mom's face turns red. "Really? All you want is paperwork? You didn't even come to console us in our time of grief. You know, your brother is missing?"

"Argh! Mom, Vinnie isn't missing! He pretended to be violently ill and persuaded the guard to take off his handcuffs and shackles. Then, he walked away from his trial. That's not the same as a missing child."

"Well, you don't know that. Your brother could be dead and you don't care."

My mom's words bring me up short. "You know, you're right. After I heard what he did to that poor teenager and Katie, he can rot in hell for all I care."

"Zoelle Dominique Hurlington, I don't even know who you are," my dad yells as he places his hands on his hips. "It's like I don't even have a daughter anymore. I should just disown you."

"With all due respect sir, if that is the way you're going to treat her, she's probably better off alone."

Phoenix quietly walks me away from the confrontation. It's a good thing his arm is around my waist. My knees are shaking so bad I'm about to fall down. He helps me get into the truck and Bruiser hops in without hesitation. As I am fumbling to put my seatbelt on, my mother knocks on the window of the truck. She has an accordion file in her hand. I roll down my window and she thrusts it at me.

"Until you can come to your senses and understand all those senseless accusations leveled against your brother are lies, you're no longer allowed in this house and you do not exist to us. Do you understand?"

I nod. "Not much room to get confused. Obviously, Vinnie can do no wrong and I can do no right. You made your choice, now I'm free to make mine." I take a deep breath and let it out before I add, "Goodbye. I hope you find the peace you're looking for." I put the file on the floorboard and roll up the window.

Phoenix throws the truck in reverse. After we hit the main road, he reaches out to grasp my hand. "I'm so sorry, Zoe. I wish things would've gone differently."

I glance out the window and watch the landscape fly by. "Yeah, me too. I guess I don't have to worry about my parents missing me if we end up in Oregon."

Phoenix lifts my hand up and kisses the back of it. "Thank heavens for small blessings."

I shrug. "I guess so. I mean, I expected it to go poorly because my parents wouldn't even look at me during the trial, but I never figured they would completely disown me for following the court order. I mean the weird thing is when all this went down with Katie, my mom told my brother to basically sit down and shut up. I wonder what has changed?"

"I have no idea," Phoenix remarks. "Remember, just because they say you're wrong, it doesn't mean you actually are."

I rub my temples to stop my pounding headache. "I don't even know what to say. Can we not talk about this for now? I still have to figure out what just happened."

"For now, it's forgotten. We have a party to go to,

right?"

I let out a shaky breath. "I'm not sure I'm in much of a party mood, but I don't have a better plan."

Jessica greets me at the front door with a big hug. "Thank you for coming. I should warn you — Mitch got a little crazy when he started inviting people. I'm still not used to people making a big deal about my birthday — but it is what it is." Jessica reaches toward Phoenix for a hug. He backs away and adjusts his backpack on his shoulder.

"It's nice to finally meet you. Thank you for doing so much for Zoe," Phoenix says as he pulls a small gift from his backpack. "Happy birthday!"

Jessica studies the small rectangular box. "Oooh … you guys didn't have to do that. Your company is enough. Lord knows, I'm exhausted. I could use some pampering. My kidlet doesn't seem to know the difference between night and day."

"So sorry," I sympathize. "Don't worry about it — we're glad to be part of your celebration. Need me to help with anything?"

Jessica giggles. "With this group? Hardly! Mama Rosa, Lenore and my grandma have it all covered. Sit down and make yourself comfortable. There is more food here than we'll ever eat."

Phoenix looks at me with his eyes wide. "It's okay, I'll figure it out. Ivy's mom used to be a teacher, she's used to dietary restrictions," I murmur softly.

He relaxes slightly. "I should've known you would think about me."

I weave my arms around his neck and kiss him lightly. "Always," I whisper.

The sound of a throat clearing behind us breaks the romantic moment. I swing around to see Stuart with a goofy grin on his face. "Gee, you get a little busy having a baby and when you reenter life, one of your friends is locking lips with someone you don't know," he teases.

My face heats as I flush with embarrassment. "Phoenix Wolf, this is Stuart Eastwood — otherwise known as Dr. Stuart. He's the vet who owns The Critter Clinic where Dr. Austin works."

Phoenix reaches his hand out for Stuart to shake. Stuart shuffles the baby around in his arms so he can return the handshake. "Nice to meet you; I've heard good things about you. Who's this little one?" he asks with a friendly grin.

"This tiny princess is Chahani. She clearly has everyone wrapped around her little finger including her big sister, Maya."

"I've met Maya. She's quite a dog trainer," Phoenix says as he strokes Bruiser's ears.

Stuart grins. "She is. Her agility coach can't believe how quickly she's progressed. Atlas is a wonder dog."

Stuart turns toward me, "Mitch tells me you might be moving to Oregon. Is that true?"

"Umm … I don't know. Phoenix got a great job offer there, but I don't want to leave Mitch and Jess in a bad situation."

"Would things look different to you if you knew someone who could take over your job?"

"Well, I guess it would depend on if they love

animals is much as I do. It would have to be a good match — not that I'm the one in the hiring or anything. But still …"

"I've got a guy, Dashonte. He's worked with me for over a year. He's probably one of the best people I've ever seen come through my clinic. His mom's health has taken a turn for the worse he could really use a job."

"What does Mitch think of him?" I ask as I try to tamp down my excitement. What if I had a way out of my dilemma? It would be perfect.

"Mitch has told me many times he would like to steal Dashonte from me if he had an opening."

"Don't you need him at The Critter Clinic?" I ask.

"He would be a loss for sure. Still, I have other volunteers. Dashonte is amazing with the animals. Honestly, it's a waste of his talent for him to stay with me. I can see him blossoming into an amazing trainer."

I try to act nonchalant. "Well I suppose it would be up to Mitch and Jess. Still, I can't see Mitch turning down a recommendation from you."

"What wouldn't I do?" Mitch asks as he walks over to us. "Stuart and I have been friends for so long he knows there's not a lot we haven't gone through together. I'm a little afraid to ask what he's got me into this time."

"Hey! I'm innocent. I'm merely trying to solve your staffing problem," Stuart replies as he holds up his hands in front of his chest in a gesture of protest.

Mitch's eyebrows climb as he remarks, "I wasn't aware I had a staffing problem."

Stuart scrutinizes me before he answers, "Well, you might not have one today — but I think it'll happen soon.

That's why I suggested that Dashonte come work for you."

"Awesome, I —" Mitch tries to respond before he's interrupted by the shrill ring of my cell phone. In order to keep from interrupting the birthday party, I answer the phone as quickly as I can.

"I heard you burned your bridges with Mom and Dad. Now, you have no protection from me," the voice at the other end of the phone threatens. There is no doubt in my mind. It's Vincent. My parents must be directly communicating with him. It's only been a couple of hours since we left their place.

"Vinnie, you have to turn yourself in. Every minute you're on the run, makes it worse for you."

"Worse than a conviction?" he scoffs. "She was asking for everything I gave her. You and everyone else should have butted out of our personal relationship. So, don't stop looking over your shoulder because I will always be there."

Shock takes over my body in a wave and I drop my phone as my knees collapse and I land on my butt in the grass.

"Darya, come here!" Stuart yells, startling the baby and making her cry. "Grab Tristan and Isaac too."

Phoenix sits down on the ground behind me and pulls me against his chest. He strokes my hair. "Whatever it is, it's going to be okay. If it's your brother, they will get him. You have too many friends who know the ins and outs of law enforcement. He won't win. I promise."

Between Chahani's wailing, and Phoenix and my unusual position in the middle of the yard, we're attracting a bit of attention. Phoenix abruptly stands up and holds his hand out for me. "Let's go to Hope's room," he suggests. "We'll have more privacy there."

As we take off to Hope's Haven to enter the room which has become our refuge from the world, Stuart hands the baby to Maya. "Need you to watch your sister for a minute, your mom and I need to deal with something."

"Okay Dad," Maya offers. "Is everything okay with Zoe?" she asks with a confused frown.

Stuart ruffles her hair. "It will be — once we sort everything out," he answers as he motions for Darya, Isaac and Tristan to follow us.

Phoenix enters the room and flips on the light switch. It is unbearably crowded with all of us in the small room. Even so, I'm grateful to Phoenix for the suggestion. I do some of my best thinking and planning in this room. Right now, I seem incapable of doing either. I sink down onto the loveseat and try to collect my thoughts.

Darya sits on the loveseat next to me. "I've been out of the loop for a little while; can you fill me in from the top?"

Phoenix pulls his iPad out of his backpack. He glances over at Darya and says, "I'm an incredibly fast typist. I can scribe if you'd like."

Darya looks surprised but replies, "That would be helpful."

"How much do you know about what's going on?"

"Only what I've learned from Cody at roll call. He gave the entire force a heads up about your brother being at large."

"That's only part of the issue. Before I testified at the trial, Vincent threatened to burn down the place where I work, and burn me alive in it."

"How … unusual," Darya comments diplomatically.

I shrug. "Not so much when you consider I am deathly afraid of fire. He knew exactly how to get to me."

"So, he made verbal threats?" Darya clarifies.

"And more, he actually came on the property at Hope's Haven at least twice and left objects behind. Once, they were all shaped like tiny campfires."

"Oh wow! No wonder Cody was concerned about you. You testified against your brother, correct?"

"I did. After that, he escaped from the guards at the trial."

"I wonder if he knows he's been convicted," Darya comments.

I nod. "I know he does. He referred to the verdict while he was threatening me."

"What did he threaten, specifically?"

"He said he was going to kill me because he has nothing else to lose."

Phoenix looks up from the iPad with a fierce expression. "Oh heck no! That's not acceptable to me. I just found you and I won't allow him to take you away."

Chapter Twenty-Three

Phoenix

I HANG MY JACKET up in Zoe's closet. I don't know why I even bother to keep an apartment. I am here ninety-nine percent of the time. I unbuckle Bruiser's harness and remove it. He shakes himself out and then crawls into his dog bed. It isn't long before I hear his soft snores. While Zoe is making herself comfortable, I make her some hot chocolate with marshmallows. I know we're in Florida, but sometimes you just need comfort food.

As she comes out of her bedroom, she is braiding her hair in a ponytail. I collect her into a hug, still marveling about how natural this feels.

"Did you have fun?" I whisper against her temple.

She nods. "I did. Or I was until my brother called. He put a damper on the whole party. It's not fair, Jessica deserved to have a happy day and I ruined it for everyone."

I shake my head vehemently. "You didn't ruin it. Your scumbag brother did."

"You're right," she acquiesces. "Trust my family to screw up everything in my life. My parents are still on my bank account and I know they'll restrict the money I inherited from my Nona."

"You know they can't do that if it's your money, right?"

She sighs. "I know. But I don't have any resources to fight them. They know it. So, they can do whatever they want to me and I can't do anything about it."

Zoe looks so shattered. The trial and the fight with her parents have obviously taken a toll on her. When we first met, she had a smile at the ready most of the time. These days, I have to practically move heaven and earth to shake her gloomy mood. It's time for me to step up to the plate as my father would say.

"I'd like to change that," I confess as I sit down on her loveseat and urge her to join me.

"You'd like to change what?" she questions with a puzzled look.

"I hate that you feel like you need to look over your shoulder to make sure your brother won't attack at any minute. It's awful to be scared to do the things you like to do."

"I was hoping you wouldn't notice."

"How can I help it? Every time your phone rings you jump and you watch the news through your splayed fingers. I know you like taking long walks with the dogs, but you've been delegating that duty to Devon and me."

"Do you blame me?" Zoe challenges.

"No! Of course I don't blame you. I simply wish it wasn't that way. He shouldn't be able to destroy your sense of safety."

"I have no idea what I can do about it. It's become my new normal. My brother is running around loose. I know he has a history of harming people. If I'm honest with myself, it probably goes back to when he was a teenager. The way he reacted to the house fire which killed Lizzie's grandmother was bizarre. In retrospect, I think he probably had something to do with it. If he was capable of that way back then, I hesitate to even think what he's capable of now."

"Do you trust me?" I say as I brushed the hair out of her eyes.

"Of course I trust you! You sat beside me every single day I was permitted to stay in the gallery at the trial. If I didn't trust you, there's no way I would've allowed you to see the ugly side of my life."

"See? That's just the thing. Before I met you, I used to have all sorts of ugly sides to my life. But, you have smoothed down those edges and helped me fit into life. Because of you, my life is less ugly."

Zoe looks at me skeptically, "I don't know if that's true. I think your parents aren't happy with our relationship. I turned what was a supportive relationship into one filled with anger. I'm not sure I'm actually making your life less ugly."

I thread my fingers through hers as I pause to gather my thoughts. "I know it seems like it on the outside because my parents are quick to pin the blame on our relationship, but that's not really what's going on. This began years ago when I first started working for Tristan. Before then, my parents were responsible for any progress I made. They monitored it, measured it, and celebrated it. After I went to college and got my degree, they didn't have much say over my life anymore. I think the fact that you are my girlfriend has crumbled the last bit of hope they had that our relationship would be the same parent-child dynamic it's always been."

Zoe smirks at me. "I'm not real great at big words, but did you just tell me being with me helped you grow up?"

"In a weird way, that's exactly what I'm saying. I had all the trappings of being a successful millennial. I had a great job, an apartment and a dog. From the outside, everything looked okay. But on the inside, I was still living with the limitations I had put on myself or allowed others to place on me."

"Phoenix, I didn't somehow miraculously fix you. Your Asperger's syndrome is still there. It just doesn't matter all that much to me."

"Are you sure?" I ask.

"Honestly, some days it bothers me more than others. Yeah, it's frustrating when you can't meet my gaze during a conversation or when you don't understand the context of a situation. But, you're not the only person who has issues in this relationship."

I scrub my hand down my face in frustration. "I was going to ask you something, but now it seems stupid. I don't want to be the person who bothers you day-in-and-day-out."

"No, that's not what I mean. It's totally not what I mean. Every relationship has stressors, we happen to have a few more. I never said I didn't want to try."

"Living with me is hard. Just ask my mom — she'll tell you all about how frustrating it is to be around me. What if that doesn't get any better?"

Zoe captures my face between her hands and plants a kiss on my lips. "You silly man, can't you see how much progress you're making? Do you remember the first day we met? You didn't want to shake hands. Today, you felt comfortable enough to shake almost everyone's hand and when I was having a crisis, you didn't think twice about wrapping your body around mine to protect me from my fear. You have never done that before. Today, you even ate a hot dog with condiments."

"Big flippin' deal! I don't know if just being able to eat food like normal people is going to be enough. What if my parents are right and I can't be in a regular relationship?"

"First of all, I'd like to have a few words with your parents. They're almost as bad as mine. In case you haven't noticed, we've been having a relationship for almost five months now. It's a pretty great one, if you ask me. You have been there for me, Bruiser and even Jessica and Mitch."

I shake my head as I admit, "I never planned to stick around so long. I guess that in itself says something, right? For the first time in my life I've been able to roll with the punches. I never expected to find you. I didn't know one person could change my life so much."

Zoe hugs me close. "You have changed my life too. Before you, I didn't know if I could ever trust anyone again. Inch by inch, conversation by conversation and idea by idea — you changed my perception of the world. I'll never forget that."

"Remember when I asked you if you trusted me? There's a reason I asked."

Zoe gives me a watery grin. "I sort of figured."

Right before I ask my question, I start to panic. What if her answer isn't what I want to hear? It would ruin everything we built together. Am I willing to risk it all?

"Phoenix?" she prompts.

I take a deep breath and expel it. Bruiser wakes up and jumps on the couch. He places his head on my lap so I can pet him. Something about touching him is phenomenally calming.

After a minute or so, I find the courage to ask my question.

"I have decided I'm going to accept the position at Identity Bank West. You've shown me I am capable of things I never thought possible. I don't know if I could always do things like this or if I can because you made me brave. Zoe, as much as I want this promotion, I don't want to leave you. Will you please come with me to Oregon?"

Zoe blinks several times. I can't read her expression. Maybe I have miscalculated everything.

"This decision will make everyone angry. Are you ready for people to give you grief about your decision?" she asks.

"I guess we'll find out. But, it's time for me to do the right thing for me for the right reasons. Tristan is right. I earned this promotion. I might fall flat on my face — but I don't think I will if I have you by my side."

A tear slides down Zoe's face. My stomach lurches. "I wish I could give you an answer, but I'm not ready yet."

"Will you ever be ready?" I demand as panic starts to set in.

"I will be, someday. You saw what happened today. I don't even have a relationship left to preserve with my parents. So, I don't need to worry about them."

"So what's the problem?" I press.

"It's a big move!" Zoe exclaims. "I can't leave Jessica and Mitch short staffed. It would not be fair to dogs like Bruiser. We have more than half a dozen dogs and various states of training. There are people like you who are waiting for service animals or protection dogs. Law enforcement agencies are waiting for search and rescue dogs. I can't up and leave simply because I've fallen for someone."

My sense of relief is so great I had to catch my breath. I thought for sure Zoe would say goodbye forever.

"So what do we have to do to make this happen?" I ask, afraid to feel hopeful.

"Without access to my money, I have to find a job. What's more, I need to find someone to take my old job. It can't be just anyone. They have to understand what it's like to work with rescue dogs and how important our mission is."

"I understand. What about the guy the vet was talking about?"

"Dashonte is my best hope. I'm going to go talk to him tomorrow at The Critter Clinic. I pray he is as perfect as Dr. Stuart says he is."

"Okay, what else is there?"

"There's a ton of stuff involved in moving clear across the nation. I'm supposed to be in Katie's wedding. I promised. I can't back out now. The wedding is in less than a month Katie and Logan decided to hold their wedding in Florida since most of her friends and family are here. So, juggling our timelines will be a challenge. Not to mention I have to figure out how I'll support myself and find a place to live."

My heart is in my throat. "Uh ... maybe I don't

understand what's going on between us. It wouldn't be the first time. I kinda figured we we'd move in together. I'm with you every day anyway. I don't want to go back to the way it was before I met you."

Zoe sighs and leans against my chest. "I don't either. But, I'm pretty short on miracles right about now. I want to believe things will work out, but I'm afraid, too."

"Why? I guess I consider our whole adventure miraculous. Why do things have to change?"

Zoe sits up and faces me. "You were honest with me about the struggles of dealing with Asperger's syndrome. Now it's time for me to face my truth."

"What are you talking about?"

"There isn't an easy way to explain all this. You might not even understand — but I think you will."

"If I don't, please explain it to me until I do."

"You know when you told me about the kids making fun of you in school for being different. That happened to me too. I was okay until about the sixth grade and someone I thought was my friend discovered I can't read very well. She started making fun of me and calling me slow. Pretty soon the rest of my classmates were saying I belonged in the special classes and I shouldn't hang out with them."

"That's awful! What did your parents do?"

"It was even worse at home. My dad went on and on about how I'd never be able to find a real job like Vincent because I was too stupid to read. I was lucky to get the job at the pet store and even luckier to get my position at Hope's Haven. I guess I'm afraid if I move to Oregon with you, I might not get lucky again. Do you know how hard it is to find a job when you can't read well?"

"No, not specifically. But I do know what it's like to feel less than everyone else because you're different. I wish you could understand what I see when I look at you. I don't see someone who can't. I see a compassionate, passionate and dedicated woman who was able to see beyond how I present myself and figure out what makes me strong."

Zoe blows her nose on a Kleenex she finds in her sweat jacket pocket. "You are too sweet for your own good. That's probably the nicest thing anyone has ever said to me."

"I didn't say it to be nice. I said it to show you how much you've helped me. Now, it's time for me to return the favor."

Zoe assures me it's all right to walk into Dr. Stewart's practice. I knew it would be a mistake. The first thing I see is Dr. Stuart giving an orange cat a shot. Although I can't see any blood, I know it's there. I sway a little.

"Are you all right Mister?" A teenager with shiny black hair nearly to her waist asks me as she helps Stuart hold onto the cat.

Zoe pats the teen on the shoulder. "Don't mind Phoenix. He doesn't like blood."

The teen swings her head around to look at me with renewed scrutiny.

"Corkscrew isn't bleeding. Dr. Stuart says he'll be fine. He just has an infection. He's going to show me how to give him his medicine. My mom is a nurse, but she works a lot so my dad would have to give Corkscrew his medicine. That would be kind of hard because my dad can't see anything."

"Okay, thanks for letting me know."

"My name is Ketki. Hey, do you ride a motorcycle?"

My eyes widen as I look at her in surprise, "I do. But how did you know?"

"My stepdad says there is somebody at his work who rides a motorcycle. The guy used to have a noisier bike but just got a new one which isn't so loud. Somebody told him the man has hair almost as long as mine. You have long hair, so I figured it might be you."

"It might be. Does your dad work at Identity Bank?"

"Yeah," Ketki confirms with astonishment. "His name is John. He helps make computer games."

I smile at her. "What a coincidence, so do I."

"Do you help my dad?" Ketki asks.

"In a way, I check the programs developed by Identity Bank to make sure they don't crash. I don't think I've ever worked on the same project as your dad — but I know who he is."

"That's cool! Tristan and Marcus work with my dad sometimes too."

"I'm very glad to meet you. I can't believe we've never met before. Lots of people have told me you are a very good gamer."

"Are you?" Ketki challenges.

I nod. "I've been playing video games since before I could talk."

"Me too!" Ketki responded. "My dad says it took me a long time to talk because of my Asperger's syndrome. So, I don't know exactly how old I was when I started.

But, I'm better at video games than almost all of my friends."

"That's something else we have in common," I comment.

"Which, friends who suck at video games, or Asperger's syndrome?"

I chuckle. "Both, actually."

Ketki does a double take. "You have Asperger's? I've never met a grown-up who is an Aspie."

"Well, you have now. I heard a rumor you're looking for people to test out your modified programming. I'm game. But I warn you I'm really good."

"So am I," Ketki announces. "Pick your time and place and we'll play. Can I see your phone? I'll give you my number. Text me whenever you want to play. It'll be awesome to have a new MMORPG player. I can't wait to beat you," she adds with a confident smirk.

Ketki takes my phone and rapidly types in some information. She could give my typing skills a run for my money — I can tell she's a serious gamer. I smile when she returns my phone. "Things are crazy in my life right now, but I'll definitely take you up on your offer. Anyway, it was nice to meet you."

Stuart places the cat back in his carrier. After he washes his hands, he turns to us and asks, "What brings you guys by today?"

"We were hoping to talk to Dashonte. Does he work today?" Zoe asks as she smooths her hair with trembling hands.

CHAPTER TWENTY-FOUR

ZOE

PHOENIX WAITS FOR ME in Stuart's quaint waiting room while I look for Dashonte. Following Stuart's instructions, I find Dashonte in the supply room checking in a new shipment. He looks up as if he's startled to see me there. "Can I help you? The waiting room is down the hall to your left if you're waiting for Dr. Stuart."

"Actually, I came to talk to you, Dashonte."

Dashonte's eyes narrow as he regards me. "Wait … you know who I am? Are you some cop friend of Darya?"

I smile at his suspicion. "I am Darya's friend — but I'm not a cop."

He looks confused. "I'm sorry. Should I know you?"

"As far as I know, we have never met. But Dr. Stuart recommends you highly."

Dashonte visibly relaxes. "Isn't Doc the best?"

"I agree. He's a great guy. He does lots of free vet care for Hope's Haven. We rely on him a lot."

Dashonte's eyes widen. "You work at Hope's Haven? That's so cool. I've always wanted to work at a place like that. My mom and I can't have any animals where I live, but I would love to be able to train animals every day. It's like my dream job. Have you seen what the guide dogs do? There's this dude with his guide dog. He's like the best dog ever. Well, maybe not ever — because Darya's dog, Dozer is fiercely cool."

"So ... you like dogs?" I ask. "What about other animals?"

Dashonte's face lights up. "I could do without spiders, but everything else is my vibe."

I laugh out loud. "I'm totally with you on the spiders. Then again, snakes aren't my thing either."

"Like I said, I'd love to have a dog, but I'm not allowed where we live."

"What if I told you there was a job opening at Hope's Haven?"

His jaw goes slack. "Last time I talked to Mitch, he said his employees are pretty much there for life and he didn't have room for more. But, if there was a job up for grabs, it would be epically sweet. I've always wanted to work hands on with animals — more than I do here."

"Do you have any experience training animals?"

A sad expression flashes across Dashonte's face. It's gone so quickly, I almost wonder if I imagined it. "I trained my brother's puppy to shake and rollover. Why?"

"That's a great start. My boyfriend got a phenomenal job offer in Oregon. I'd like to go with him, but I have a responsibility to the animals. So, I don't want to leave until I find someone as passionate about animals as I am."

Dashonte's chest puffs up. "You wouldn't find anyone who loves animals more than me. I mean, look at what I've done here. My job is mostly cleaning up after Dr. Stuart and all the animals. Some people might think my job is boring and not worth much. But, I think it's important. I help Dr. Stuart give all the stray dogs an opportunity to get well and be able to be placed in good homes. I don't mind hard work."

"Trust me, you'll be doing some of the same routine work at Hope's Haven. I still have to clean dog runs, fill food dishes, and wash out dog kennels. But, it's rewarding to change someone's life with a dog. If you're interested, you can come follow me for a day. I have about six weeks before I need to move to Oregon. If you want the job, I could start your training before I leave."

Dashonte's brow furrows. "I'd love to, but I don't want to leave Doc hanging."

"Somehow, I think Stuart would be okay with that. After all, he is the one who recommended you for the position."

"Wow! To think all this started because I rescued a puppy who was being hurt."

"What can I say? Sometimes karma rocks!" I respond with a chuckle.

"Boy, these dogs would gladly compete in a marathon. They sure do like to walk." I adjust my hold on Jolie's lead so I can hold Phoenix's hand.

Phoenix looks down at Bruiser. "Yeah, this guy will be good for my fitness regime. No more vegging out on the couch with video games. Although, I did promise Ketki that I would join her massive multi-player role-playing group. She's been reminding me almost every night. Ketki is a fan of text messages."

"How did your meeting go? According to Tristan, she is one of the most gifted gamers he's ever run across."

Phoenix looks over at me. "Let's just say I recognize a lot of myself in her. I think we could relate on a lot of different levels."

"I'm sure you can. If you run out of things to talk about, Ketki will have you covered. She is one of the most inquisitive kids I've ever seen in my life."

Phoenix smiles, "I can see that. How did your meeting with Dashonte go?" Phoenix asks me as we sit down on a park bench.

"Good! He didn't even wait two days to come visit Hope's Haven. He showed up yesterday ready to work. If he catches on to dog training as quickly as I think he will, I've found my replacement. Remind me to thank Stuart for the lead."

Phoenix takes a chug of his water. When he's finished, he looks at me directly. "Does this mean what I think it means?"

"Probably — if you're thinking it means the coast is clear for me to move to Oregon."

"Is this something you really want to do? I thought about our conversation and I want to make sure I didn't pressure you into moving if you don't want to."

"That's sweet, but I'm not doing anything I don't want to do. I will miss my friends — but if you moved to Oregon and left me behind, I would miss you much more."

"This is the best news ever. I'll text Kendall and take

her up on her offer to help us find a place."

I wrap my arms around myself defensively as I admit, "I'm more than a little scared. I've never lived so far away from home and I'm afraid I won't be able to find a job or friends in Oregon."

"I have an idea. I've been thinking about this for a while. Remember when we stopped in and got coffee at Tough Break?"

"Yeah, I remember their mocha iced coffee. It was amazing."

"That too — but the thing I remember was your conversation with the barista."

"I don't follow. We were simply talking about what I do at Hope's Haven —"

"Right, but remember the comment she made? She said, 'I wish you could come out to my house and fix my dogs.'"

I shoot Phoenix a puzzled look. "Uh-huh. People say those kinds of things all the time."

"Well, why can't you?"

"Why can't I what?"

"People hire concierge services all the time — for everything from cooking, massage, computer set up, lawn services and medical care. Why couldn't they hire you to be a dog trainer in their homes?"

The simple eloquence of his solution is stunning. "I could totally do that! I can't tell you how many times I've helped Mitch teach his classes and people have told me their dogs behave differently in class than they do at home. Now, I could fix people's issues with their pets right in their home environment. Your idea is brilliant!" I practically squeal as I throw my arms around his neck.

Phoenix shrugs and blushes. "I try. Sometimes, my overactive, analytical brain does me some favors."

"Well, I for one am happy for the way your brain works. I was feeling so stuck and you just came up with the perfect answer. Hey, I could even die my hair rainbow colored again and no one would care. I could choose to work in scrubs if I wanted to. That's what I did in high school when I worked at the vet clinic. They are the most comfortable clothes on the planet. I'm so excited. I could have some made with my business name," I ramble. "Wait a minute! I don't even have a business name. What am I thinking? There would be so much to do to set up everything," I add with a sigh.

"Whoa! Take a minute to catch your breath. You might want to hold off on dying your hair until after Katie's wedding. Don't worry about figuring out everything all at once. I make enough money right now to support the two of us. I'll make even more with my promotion. So, you can take your time and design whatever type of business you want."

"But ... moving across the country will be outrageously expensive. Are you sure? I mean, I don't want to be a burden."

Phoenix turns toward me and cups my face. "I thought I made it clear. You're not a burden. Ever. You are my key to freedom."

"Freedom?" I ask.

Phoenix nods solemnly. "Yeah, freedom. At first I thought freedom was being able to ride my bike across the country. It would've been fun, but I don't think I would've experienced freedom the way I feel it with you. I have the freedom to be myself and not hide who I am. I have the freedom to be braver than I've ever been. I'm free to pursue my dreams without feeling like I'm going to disappoint everyone. What you've given me is priceless."

"I don't even know what to say. I don't think I did all that much, but I'm glad your life is better because I'm it."

Phoenix stands up and pulls me to my feet. He takes a few moments to straighten out dog leashes and then kisses me soundly.

"My life is amazing because you're in it. Please never forget that. For the first time in my life, I am looking forward to a new adventure. I'm glad you're going on it with me."

Katie holds a dress up against me and frowns. "Why does this have to be so hard? I like it on the hanger, but it clashes with your hair."

"Don't ask me! The last time I was supposed to be a bridesmaid in a wedding, it was yours. You're lucky I like you. Otherwise, I wouldn't even wear a dress. They're kind of not my thing. I did like my dress the last time though."

"What color was it?" Niana, one of Logan's sisters asks.

"It was probably the best thing to come out of that debacle with my brother. For once, I had a sophisticated LBD."

Sonia, another of Logan's sisters, responds. "I hate to break this to you, but black is a no go. It's considered bad luck in our culture."

Logan's little sister, Riya playfully slaps Katie on the forearm. "Yeah, you had your share of bad luck during your last wedding. You don't need to tempt fate."

Katie is quiet for a moment. "When my whole wedding came crashing down, I was devastated. But, meeting your brother and falling in love with him is the best thing to ever happen to me."

"Good point. But, you guys are so much in love that it makes us single ladies a tad nauseous. Isn't that right, Zoe?" Riya asks me with a playful grin.

Katie chuckles. "Oh, that's right you guys don't know. Quiet little Zoe has landed herself a sexy motorcycle dude. She is going to move to Oregon with him. I'll finally have some of my friends in my neighborhood for a change."

All the women in the wedding party focus their attention on me. For a moment, I don't know what to say. Finally I admit, "Yeah, he's pretty sexy. But, he's more of a computer nerd than a motorcycle dude."

"Well, he's hot enough he could be on the cover of any bad-boy romance novel," Katie jokes as she fans herself. "Seriously, how is it going?"

I look down at the floor and let out a breath. "It's hard. I hate to say it, but it's way more complicated than I ever expected. Everything about my life is up in the air. I'm in love with a guy who has a hard time with relationships. To make matters worse, my parents have disowned me. I don't know where I'm going to live or how exactly I'll support myself."

Katie reaches out and hugs me. "Oh, honey. I totally know what you mean. I felt like that when I moved to be near Logan. But it all came together fabulously. Give it a chance. I think it will work out for you too."

Chapter Twenty-Five

Phoenix

"These cufflinks are the definition of pure evil, I swear," Logan mutters as he tries to fasten mine. "My hands are just too big for this kind of stuff."

"Can't say I've ever worn them before," I answer.

"I don't know how to thank you for being in the wedding."

I shrug. "Standing up in front of a group of people is not my favorite thing to do. But, if it makes Zoe happy then it's worth it."

"I have a feeling our women are going to think we look like rock stars," Aidan predicts as he straightens his tie.

"Says the actual rock star," quips Cody. "The rest of us may not fare so well."

Logan's coworker Nick looks up from where he's polishing his shoes. "Speak for yourself. Sonia was eyeing me before I even put on this monkey suit."

Logan grins. "I hate to burst your bubble, buddy. Knowing Sonia, she was just calculating how long it would take the two of you to walk up the aisle based on your height. She is an engineering student on the honor roll. It's kinda what she does."

Cody laughs out loud at Logan's statement.

"I might not laugh so loud if I were you," I caution. "I met Niana in the parking lot. I understand she's a psychologist."

"Funny, from a guy who gets to walk his actual girlfriend up the aisle."

Dylan Palmer, who served with Katie on the force snickers at Cody's remark. "Hey, I'm not complaining. I got the hot musician."

"Dude!" Logan says. "Those are my little sisters you're talking about. I don't need to know that you think they're hot."

"Newsflash - your sisters are hot," Cody says. He holds up a can of pop and salutes Logan. "Here's hoping your wedding is less dramatic than Katie's last attempt at this."

"I wouldn't bank on it," mutters Aidan.

"What do you mean by that?" Logan asks with alarm.

"It's probably nothing but when Tara was on the phone with Katie, it seemed like they were plotting something. When she realized I was reading her lips, she turned away. So, I wasn't able to eavesdrop."

I always forget Aidan is completely deaf without his cochlear implants. "How does that work? Do you always lip read her conversations with people?"

Aidan winks at me. "Only when Tara's being

secretive and mischievous."

"I see," I answer, even though his answer isn't very clear.

Logan sets down the lint brush he's been using on Cody's jacket. "Okay, is everybody ready? I probably need to go rescue my lovely bride before she starts remembering what a nightmare her last wedding was."

The urge to fiddle with my collar is almost irresistible. Fortunately for me Katie and Logan thought it was a great idea to include Bruiser in the wedding so I am able to focus on the sensation of his weight on my foot. Actually, it's the most unusual wedding I've ever attended. Not only do I have Bruiser with me, Darya has Dozer with her and John, Ketki's father brought his guide dog, Tuffy. In a testament to Zoe's training prowess, all three service dogs are staying on task. In fact, I think Bruiser is handling this high stress situation far better than I am. I hate people looking at me and the whole audience is watching Logan and his groomsmen.

Before I can unravel further, Jude starts to play the acoustic guitar. I smile when I see Tara coming up the aisle holding her daughter Madeleine. Maddie has a difficult time walking. Her birth mother had a stroke while Maddie was being born and as a result Madeleine has cerebral palsy. As Tara is walking down the aisle Maddie is throwing petals from a small basket. Inexplicably, Tara stops about three quarters of the way up the aisle. She appears to be waiting.

Riya walks up the aisle followed by her sisters Sonia and Niana. As Riya reaches up to brush her bangs out of her face, I notice her hands are beautifully painted with *mehedi*. The intricate design is stunning. I am so captivated by the artwork I almost miss the fact that all three women stop beside Tara.

I have to catch my breath when I catch sight of Zoe. I'm used to her wearing casual clothes. Her dress today is anything but casual. Its deep jewel color accentuates her beautiful eyes and athletic build. When she catches my eye, she smiles broadly. I can't wait until she gets up here with me. Yet, like the others she stops.

Mindy, Aidan's honorary niece sits at the piano and plays the traditional wedding march. Katie starts to walk up the aisle. She is wearing a strapless dress and her *mehedi* trails up her arms in a dramatic pattern. When she stops in the middle of the aisle, Logan lets out a groan.

Katie grins as she stands there quietly.

Out of the corner of my eye I see Jude, a member of Aidan's band wink at Mindy and they began to play the classic hit from the Rolling Stones, *Wild Horses*. All of us look around and try to figure out what's going on.

Madeleine pulls a rolled up piece of paper from her basket and hands it to Riya. She starts to unfurl it and hand the other end to Sofia. They hold the banner up so Logan can see. When he reads, "Wild horses couldn't drive me away from this wedding! — Love Katelyn", he laughs out loud and yells at her, "I love you too". The sisters turn around and show the audience what he's laughing at. Then, they put the banner down on a chair and all five women sprint toward the stage.

Zoe stops in front of me for a moment. Then she seductively slides her hands up my body and cups my face as she gives me a theatrical kiss. As I return the kiss and pull away, I notice Aidan and Tara are still in the middle of a passionate kiss. Cody looks amused while Nick and Dylan look like they've been struck by a Mack truck.

Sonia pulls a compact mirror and lipstick from a pocket in her dress. She begins to make a big show of fixing her smeared lipstick while Nick looks completely befuddled. I'm tempted to laugh at him — but I suppose I have the same expression on my face. Sonia turns toward the audience and quips, "Well, that was a bit messier than I expected but I have to say this is the most fun I've ever had at a wedding."

I lean down and whisper in Zoe's ear, "Funny, I was thinking the same thing."

"That was quite a number you pulled on us." I sit behind Zoe and place my arms around her waist. "You took all of us by surprise."

"I know. Wasn't it the craziest thing? We came up with the idea while we picked up our bridesmaids' dresses. I guess Logan used to tease Katie that he was planning to handcuff her to the pulpit to make sure she didn't run away from her wedding this time."

"Oh right … I remember now. When Katie was on the run from your brother after he went crazy at the wedding, she met Logan at a bar, right? I think I remember reading about the way they met. I didn't put two and two together."

"Yeah, she was wearing a wedding dress the day Logan met her. She drank so much Jack Daniels that night to try to forget my brother, she almost didn't recognize Logan. So, they started using Katie's status as a runaway bride as a running joke between them.”

“It makes perfect sense, if you know the whole story. But still, this is the strangest wedding I’ve ever been to.”

“According to Tara, all of her friends specialize in bizarre weddings. It’s funny because Jessica said the same thing about her friends.”

“Someday, I hope someone tells us our wedding was the most entertaining thing they’ve ever been to.”

“Seriously, it would be hard for anyone to do better than this. I mean look at the dance floor. Aidan O’Brien and his whole band are the entertainment. I never thought I would see anything like this.”

I smile. “I guess there are perks to being Aidan O’Brien’s personal bodyguards,” I remark as I stand up and brush off the back of my pants. I loosen my tie and shed my jacket. I stick the cufflinks in my pocket and roll up my sleeves.

“I guess so, but I’ve heard that Aidan is right up there with Tristan on the nice guy scale.”

I tie Bruiser’s leash to the base of the tree behind us and extend my hand to Zoe. When she wobbles as she tries to stand, she kicks off her high heels.

“Would you like to dance, milady?” I ask as I bow a courtly bow.

“Umm … sure … I guess so. I’m a little nervous because Tara used to be a professional dancer. The dance moves I learned in high school are not very impressive, trust me.”

I glance over at the makeshift dance floor. “Judging by what I see, I don’t think it’ll be an issue. There appear to be lots of different experience levels having fun.”

Freedom

As we start to walk toward the dance floor, Bruiser growls aggressively. I hold up my index finger to Zoe. "Hold on a second, I think I better let Bruiser do his business before we get lost on the dance floor."

Zoe puts my jacket over her shoulders and leans against the tree. "That's okay. I'm probably more comfortable watching everyone else."

When I unhook Bruiser from the tree, he takes off running toward the sheds. He is dragging me behind him like a trailer with a broken wheel.

As we approach the outbuildings, I notice the shed door where I keep my motorcycle is propped open slightly. My stomach drops to my toes. This cannot be good. Bruiser drops down and army crawls until his nose is right under the door. His hackles raise, and his growl becomes even more commanding. I cautiously approach the door to the shed while I use the building for cover. As I peek through the crack in the door, my heart about stops when I recognize the man vandalizing my motorcycle. How in the heck did Vincent know Zoe was going to be here today?

Out of the corner of my eye I see a piece of two by four. I reach out and catch it with my foot and drag it toward me as I keep an eye on Vincent. Quietly, I slide the door shut and slide the two by four through the handles.

I don't know how long that will hold. Out of desperation I drag a heavy meat smoker in front of the door. I grab Bruiser's leash and run back to the wedding party as fast as I can.

As I pass the beverage table, I see Darya standing with Dylan and Cody. Darya is the first to notice my panicked expression. "What happened? Is Zoe hurt?" she asks me in short staccato questions.

I shake my head as I try to catch my breath. "Call 911. Have them send as many officers as they can spare."

"Oh man! Please tell me this doesn't involve Katie again," Cody says.

I shake my head as I blurt, "I've got Vincent trapped in the shed. I think he was messing around with my motorcycle."

"Vincent Hurlington as in Zoe's brother, convicted felon and suspect at large?" Dylan asks me as he takes off running toward the sheds. Cody follows close behind.

"The very one," I answer with a labored breath.

"Oh man! Katie's going to hate me. I promised her there'd be no official police call at this wedding," Cody laments as he pulls his cell phone out of his pants pocket and calls 911.

My knees are shaking so violently I can barely stand as I hold Zoe to my chest. I don't think I've seen so many law enforcement vehicles in my whole life. I guess that's what happens when you go on the lam in the middle of your trial.

Zoe slumps when she sees the tactical team running across the yard. "This won't end well for my brother, will it?" she whispers tearfully.

"I think everything will be resolved quickly. There are enough ex-military and current police officers here to ensure a good outcome," I respond with more conviction than I feel. I place my arms around her waist and give her a light squeeze. "Everyone is a professional. No one wants anything to happen to your brother. He needs to face justice for all the things he's done."

Just as I comment, Vincent is being escorted across the lawn against his will. His arms are handcuffed in front of him, Cody and Dylan flank him. Darya has a gun trained on him from behind.

When Zoe sees her disheveled brother, she lets out an involuntary cry. Vincent starts yelling profanities and death threats at Zoe. He takes advantage of the momentary distraction and swings his arms around to hit Dylan in the face with his shackled hands. The metal in his cuffs slice a gash in Dylan's face. Vincent takes off running. Darya issues a command in German and Dozer transforms from a lackadaisical couch puppy to a lean, mean weapon. He takes chase and tackles Vincent a few yards away from where he broke away. Vincent is screaming for his mama as Dozer clamps his jaw down on his arm.

Between the blood on Dylan's face and the lacerations on Vincent, it's amazing I'm still upright.

Darya issues another command as the tactical team reaches them and subdues Vincent. Reluctantly, Dozer releases the perpetrator and walks quietly over to Darya and sits down at her feet.

Zoe has had enough of the scene in front of her so she turns around and buries her head in my chest as she sobs.

"What's wrong Zoey-Pie? Is this a little too much truth for you? Are you embarrassed to be my sister?" Vincent taunts as he charges toward her. Three or four burly officers in dark clothing restrain Vincent as he struggles to get at her.

Zoe's stands up straight and marches closer to her brother. "You want my truth? I'll give it to you. I am embarrassed to be related to you. You had the best of everything and you threw it away so you could pretend to have power over someone else. Well, I'm done giving you power over my life. You can rot in hell for all I care."

"I should have burned down this place with everyone and everything in it! I didn't get you this time, but I will kill you the next time I see you," Vincent threatens as the tactical team marches him across the lawn toward their vehicle.

Zoe and I walk to the front lawn to watch what happens next. Katie walks up behind us, still wearing her ivory wedding dress. "Some days, I wonder why I gave up police work. Today is not one of those days."

The tactical team stuffs Vincent into a nondescript SUV and drive off.

Katie looks around at all the stunned guests and the tables which were upended during the struggle. "I'm sorry my brother ruined your lovely day," Zoe tells Katie as she gives her a tearful hug.

"Don't worry about it. You are not him or the things he's done. That's all on him."

"Still, it's your wedding day —" Zoe argues.

Katie shrugs. "After the news media gets wind of what happened today, my runaway bride story will seem like nothing. Maybe we should throw a wedding every year and see how dramatic it can be — it'll be like dinner theater," she finishes with a chuckle.

"Funny, but I'm not at a point where I can laugh just yet. I almost lost the love of my life today. That call was too close for comfort," I confess.

Zoe looks at me with wide eyes and a slack jaw. "Wow! I didn't know we were this far along. You said the L word. I mean, I've been in love with you for a while. But I never knew if you felt the same way."

"What did you think I meant when I asked you to move to Oregon?" I incredulously reply.

"I don't know. That's part of what made this move to Oregon so difficult. I didn't know where I stood with you."

"As you know, finding words is not a natural talent for me. If I ever forget to tell you how much I love you and what you mean to me, just remind me."

Epilogue

Zoe

I throw the oversized tote containing toys, treats and grooming equipment onto our couch as I walk by. I lean down to stretch out my back and twist around to see if I can loosen the tension. I don't see Phoenix in the kitchen where he usually is at this time of day, so I kick off my shoes and walk into our office.

Phoenix has his headphones on and is rapidly typing on the computer. I take a moment to admire his dogged determination. He has been working on this project for several days. It's a different sort of project than he usually does. This time, he's trying to reverse engineer a competitor's software to find the security glitch which is allowing the company to glean personal information from each user's personal contacts. Even though today is Saturday, he's hard at work trying to unravel the puzzle.

I walk up behind him and kiss him on the neck. He startles because he didn't hear me coming over the music playing through his headphones.

"What are you doing here? I thought you were working with the Ferguson family today."

I run my fingers through his hair and massage his neck. "You must be buried in code. I've been gone for three hours."

Phoenix glances down at his cell phone. "No kidding? Wow, it seems like I was just kissing you goodbye this morning."

Sighing, I remove my Critter Coach apron. Stuart helped me choose the name and I drew the logo. Most days, I'm really proud of what I've accomplished in a few short months, but today I'm just exhausted.

I flop down in my favorite chair — a big round papasan. Well, it used to be my favorite chair but at the moment, it has flipped over on top of me as I sprawl on the floor. It's pretty symbolic of how my day has gone.

Phoenix springs into action. He pulls the chair off of me and sets it upright. He squats down beside me as he asks urgently, "Are you okay? What happened?"

"It's just one of many misses in my life today. I can't even say I'm surprised. I landed off-center and got dumped."

Phoenix examines me carefully. "Do you hurt anywhere?"

I shake my head. "Only my pride."

Phoenix stands up and offers me his hand. After I make it to my feet, he scoops me up and carefully sits down in the chair as he holds me on his lap. "So, tell me, what was so awful about your day?"

I burrow deeply against his chest and take a deep breath. "I feel stupid even complaining. Critter Coach has grown faster than I could ever imagine. Still, sometimes people drive me nuts."

"I thought you liked the Ferguson's dog."

"I do. Willie is an awesome whippet. But, the people

in his life could use some help."

"What do you mean?" Phoenix asks as he brushes some hair out of my face.

"Well, Frederick has a good head on his shoulders — especially for being twelve. But, Willie is his first pet and he doesn't quite understand Willie isn't an action figure he can put down and ignore whenever he wishes."

"What about his parents?" Phoenix asks.

"Oh, don't get me started. The dad is a field producer for a television show. He's gone a bunch. So, Teresa, Frederick's mom, treats Willie like he's a baby. She even has a special purse she carries him around in."

"I'm not an expert on dog breeds, but didn't you tell me Willie is a whippet? Don't they need huge amounts of exercise?"

"Bingo! You get it. Unfortunately, I can't seem to reach either of these clients. Frederick is open to new information, but he doesn't want to take the time to learn about the responsibilities of having a pet. Teresa should know better, but she thinks it's 'cute' to treat her dog that way. Poor Willie doesn't know what to do because the rules are different. I don't have a good way to teach them this information. They can't afford to have me follow them around for days on end to correct their bad habits."

Phoenix is silent for a couple minutes. Finally, he replies, "You said Frederick likes to treat Willie like a toy, right?"

I nod, puzzled at his question.

"What if I could develop a video game which would educate kids and teenagers about proper pet care?"

"That sounds like a fabulous idea. Can you make one

for his mom too? Honestly, she lacks even more skills and common sense than Frederick."

I can feel Phoenix shrug as I cuddle up against his chest. "I don't see why not. We could design some software for adults. It would be cool to develop a mobile app. I think now people spend more time on their phones and tablets than they do in front of a computer these days."

"Are you just saying all this to make me feel better?" I ask skeptically. "Do you think Jameson would allow you to do that on the side? Some companies are picky about what their employees do during their off hours."

"I'm sure he would think it was a great idea. Just the other day, he was telling us not to get pigeonholed in our jobs and to continue to be creative. He was stressing that one of Tristan's core values is to challenge ourselves to do what scares us."

"We've been doing a pretty good job of living up to his motto recently, haven't we?"

"You can say that again. But, we kind of prove Tristan's point. We have been living outside our comfort zone for months and look how much better our lives are now."

"Okay, you've convinced me. You provide the computer skills and I'll provide the knowledge about training dogs. Together we'll conquer the world."

"Maybe just a small corner of it, but it will be great fun to try."

"Can you believe we're actually doing this?" I check the

thermometer on the turkey.

Phoenix chuckles softly. "It's dinner with my parents, it's not like we're finding the cure to cancer or anything."

I playfully bop the back of his head with an oven mitt. "You don't understand. This is a huge deal. This is the first formal dinner we've had in our new home."

Phoenix grins. "I know. My parents are never going to believe how domestic we've become. We are like an old married couple. Did I tell you I spent twenty minutes the other day trying to figure out which brand of laundry detergent would work best? I even opened the lids and sniffed the detergent. I felt like such a rule breaker."

I laugh out loud. "You are too funny. If someone was to look at you, they would never guess you like to live life on the straight-and-narrow. You are the quintessential rebel without a cause."

"I've heard a rumor you think my motorcycle gear is sexy. So, why would I mess with success?"

"Good point," I reply as I stand on my tiptoes to give him a thorough kiss.

After I pull away, a sad thought crosses my mind. My mom used to kiss my dad all the time in the kitchen when they were cooking together. The memory is enough to make me a little lightheaded. "I'm so happy things are working out with your parents, but I can't help but miss mine."

Phoenix hugs me close. "I'm so sorry Zoe. I'm still trying to wrap my brain around the fact that they embezzled money from their social club to help finance your brother's time on the lam. They seem so uptight about law and order — I figured they would turn him in.

Instead, they made it easier for him to escape and continue to torture you."

"I know. It's like I don't recognize any of my family members. They've all become cruel distorted versions of themselves. All I have left are a few touching family memories. It's not fair."

"I know it's not, Zoe," Phoenix murmurs against my temple as he embraces me. "Look on the bright side. Maybe you can adopt my parents."

I pull away and give him a skeptical look. "I think you're forgetting something. Your family doesn't care for me much. I think your mom disagrees with nearly everything I do — especially when it comes to you."

"I don't know about that. It seems the longer we are away from home, the bigger fans my parents have become. They appear to be looking forward to this visit."

Bruiser gives a puff of a woof a second or two before our doorbell rings. I reach down and grab Phoenix's hand as we walk hand-in-hand to the front door. "You ready for this?" I whisper.

Phoenix smiles. "I have no earthly idea, but I know if you're next to me I can handle almost everything."

As soon as I open the front door, Phoenix's mom envelops me in a hug. When she's finished, his dad shakes my hand. "Mr. and Mrs. Wolf, we're so glad you're here. Welcome to our home."

Phoenix's dad pats me on the shoulder. "Oh, don't be silly. We are just Moon and Clarence here. It's nice and green here in Oregon. There are mountains almost every place you look."

I smile. "I know! It's great, isn't it? I had the same reaction when I first came here. It's like an enchanted forest of green. I'm surprised you guys could come all the way out here. It's a long trip."

"It sure is! We are happy to be here, but it's even better because it's on my company's dime. They offered to train me in either Minneapolis or Portland. So, since you guys were here, it was an easy decision," Clarence explains.

"Phoenix, you have such a nice home," Moon comments as she looks around. "Your job must be going well —" she probes, clearly seeking an answer.

"Thanks, Mom. Come on in and sit down," Phoenix instructs as he escorts them to the sectional couch in the living room. I make myself busy as I carry food to the table. Phoenix continues, "My job is fine. Actually, it's better than fine. My boss is really creative about meeting my needs."

"What do you mean?" Clarence asks as he grabs a handful of salted nuts off the coffee table.

"Well, Jameson is excellent about thinking outside the box. He allows me to issue a video every week to my staff talking about our goals, upcoming tasks, accomplishments and any concerns. Then, there is an online forum for our little section of Identity Bank West. Anyone can post any questions to me and I will address them in the next video. It's so much easier for me to deal with problems and conflict if I can think about what I want to say ahead of time. It's great that I don't have the look people in the face while solving conflicts. The pre-produced videos are almost a perfect accommodation for me," Phoenix explains

"Well, that's just good problem-solving. Sounds like you found the ideal work environment. I hope they're paying you plenty for your skills because they are second to none," Phoenix's dad announces as if any of us need any convincing.

"Let's say Tristan willingly invests in great talent. They're even letting me work on a side project to help people become better pet owners."

Moon is studying my every move. Eventually, she pipes up and asks me, "Need any help?"

I set the mashed potatoes on the table. I point to the dishes I left on the counter. "You can help set the table, if you want. It took me longer than I expected to make the gravy and I just haven't had a chance to get to the table."

Moon walks over and picks up a stack of dishes. When she takes a closer look, she gasps. "Phoenix must love these. They are perfect for him."

"Aren't they great?" I concede. "I found some similar ones, but they weren't quite big enough for what we needed. So, my friend Ivy, who works with ceramics, made us a set as a going away present."

"Oh well, that was nice of her. But, I can't help but wonder if it's such a good idea to cater to Phoenix and all his oddities. He has to be able to function in the real world," she pontificates.

I shrug. "In the grand scheme of things, I'm not sure it matters all that much to the rest of the world whether Phoenix's mashed potatoes and peas touch. Still, it matters a ton to him. I don't see the harm in making his world more comfortable. Look around you Mrs. Wolf. Your son is doing a phenomenal job adapting to the real world. He's one of the most valuable employees at Identity Bank West and he is working on the thoughts and behaviors which hold him back a bit. I mean, come on … he is able to fly without me these days. That's a big deal."

"That's nice dear. Do you understand life with Phoenix will be hard? Are you prepared?"

"I am. You're right. Being with Phoenix is probably the hardest thing I've ever done," I confide. "But —"

"I told Clarence you probably weren't cut out for this," Moon interjects in an acerbic tone.

"You didn't let me finish." I assert. "The rest of what I was going to say is although being with Phoenix is the hardest thing I've ever done, it is also the easiest. We are free to be ourselves and love each other openly and honestly. Phoenix can't change who he is, but neither can I. The fact that he's different is one of the reasons I fell hard and fast for him. If he was just ordinary, I would've paid your son no mind. I love Phoenix for who he is and I don't think it'll ever change."

Phoenix comes up behind me in puts his arms around my waist. He gives me a light squeeze before he asks, "Do you really mean it?"

I turn in his arms to face him. "I do. Sorry to tell you, you'll have to kiss your precious freedom goodbye because you're stuck with me forever. I'm not going anywhere."

"I think you misunderstand the situation," he says with a bemused smile. "I have the freedom to soar because you love me. I love you so much, Zoelle Dominique Hurlington. I don't know what I would've done if our fates would've gone in a different direction."

Clarence walks up beside us. He points at Moon. "See? I told you. Phoenix has found his match in Zoe the same way I found mine with you. You can stop worrying. They are obviously thriving without us."

Moon gets a little misty eyed. "I don't know if I can do that, Clarence. I think there's a part of me which will always worry because I'm his mom."

I turn and hug Phoenix's mom. "I expect nothing less. A mother should never stop loving her child no matter what. I just hope someday you consider me to be part of your family too."

Phoenix hands his mom a paper towel as she starts to cry. "I never thought I would see the day my son would fall in love with someone who loves him just as much. It'll take a bit of getting used to, but I am happy to include you in my family."

"Mom, that would be perfect. Zoe's family seems to have trouble figuring out what it means to love someone."

Moon looks at me for confirmation. "Sadly, Phoenix is right," I reply.

"Well, that just makes your love all the more miraculous," she says as she hugs me again.

Clarence picks up three glasses of water from the table and hands one to each of us while he takes the last one. He holds it up as if he's about to give a toast.

"Here's to having the freedom to love who you choose."

I take my glass and clink it against everyone else's glass. "I'll drink to that."

THE END (for now)

For more information about Tara and Aidan's daughter, Madeleine O'Brien, please check out <u>Dreams Change</u>.

Note from the Author

Dear Reader,

Thank you for reading *Freedom*. I hope you enjoyed it.

For the moment, *Freedom* is the last book in the Hidden Hearts Series. However, if you are a fan of the characters in this series, you may want to try my new series Hidden Hearts — Protection Unit. These books have the same friends you've grown to love and root for, but the stories are a little more suspenseful with police procedure.

If you would like to start my first series, it begins with *Until the Stars Fall from the Sky*.

Jeff had a plan.

In an instant, he forgot it.

Who is the woman with the red hair?

Jeff knows what he wants from life. Finishing at the top of his law class isn't just a goal, it's a real possibility. He can see the finish line. The competition is fierce, but is it worth sacrificing his whole life?

Will his heart get in the way?

Mary Crawford

Kiera knows a thing or two about discipline. As a former Paralympian, she spent hours in the pool. Now, she takes that same focus into her job as a social worker as she finishes her Master's degree.

The last thing on her mind is meeting someone new.

With every twist and turn, everything is working against them.

Can love find its way?

You will adore this emotionally-charged contemporary romance.

Get *Until the Stars Fall from the Sky* now!

~Mary

Because love matters, differences don't.

ACKNOWLEDGMENTS

IT WOULD BE EASY to make assumptions if you follow social media. These days, fashion and makeup choices seem endless. People have piercings, tattoos and long hair. For the most part, these things get little notice in today's society. The message is different is good.

The problem is that when difference is hidden — as in Asperger's syndrome, sensory dysfunction or dyslexia — people are much less accepting. People with invisible disabilities experience the same hopes, dreams and aspirations as everyone else. They just have more barriers to overcome to reach them.

Someday, my sons may choose to read this book. I pray they come away with a message that everyone regardless of disability, economic circumstances, or family background, everyone deserves to be loved.

Difference is good. The world would be a very boring place if we were all the same. Diversity should be celebrated in all its forms.

I love you Brandon and Justin.

I've shared my story with my readers before. Yet, I never grow tired of telling the story of a man wearing green polyester pants and a white snap-up cowboy shirt who fell in love with a young college student with a service dog and a wheelchair. He has always made me feel like the most beautiful woman on the planet despite my disability. He is the person who embodies my tagline. Because love differences don't. Happy 29th anniversary Leonard! Thank you for seeing me for who I really am.

I would like to thank several people. Actually, I would like to think so many people I cannot possibly name them all. I would like to express my appreciation to the Indie Author community. You are all amazing. Whenever I assaulted you with endless questions, you willingly answered me with grace and good humor. When I feared my writing career would be completely derailed by three lung surgeries this summer and several weeks of hospitalization, many of you took the time to give me personal encouragement to work my way through my pain and frustration.

I'd like to thank Kathern Watts for brainstorming with me to come up with the ideas for this book. Your unfailing support and help with research and story continuity are appreciated more than I can say.

Thank you to Kathy Faltinson for stepping up and tackling the gargantuan task of editing my work. Thank you for your careful, thoughtful feedback. You have made this book stronger.

I also wish to thank my beta readers and my street team for helping me keep my stories grounded and real. You are amazing.

About the Author

I have been lucky enough to live my own version of a romance novel. I married the guy who kissed me at summer camp. He told me on the night we met that he was going to marry me and be the father of my children.

Eventually, I stopped giggling when he said it, and we've been married for more than thirty years. We have two children. The oldest is a Doctor of Osteopathy. He is across the United States completing his residency, but when he's done, he is going to come back to Oregon and practice Family Medicine. Our youngest son is now tackling high school and where he is an honor student. He is interested in becoming an EMT.

I write full time now. I have published more than thirty books and have several more underway. I volunteer my time to a variety of causes. I have worked as a Civil Rights Attorney and diversity advocate. I spent several years working for various social service agencies before becoming an attorney.

In my spare time, I love to cook, decorate cakes and of course, I obsessively, compulsively read.

I would be honored if you would take a few moments out of your busy day to check out my website, MaryCrawfordAuthor.com. While you're there, you can sign up for my newsletter and get a free book. I will be announcing my upcoming books and giving sneak peeks as well as sponsoring giveaways and giving you information about other interesting events.

If you have questions or comments, please E-mail me at Mary@MaryCrawfordAuthor.com or find me on the following social networks:

Facebook: www.facebook.com/authormarycrawford

Website: MaryCrawfordAuthor.com

Twitter: www.twitter.com/MaryCrawfordAut